A Scandal at Delford

A Regency Romance

Kate Westwood

Published by Kate Westwood
www.katewestwood.net

ISBN: 978-0-6484007-0-7

Disclaimer

This is a work of fiction. Names, characters, places, organisations, events, and incidents are either products of the author's imagination or used fictitiously.

Books by Kate Westwood

A Scandal at Delford

Beauty and the Beast of Thornleigh (Coming Soon)

A Bath Affair (Coming Soon)

Acknowledgements

A big thank you to Beverlee Swayzee for beta-reading, so much appreciated, to Kim Lambert for her unending patience and help with publishing, and to Alex Aislabie for saving my sanity by doing the social media stuff. I would also like to acknowledge the help of Steve Wright, who beta read for me. Steve, wherever you have passed over to, I hope you know how much your input was valued. Thanks.

Dedicated to my sister Rae, who is a true friend

in every sense of the word.

Table of Contents

KATE WESTWOOD

x

'A woman especially, if she have the misfortune of knowing anything, should conceal it as well as she can.'
-Jane Austen, *Northanger Abbey*

KATE WESTWOOD

One

'A letter came from Cousin Lavinia yesterday, Papa. She has invited me into Hertfordshire, to Delford, for the summer. I ought to go, for I have not seen my cousin since Aunt Jane died. Since you and my step mama will be abroad in Italy, may I not go?'

Charlotte Milton directed this address to her father rather anxiously, over a laden breakfast table, at the head of which sat Dr Milton, his mouth working up and down in regular fashion, like pistons in a steam locomotive. Before him sat his plate, half emptied of its rolls, cold cuts, and pound cake, the missing contents of which had disappeared between the thick, ruddy lips of its owner only minutes before.

His new wife of only four weeks sat at his right hand, opposite her stepdaughter, sipping tea and playing idly with her cake. Her black eyes flickered briefly in the direction of her stepdaughter when Charlotte spoke, but she kept her countenance neutral, and if any ill will was perceived by Charlotte in that flickered glance, she gave no sign of recognition.

Dr Milton doggedly finished his masticating and put down his fork with an air of vague annoyance at being interrupted in the pursuit of his breakfast. 'Lavinia? So, Markham's got her there, has he? Never liked the man, myself. But I will say the invitation is excellent timing.' He scraped more meat onto his fork and turned to Mariah. 'We shall not want her here, my dear. She had better go into Hertfordshire and be done. It answers the problem neatly. We can write to her from Italy. What say you?'

The silent little woman at his side flickered another glance in the vicinity of Charlotte's person, without meeting her eyes, and tilted her dark head to look at her husband. Her voice had a breathless, flimsy quality, like a thin reed buzzing in a breeze.

'Why she can have nothing to do here, when we are away! It had better be arranged at once, for we are to leave Saturday. Now we will not have to get Nanny Scrutch in to chaperone.'

She looked at Charlotte from under low, dark brows and their eyes briefly met at last. Charlotte perceived relief in her look, and something else she preferred not to dwell upon. There is little use in pursuing the good will of someone disposed to dislike you on sight. Charlotte, having applied all her arts of persuasion and cajoling forces, had quite given up the idea of making her new stepmother like her. From the first, she had sensed the woman's resentment and done her very best to counter it with her kind attentions, to no avail.

Mariah Milton, a petite woman of years closer to Charlotte's own than to her husband's, had a tidy income and a pretty face. Charlotte knew her father's character and understood that he had married Mariah as much for her money as for her face and, although she loved her father, the thought left a bitter taste in her mouth.

Her father, pronouncing loudly to his friends the need for 'some company and motherly advice for Charlotte', had forgone all gentlemanly decorum, and all the conventions of good society, by choosing to marry Mariah eleven months after the death of his first wife, installing her in his home post-haste. This event provided ample fodder for rumination by the town gossips and ensured that Charlotte had endured numerous prying questions.

To add to her distress, Charlotte had quickly found that Mariah, as docile and dutiful to her husband as she might be, showed little inclination for her new stepdaughter. If Charlotte suggested a walk together, or even entered Mariah's private parlour, her stepmother frowned and offered little encouragement. In company, Mariah resorted to resentful looks cast secretly, and an affected, apathetic interest.

Dr Milton, never having taken much of a personal interest in his daughter, having left that to his now departed wife, had not been in her company enough to observe this lack of intimacy between his new wife and his daughter. It was not that her father was unkind, and he was, perhaps, a trifle more attentive in the wake of his first wife's death, but a feeling of real intimacy, of being loved dearly, was the loss that Charlotte felt all the more lacking now that her mama was gone.

After the shock of finding that her father had planned to remarry so soon after the loss of his first wife, Charlotte had comforted herself with the hope of finding a friend in the new addition to their family, but instead had found only apathy and resentment.

Her guilt at being disinclined to like her new parent had obliged her to repress bitter disappointment in her new domestic circumstances, but still, it rose up in her; not only had she been forced to suffer patiently the gossip of the village over the hasty remarriage, she'd also had to endure a seeping, grey loneliness in her own home. Her spirits had sunk even lower at the appalling prospect of remaining for life in the house of her father and his new wife, and when Lavinia's letter had arrived, she had been anxious that her father might agree to the stay, releasing her at least for the summer.

Dr Milton now nodded in agreement with his wife. 'She can take the carriage and it can return the following day. I will leave it to you to arrange the particulars, my dear.' He took a large mouthful of cake and continued in between piston strokes. 'It will be just the thing, for her to spend summer in the country. It is cooler there than here, and she will find it refreshing.' He turned to Charlotte. 'You have been so pale and thin I have quite had in mind to give you a tonic. But perhaps two months or so in the country will do just as well. Yes, well, well! So, Markham has her, does he?'

'Yes. Lavinia is under the guardianship of her uncle. Her parents died about two years ago. You remember? First her father's heart gave out, then Aunt Jane died soon after. Mama always said my aunt died of a broken heart.'

Her father snorted. 'Broken heart? Consumption it was, the devil take it! Broken heart is it? Fustian nonsense!'

Charlotte said nothing, used to her father's blustery ways and unsympathetic heart, which she thought was not the best quality for a medical man, but she sipped her tea, quietly rejoicing in her father's ready acquiescence to the proposed visit. Her stepmother's stony little eyes observed her from under their half-closed lids, her thoughts flittering about darkly behind them. Charlotte looked away.

'I recall the girl here several times, with your mother's sister,' continued her father. 'Pretty little thing. Summoned into Hertfordshire to be married off, no doubt. Heiress, isn't she? Well, she will be quite a different girl now to what she left you, ho?'

Charlotte recollected the high-spirited young cousin with whom she had spent many hours in years past. The death of Lavinia's parents must have had a somewhat sobering effect on her in the last few years. And Lavinia was much grown now and would be quite a young lady. Still, her cousin had been a flighty, silly creature at fourteen.

'I do hope Lavinia is a deal less silly about fashion and young men than she used to be,' she replied. 'But I am sure she is a grown-up young woman now, with more sensible manners. After all, it is very hard to lose two parents in the same year. She will be quite altered by it, I expect.'

Charlotte keenly hoped and expected now to find a more mature and sober young lady, one in whom she could find a friend and confidante, and in whose society the two months of her stay would pass pleasantly.

To share her thoughts and feelings with another female who would not ask indelicate questions about her father's remarriage would be a comfort to her after being so long burdened with grief and disappointment, with no outlet for release. She was also relieved to be away from the home that held so many memories of her own dear mama and which were now made more poignant by the addition of a new female.

She thanked her father and her stepmother politely and left the room, conscious of Mariah's never once having addressed her during the course of breakfast.

Two

Charlotte smoothed her grey silk traveling dress over her knees with a slender, gloved hand and tried to focus on the scenery outside the carriage window. She had been jolted and rattled along in her papa's carriage for five hours and she was more than a little fatigued with the journey. Earlier, they had stopped at an inn where the driver had watered the horses, and she, and Jane, her maid, had taken a light meal in the parlour there, but now they were another three hours on, and Charlotte was feeling the effects of inactivity. She stretched out her limbs and let her thoughts drift.

She was keen to see her cousin after a lengthy separation, feeling sure that they would each be a source of consolation to the other, having both suffered losses within the last twenty-four months. She felt that a long stay in the country would be just the cure wanted by her low spirits, and the thought of long walks, and picking wildflowers in the hedgerows with her cousin, lifted the corners of a mouth that had not smiled as often as it should in the past year.

She was also curious to see her cousin's new home, but was not so sure about meeting Sir Benedict Markham, her cousin's uncle, and guardian of her fortune. Lavinia had not written much about her father's older brother, except that he was 'an old fossil with greying hair, a large income, and an intimidating manner to match'. Charlotte hoped that he would not be too intimidating or she would spend the summer nervous of her host!

~~*~~

The carriage passed into a dim, wooded area, where the road ran beneath some towering oaks which were decked with new greenery and the promise of summer. Charlotte found herself moving through a cool, leafy lane bordered with fields. Workers dotted the pale green and gold pastures, moving slowly in the lazy afternoon warmth.

'Is this Delford, Miss?' Jane roused herself to peer from the window.

'I collect it is, Jane. It is rather large, is it not?' Her cousin had told her that the estate was very large, and Charlotte scanned the countryside with interest, eager to take in all of the details she could of her home for the summer.

As she peered from the window, she perceived a man on horseback on the road ahead, deep in conversation with a young lad of twelve or thirteen years. The figure on horseback was upright, and very tall, so that the boy below was forced to crane his neck to answer the fellow's questions. Dressed in a dull waistcoat and breeches, his tall riding boots splattered with mud, the man on horseback looked to be an overseer of sorts, and the lad was very surely one of his workers. As they drew closer, Charlotte heard the figure on horseback curse at the lad below.

Charlotte had always been acutely sensitive to the distress of others, and quick to respond. Her kind and passionate nature meant that she would always take the part of those needing a defender. Now, she could not help herself and she glared at the man from her open window as they passed, feeling keenly the discomfiture of the lad, who bowed his head and seemed to be taking the verbal barrage meekly.

The man glanced up as the carriage passed, anger etched into his features, and his eyes at once picked out the angry young woman who glared at him from the open window of the carriage. His eyes were very dark, and his well-cut, yet unruly dark hair did little to soften the intensity of his return glare at Charlotte.

As his eyes met hers, time seemed to slow. She felt a little shock, as if a charge of lightning had surged between them. At once, a total stranger seemed to know her secrets, her fears, and her hopes, and worse, to understand the intense feeling that he had evoked in her. He held her gaze, a small smile forming on his lips. She could not pull away from his eyes. The world spun slowly around her. Then the carriage passed and he was gone from her view.

Charlotte drew back from the open window, aghast, and ashamed at the sudden awareness of her femininity on receiving that stare.

'Are you ill, Miss?' enquired Jane, who had seen nothing from her side of the carriage.

'Oh no, I'm very well. It is nothing!' And yet, an unexplained rose colored her face and she breathed deeply, willing her nerves to calm. It was ridiculous to react in this way to the stare of a stranger. And a labourer at that!

Anger mingled with shame rose up in her, to think that a mere estate worker could be so blatantly insolent to a woman, who was, very obviously, a guest of his master's. Charlotte decided at once that if she found the chance, she would mention the incident to her host. Let Sir Benedict Markham deal with the man! And she would certainly take good care to avoid the workers on her host's estate, lest she meet him again! And the poor lad! She was certain he could have done nothing to deserve such a censuring. She would certainly mention it to her host; she was determined!

As the fields and lanes sedately passed by her window, her anger dissipated. She blushed at having allowed the man to affect her so entirely! He had incited sensations in her that she was unused to feeling. At two and twenty, Charlotte had little experience of the world, and even less experience of vigorous young males who made her blush and wish to hide her face. Yet, despite her self-reproach, Charlotte felt inexpressibly drawn to the dark and boding countenance she could not erase from her mind, and continued the last few minutes of her journey, not enjoying the views of the great house as they drove in, but in discomforting memory of a pair of dark, soul-piercing eyes.

Three

Within a few minutes, the carriage had pulled up in front of an imposing and stately house. Delford seemed to boast two great wings, one to the west and one to the east. The driveway circled up to the front entrance, which was guarded by two formidable griffins and a great stone stairway. Either side of the house stretched rolling green hills and colourful gardens and, in the distance, there sat a little church, and a lake she could just make out through the window of the carriage. The footman swung the door open, lowered the steps, and handed Charlotte down onto the gravel driveway. Her maid followed with several hat boxes.

A young woman in fine, white India muslin came running down the steps to welcome her. Pink ribbons flailed gayly in her wake. 'Oh, you are here at last! I waited ever so long, Charlotte! Aunt Eliza is lying down in her room with the head-ache, and she says to tell you she is very sorry not to welcome you. But she will be down for dinner. My uncle is out on the estate, or doing business or something, so all you have is me.'

Charlotte laughed delightedly and greeted her cousin with an embrace and a kiss on the cheek. 'Just you will be quite acceptable for now. It has been a long journey. My dear cousin, you look well. How lovely it is to see you again.'

Servants trouped out of the front door to collect her luggage, while Charlotte followed her cousin up the steps and inside, and was ushered into a small, cosy parlour decorated in a tasteful bird's-egg blue with subtle gold trims.

'This is my own sitting-room. Do you not think it very handsome?' Lavinia waved her into a doorway without waiting for a reply. 'Now please, do sit down. No, here, this is nearer the fire,' she directed her cousin. 'Not that we need one, but I always have the servants make one up, for it looks so cosy. You must be fatigued to death! I hope your journey was not too horrid? I do hate a long journey, myself. So tedious!'

Smiling, Charlotte obligingly sat in the nearest chair, removed her bonnet and gloves, and studied the face opposite hers. Lavinia's colouring was very fair to Charlotte's darker golden brown, and her face was glowing and excited. Her figure had filled out since Charlotte had last seen her and she was looking delightfully plump and rosy cheeked.

Lavinia rang for some tea, then turned soulful blue eyes to Charlotte's hazel green ones. 'I was sorry to hear of your mama's passing. It seems only yesterday, yet it is past a year! I hope you are over the worst? But you are so thin, Charlotte! You are quite wan and pale. You are not in your usual looks at all!'

Charlotte looked away momentarily, not quite expecting this indelicate attack on her complexion and figure so soon after arriving. The loss of her looks in the last year had corresponded with the loss of her spirits, but she did not mention this to her cousin.

'I am sure I will gain some colour once I am outdoors again,' she assured her cousin. 'I shall walk as much as I can, if we are not engaged elsewhere.'

Lavinia shrugged. 'I shan't walk much with you, if it is still your habit to take such long walks. I cannot abide long walks! I am sure it is not good for one's ankles.' She looked Charlotte up and down critically. 'That is a rather pretty travelling dress,

Charlotte. But the colour is too sombre on you! You ought to wear rose, or jonquil, for they are very much in fashion this year! I have a new gown in jonquil. Do not you think it a divine colour? Did you bring many gowns? And tell me, how do you find your new stepmother? What is she like? Is she a woman of fashion? Is she very pretty?'

Charlotte was unsure whether to laugh at her cousin's ability to lead polite condolences so quickly around to the subject of fashion, or frown at the insensitive mention of her father and new mama. She repressed the urge to reprove her cousin and decided the difference of a few days might improve Lavinia's insensitivity. She remained silent, and Lavinia, oblivious to her cousin's subdued mood, continued to pepper Charlotte with trivial chatter regarding the local card parties and balls which she had attended, the gowns she had worn and the horses owned by her uncle, which she rode frequently.

Charlotte then recalled the mention of Sir Benedict Markham's sister. 'Is your aunt quite agreeable and pleasant, Lavinia? Does she suffer from headache frequently then?'

'Oh, she is pleasant enough, I suppose. I never met her when I was a child, for Papa and she did not get on, so we never visited them. Uncle asked her to live here as housekeeper after her husband died, but she is quite as tedious as an old maid! Besides, her health is quite indifferent, you know. She is an invalid, and abed half the time with some illness or other. But you will like her, I am sure. She is very prim and proper and boring, just like you, Charlotte!' Lavinia giggled.

'I may be accused of being "proper", just as a young lady ought, Cousin, but I do hope I am not so very boring,' Charlotte smiled.

Lavinia was contrite. 'Oh no, indeed, well, just a little, perhaps! You do always have your head in a book, and you care not for fashion and balls and society! I don't know how you will find yourself a husband, if you insist on refusing to show yourself off and engage young men in conversation!'

'You well know, Cousin, that I do not dislike balls, nor do I mind a pretty dress,' Charlotte remonstrated. 'But I choose not to parade myself around at parties and dinners, and would much prefer the company of a good novel or some great poetry, to engaging in silly banter with young men that have nothing solid in their heads and no great wisdom to impart.'

'You must marry sometime! You don't want to be a burden to your father and stepmother forever, you know,' warned her cousin.

Charlotte's stomach fluttered uncomfortably. The burden of a long year of loneliness weighed on her heart, and she had more than once considered that an offer of marriage, from the right man, would be the answer to her situation. But she was adamant she would never marry only for the sake of it and was determined not to be drawn into matrimony with the first brainless gentleman that asked her. Perhaps a less scrupulous woman would accept such an offer, if they didn't mind a witless creature for a husband, with no sense and even less personal appeal. But for herself, Charlotte determined never to accept an offer from anyone she did not love. Unbidden, the memory a pair of dark, piercing eyes arose, and she shook her head, annoyed with herself.

'Well,' she laughed lightly. 'If I can find a husband that can satisfy my very particular wants, then I shall be well satisfied.'

'And he should be a person of some rank, Charlotte,' her cousin noted. 'Rank means a title and that means the best society and balls and to be seen by the most important people!'

Charlotte raised her brows. 'Do you mean that, Lavinia? I would, for all the world, rather marry for love than for a title alone, and so should you, if you wish to be happy.'

Lavinia shrugged indelicately and shook her blonde curls. 'I wouldn't care,' she said. 'I only want to move in the best circles and be seen in the latest fashions. If I love my husband or do not, I shouldn't think it would matter much if I am satisfied in those things.'

Charlotte sighed and wisely pursued the topic no further. Diverting her thoughts, she turned the conversation to her absent host. 'And what is your uncle like? Is he kind to you?'

'I am sure I cannot complain,' replied her cousin. 'He provides for me very well. After all, Mama and Papa left me thirty thousand pounds, so I am not poor you know! I can have nice gowns and a good horse and all sorts of nice things. But he is a veritable old grump, and he is extremely vexing,' added Lavinia, frowning. Her eyes glinted. 'When Papa and Mama were alive, why I did not have ever so many rules then as I do now! My uncle does not understand that a young lady must be in society and not kept shut up at home. I must catch myself a husband!'

Charlotte sighed. Clearly, her cousin was still as silly as she was three years ago. If Lavinia was husband-hunting, then at this rate, no sensible man would have her!

'Does Sir Benedict really live here alone with his sister then? Are there no wife, no children?' asked Charlotte, eager to divert the conversation.

'Uncle spends all his days roaming about the estate, seeing to the animals. His lady friends are all the four-legged kind,' Lavinia laughed.

Charlotte was all amazement. 'But, is not your uncle quite advanced in years? Did he never marry at all?'

'No, never! I believe there was a lady once, several years ago. She jilted him. Or so Aunt Eliza told me. She said my uncle was very much in poor spirits after the event. I vaguely remember Mama and Papa discussing it when I was hardly ten years old. But I do not remember any details, and when I pressed her, Aunt Eliza was quite sharp with me and said it was not my business to know more. They must have had a frightful quarrel!'

'Who?' asked Charlotte, astonished. 'Your aunt and uncle?'

'No, silly, my uncle and the lady! Who *wouldn't* quarrel with him? My uncle is so disagreeable that I can hardly imagine any lady would want to be shut up with him for life!'

Charlotte wondered that a man of advancing years could have attempted to marry only once in his life. Perhaps Sir Benedict was too fastidious to find a wife suitable for his personality, she surmised. 'Do not your uncle and aunt have many acquaintances here then?' asked Charlotte.

'Why, we see so few families here that it is vastly dull!' complained Lavinia. 'The Lathams, our neighbours, are the only regular society I get. The Latham sisters are very stylish, and wear nothing but the finest gowns! But, stay, this will amuse you Charlotte; I think my uncle has his eye on one of them! She is always monopolising him at dinners! It is very droll to see. But you shall see it yourself, for they are to dine here tonight, to meet *you*, Charlotte. Miss Annabelle Latham is very fine-looking. She is reckoned the one of the most handsome ladies in the county, even though she is past her youth.'

Charlotte was intrigued. 'And you think your uncle will marry this Miss Latham? But he must be much older than the lady!'

'Oh yes!' cried Lavinia, 'she is only ten years older than I! It is quite shocking! But she seems to encourage his attentions. But I suppose at her advanced age, she must do what she can!'

'I hardly think that seven and twenty is so very advanced an age, Cousin,' laughed Charlotte. 'But I own that any woman might not be blamed for advancing her interests as best she can, especially if the gentleman is willing!'

Charlotte pondered on her own father's recent marriage and could understand that an older gentleman without a wife could become quite lonely, even with a lively niece to care for. Perhaps he would choose this Miss Latham. She sounded witless but beautiful, Charlotte thought, smirking to herself. The perfect combination for every man!

They finished their tea and Lavinia took Charlotte up to her room. She was in the east wing, alongside her cousin, and was shown into a very comfortable room with a window over the grounds at the front of the house.

'Dinner is at six o'clock promptly, Charlotte. We dine early here, for it is the country manner, you know! Do not forget we are to have guests. Put on a nice gown, for the Lathams will be in their finest!'

After her cousin left, Charlotte was relieved to sit for a while and take in her surroundings. Her room was tastefully decorated, and the view from her window enchanted her. For some time, she sat at the window seat, musing. She was a good deal disappointed to find her cousin just as silly as she had been three years ago, but she hoped her own influence, felt over the two months which she was to stay, would help Lavinia form less frivolous opinions, and gain a steadier character. Charlotte thought then of her mother, whose own kind and sensible character and reasonable opinions had influenced Charlotte's. She dabbed gently at her cheeks, where two tears had fallen, and she put such melancholy thoughts aside to dress for dinner.

For dinner she chose a plain white-on-white muslin, of good quality, not ostentatious, but soft and becoming to her slender figure. Conscious of there being other ladies present at table tonight, Charlotte went to some pains with her hair, adding in some small gold and mother-of-pearl pins that had been her mama's, and added finally a small gold cross. Satisfied that she would meet her host and his guests with dignity, she made her way downstairs to the drawing room where she could hear voices murmuring from within.

She had just stepped forward to grasp the door handle, when a slight movement to her left caught her eye and turning her head, she found herself looking straight into a very familiar pair of dark eyes.

'You!' she gasped.

He stood six feet away in the shadows of the hall, that same half smile curling his lip, the same knowing glance seeming to read her inmost thoughts. Charlotte at once realised her error, and dismayed beyond measure, tried to piece together her scattered thoughts, the clues she had missed. But there had been no clues, and Charlotte had made an honest mistake.

Her host paused, then came forward from the shadows, never taking his eyes from Charlotte's face, which was now suffused with a rosy red.

Annoyed with herself, Charlotte struggled for composure. "Why I— Please forgive me, Sir. I was startled for a moment. I did not see you there.'

He bowed briefly. 'Benedict Markham, at your service.'

She curtsied politely, a rosy blush colouring her cheeks. Glancing at her host's face, she quickly saw that he was taking his amusement at her expense and knew the effect he was having on her. A small flame of irritation lit in her breast.

He continued. 'Miss Milton, I presume. Welcome to Delford. It is a pleasure to make your acquaintance. I hope you had an — uneventful — journey?'

There was laughter behind his eyes and Charlotte could see he was enjoying her discomfiture. She struggled to repress the vexation rising in her breast. She did not know whether to laugh or cry, or stomp her foot! She attempted, finally, to answer civilly and make no mention of the incident which was the cause of her heightened colour at this moment.

'Thank you, Sir. My journey was... mostly uneventful. You have a beautiful home.' Pleased with herself for showing no emotion other than polite interest, she added, 'I am on my way to find my cousin. I think this is the drawing room?'

Sir Benedict stepped forward, his eyes still on her, opening the door for her, and she moved ahead of him into a large, well-appointed room. In various positions about the room were a young man and several ladies, two of whom were quite tall, and dressed in what Charlotte thought was quite overstated finery, much more stylish than her own modest gown, and were both decked with fine-looking gems and gold chains. Another lady, of mature years and dressed in a less showy gown and a mob cap, sat quietly at the window some distance away, and looked up in welcome as Charlotte entered the room with her host.

Sir Benedict's breath was warm on her neck. Before she could gather her wits and find Lavinia, she felt a warm hand press lightly on her back, and she was guided firmly toward her cousin. Then the warmth on her back was withdrawn as imperceptibly as it had appeared and, in its place, cold shivers ran along her skin. All eyes in the room turned toward herself.

Sir Benedict made general introductions. Charlotte dropped a polite curtsey to the room. One icy set of brown eyes turned away immediately, while the others looked on in curiosity and varying degrees of welcome. Lavinia claimed her arm at once and led her away. Sir Benedict stepped back and began talking to the fine young woman who had disdainfully ignored Charlotte's entry. She had her hand on his arm and was talking intently, smiling into his eyes.

Like the other ladies, Lavinia was dressed in a modish gown of excellent quality, Charlotte perceived. The deep jonquil silk suited her cousin's fair hair and she glowed in the firelight. Charlotte felt suddenly drab beside her.

Her cousin led her first to a very fine, although foppish-looking, gentleman, whom she introduced as Sir Frank Latham. Charlotte noted that he had made a most liberal use of powder in his ginger coloured hair, and wore his sideburns fashionably long.

She stifled a smile and curtsied politely. 'How do you do, Sir.'

'How do you do, Miss Milton,' replied the foppish young man. He made a clumsy bow with much flourish. 'Your cousin tells me you stay with us at least a two-month visit! I hope we will have the pleasure of your company before long at Highview. We always give many dinner parties, you know, that sort of thing, and picnics in the summer. Your fair cousin, you know, is always kind enough to honour us with her presence,' he added, bowing deeply once again toward Lavinia. 'You must be of the party when next we give a dinner.'

Charlotte gently smiled her thanks. 'I would be honoured Sir, if your sisters would be so good as to invite me.'

The ginger-headed gentleman smiled broadly and bowed

once more. 'Yes, indeed, yes, Capital! We shall look forward to it. Any friend of your fair cousin's would be welcome, you know!' To this he added another bow toward Lavinia, who blushed prettily and half-hid her smiling mouth behind her hand.

Sir Frank retreated briefly to answer the summons of his sisters, and Charlotte watched him flounce across the room with amusement. 'He seems an amiable gentleman,' she smiled, and Lavinia laughed.

'Oh, he is pleasant enough, I suppose. He is very attentive to me, you know. So, you have met my uncle,' she added brightly, glancing at Sir Benedict, who was listening attentively, raptly, to the tall young lady who was still grasping his arm. Charlotte supposed that this was the much talked of Annabelle Latham. She appeared to be around six or seven and twenty, and was what was commonly called "a great beauty". With her fine, tall figure, dark hair, and handsome features, she was a striking woman. But her demeanour was one of hauteur and disdain when she glanced at Charlotte, and Charlotte turned away, somewhat piqued at the sight of Sir Benedict clearly enjoying this woman's conversation.

Lavinia continued. 'And how do you find him? Is he not a stern and severe-looking creature? I will ask him tonight if we may make a picnic party next week. I'm sure he will say we cannot! Uncle always takes pains to ensure I have no pleasure at all, I declare!' She said this loud enough for Sir Benedict to hear, and he glanced her way.

'If you were more demure in your attitude, Lavinia, and less scatter-brained, I would allow more occasions for your pleasure. As it is, you need to curb your tongue and act in a way that is more ladylike. Perhaps your cousin will set a much-needed example for you in this regard.' His eyes caught Charlotte's own, and she quickly looked away, confusion muddling her thoughts.

Lavinia sighed. 'See how vexing he is, Charlotte! I do think

Papa made a dreadful mistake sending me here!'

Sir Frank rejoined the ladies just at this moment, and hearing Lavinia's remark, shook his head in mock sternness. 'How could your dear father ever be accused of making a mistake, Miss Markham, which would bring into our company beauty of the highest degree and manners of the softest, and most feminine aspect imaginable. You do yourself no credit at all, and in fact, as much as it gives me pain to disagree with one so eminently agreeable, I do disagree with you, absolutely. It is too harsh, *too* harsh indeed, to say that your father, God rest his soul, made a mistake in sending you to us!' He punctuated this speech with a deep bow, furnished with all sorts of flourishes.

Lavinia cast her eyes demurely downward. 'You are too kind, Sir.'

Charlotte resisted the urge to roll her eyes heavenward, but she did not need to, for Sir Frank had at that moment accosted a nearby servant regarding the fire, which was not built high enough to keep Miss Markham from feeling the cold, though Charlotte thought the evening warm. He left, to follow this through with the servant, and Charlotte sighed.

She gathered her thoughts, which by this time were divided over two subjects, one of which involved the young man who had just left them, the other of more pressing urgency. She leaned toward Lavinia and scolded in low tones. 'You misled me, Cousin, and I do not thank you for it! You made your uncle out to be an elderly gentleman in his dotage and near death! He is not nearly so old as you pretended! He does not have even a hint of grey hair!' she accused, half-amused and half-vexed.

Lavinia had the grace to look chastened. 'Well, if I did say *something* like it, it is only because he acts like an old fossil from his collection,' she returned with spirit. 'And besides, he acts like a doting old father, trying to keep me from society. Conversation with Sir Frank is all I can look forward to for the next hundred years, if my uncle had his way!'

'Dearest, I am sure your uncle has firm reasons for attempting to keep you in check. In fact, I am sure I have no sympathy for you at all on that score! Keeping you out of trouble is probably going to be his constant employment,' she said wryly.

Only partially attending to Lavinia's tart reply, Charlotte was watching the object of her cousin's derision, in case he should come this way. He caught her eye, and delivered her a slight knowing smile. He was still laughing at her! Insufferable! She turned away at once, her cheeks suffused with a becoming pink blush. He was obviously determined to make her suffer for her mistake earlier in the day, and she regretted her impulsive glare from her carriage window. He was no doubt amused by it, at her expense! She repressed her irritation and returned her attention to Lavinia who was pulling on her arm.

'Now, Charlotte, do come and meet Sir Frank's sisters, and my Aunt Eliza.'

Lavinia's aunt, whom Charlotte supposed was the quiet lady sitting down, seemed eager to make her acquaintance. Lavinia obligingly drew her cousin toward the lady who was now standing with some effort, to receive her brother's guest.

Immediately, Charlotte liked the look of Elizabeth. The older woman had a fine, clear complexion and dark hair and eyes like her brother, although there was also more than a hint of grey at her temples. But, Charlotte thought, there was an open and pleasant look on her face, very dissimilar to that of her younger sibling.

'I am very pleased to meet you, Mrs Granger. I am most sorry to hear of your loss.'

'Oh, please make nothing of it, Miss Milton. It was many years ago now, and I have no excuse not to be a cheerful widow! I am very content here. I am a partial invalid, as you see, and frequently unwell, making it inconvenient to leave my room, for which dear Benedict makes great allowances.

Because of my brother's kindness, I have a home and company around me which I would not have but for him.'

'And how do you find my cousin? Is she impossible to manage?' asked Charlotte with an arch smile at her cousin. Lavinia laughed and made a face.

'Aunt Eliza has given up trying to manage me, I think! But I do *try* to be good, Aunt!'

'I know you do, my dear. I am trying to teach her to run a household, Miss Milton, although she does not attend very seriously,' Elizabeth added. 'I may just as well try to teach Daisy the cow to do it!'

'Oh, do not make sport of me just now, Aunt Eliza, for I cannot reply in kind, as I must introduce Charlotte to Miss Latham and her sister. Excuse us, Aunt.'

Eliza, laughing, bid them go immediately. Pulling her by the hand, Lavinia led Charlotte over to the ladies, who were now seated with Sir Benedict on the sofa by the fire. The latter was sprawling, quite relaxed, on the sofa by the younger sister, but he stood at their approach. Feeling his eyes upon her, Charlotte tried to focus on the young women before her. They looked less than interested to meet her, but the two women both stood also, and made polite curtsies before looking her up and down.

The women were very fine-looking, and beside them, Charlotte again felt quite drab. Miss Annabelle Latham wore a rich ruby satin gown of the highest quality and latest fashion. The younger sister, Sophia Latham, was as ginger-headed as her brother, but had less obvious beauty, with her pale blue eyes and sallow skin.

The sisters made a few desultory comments about the weather and the length of Charlotte's stay at Delford, then turned quickly to conversing among themselves again. Charlotte could not but help notice a look of speculative dislike on the face of the older sister, and her quick glance at Sir Benedict. Gathering quickly that the older sister probably considered Sir Benedict the property of herself, Charlotte laughed inwardly. Miss Annabelle Latham need have no qualms about Charlotte entertaining any thoughts of becoming Lady Markham, she thought cynically.

'He is all yours, and welcome to him,' she thought, as Lavinia led her back to the young gentleman standing at the fireplace, who was watching her cousin with adoring eyes. She was aware of the tittering laughter behind her which came from the ladies to whom she had just been introduced, and the deeper, masculine tones of the man who was her host. She thrust down her feelings of mingled anger and shame and tried to attend to her cousin as she chattered on about the picnic they were planning in a few days.

Sir Frank was very attentive to Lavinia and seemed somewhat taken by her youthful beauty. He stared at her as she chattered on, with a smile on his full, pink lips, and nodded and bowed every other moment, agreeing with every item that came from her cousin's mouth, whether it was contradictory to the last comment or not.

'As silly a gentleman as ever there was,' thought Charlotte wryly. 'No doubt he is charmed by my cousin, and she by him, it seems. Well, if they are both as silly as each other, it will be a perfect match, I do not doubt.' Charlotte smiled to herself and wished that she could teach some sense to her cousin. In the course of her visit, she would certainly try.

Dinner was announced, and Charlotte found herself seated between Sophia Latham and Lavinia. Miss Latham was seated to Sir Benedict's left, at the top of the table, affording Charlotte a view of all the latter's coquettish glances and smiles at her host. Happy to find that she would not have to make more polite conversation with a man who alternately made her more aware of her femininity than she had ever been before and agitated her with his knowing look that seemed to divine all her secrets, she turned to her companion and made stilted, polite conversation for the duration of the meal. Miss Sophia was not as haughty as her older sister, and made tolerable company, if Charlotte had been disposed to enjoy it. She managed to keep her eyes averted from those of her host, except once, when she happened to glance up and see that his eyes were on her. Disconcerted, she looked away immediately, quite shocked at how a simple glance could make her feel so self-conscious.

After a pleasant and simple dessert of iced fruits, the party retired to the drawing room and Sir Frank immediately prevailed upon his older sister to play the pianoforte and sing for them. Miss Annabelle Latham needed no second encouragement. She almost pranced to the piano, whereupon she took up some music and began to play and sing. Admitting the older woman to be an accomplished musician, Charlotte was nonetheless amused to observe that Miss Latham's audience seemed comprised of one person only. The lady cast simpering looks in Sir Benedict's direction whenever she lifted her eyes from the instrument, and seemed to perform for him alone. Sir Benedict, however, seemed little intrigued by the coquettish looks she was throwing his way, and engaged himself in conversation with Sophia Latham. This development obliged Miss Latham to sing even louder, shrilling uncomfortably on the high notes, and to glare at her sister whenever she thought the party was not sufficiently admiring her. Secretly, Charlotte chuckled to herself, her spirits somewhat revived after watching such an obvious display of attention seeking, and wondered which of the sisters Sir Benedict was really interested in.

Eliza interrupted her reverie with much the same thought. 'Annabelle is in very fine voice this evening,' she observed smilingly, throwing a knowing look at Sir Benedict, 'and my brother is doing a very admirable job of inciting her to even higher notes.'

Charlotte laughed, then covered her mouth, ashamed of her unkind response, and glanced at her host's sister. 'Please forgive me. I did not mean to laugh at your brother or Miss Latham. But the lady does seem somewhat piqued at the lack of attention from certain members of the audience. Is it true they will marry? My cousin mentioned that your brother has been courting the lady.'

A look which Charlotte could not interpret passed over Eliza's face. 'I think your cousin may be misinterpreting my brother's attention, although I am not privy to his thoughts. I suspect it is by no means his intention, although the lady herself might wish it otherwise.'

A feeling arose in Charlotte that was entirely unexplained, and suddenly her enjoyment of the song increased. But before she could explore such feelings, the song ended and her thoughts were interrupted first in applause for the lady's performance, and then by the advance of a tall, lean figure who came and leaned casually on the mantel piece beside them. Charlotte was once again aware of a slight colour in her cheeks and a warmth spreading through her as he stood next to her. She was very close to his person, and he seemed deliberately to lean in and exacerbate her discomfort.

'Miss Milton.' His voice was like melted chocolate. She breathed in a slight scent of pine and cinnamon. Her heart pounded. She struggled not to turn and walk across the room.

'Sir Benedict.' She kept her eyes averted.

'Your cousin tells me you are not a keen horsewoman.'

Charlotte was somewhat startled at the choice of subject, and looked up at him in surprise. 'No, Sir. Although I was taught to ride, I do not get much practice at home. I own I prefer both my feet on the ground,' she added with a self-deprecating laugh. 'I much prefer to walk.'

'That is a great pity. I am of the opinion that every lady should ride. While you are here, it would be an opportunity to improve your skills. Lavinia is a fine horsewoman. You can ride out with us tomorrow, before breakfast. You may have Eliza's mare, Ariadne. My sister does not ride at all now, due to her indifferent health, so she will not mind.' It was more of command, than a polite offer, and Charlotte felt both coerced, and alarmed at the thought of spending a morning in this man's company. She determined at once to refuse. She turned to him and opened her mouth. His knowing glance caught and held her own gaze.

'I am much obliged to you Sir, but I cannot — that is, I must — I wish to write letters tomorrow morning. Letters home. I must write to my father and stepmother,' she stumbled in a little rush.

His lips curled in a slight smile. 'I understand that your father is abroad, Miss Milton? You would do much better to wait to write your letters, for he will be unable to receive them very promptly. I will have your mare saddled and ready at eight o'clock. Do you have a habit? You may borrow one from my sister if you need it.'

Charlotte gaped at him, then turned her head quickly. The audacity of the man! However, he had discovered her ruse and she was both annoyed and defeated. She tried again. 'Thank you, Sir. But as I said, I am not a keen horsewoman and rarely ride. I prefer to write my letters, as I have friends to whom I must write to in addition to my father.' Hoping he would leave her side, she waited quietly, willing her nerves to stop jangling about so, and cast a quick look in Miss Annabelle Latham's direction. The lady had remained at the pianoforte and was eyeing Charlotte and Sir Benedict in a most unfriendly manner. Charlotte dropped her gaze.

'I did not intend to force you to ride out with us, Miss Milton, but certainly, I would not wish to detain you from your letter writing, if it is so urgent. Another time perhaps.'

A quick, furtive glance confirmed her suspicion. He was once again laughing at her! Angrily, she turned her head and stayed silent. Bowing politely, he took his leave and moved smoothly away to the side of his niece and Sophia Latham. Watching them covertly, Charlotte felt bereft, and a sudden depression of spirits rose in her. Confused and puzzled at herself, she calmed her nerves and tried to feel the proper amount of relief at her dismissal. A morning in the company of Sir Benedict was not likely to soothe her already upset nerves. As much as she might have welcomed the fresh air, her decision was prudent, given how she felt most unsettled around him. Tomorrow, she would avoid Sir Benedict until she could face him with equanimity and her nerves were under control!

The next day she arose very early and went to the window to admire the early morning scene before her. She washed, helped herself into her pale blue morning dress, and went downstairs to see if there was tea available. No one else was about in the morning room, and she sighed with satisfaction. She had always delighted in solitude before breakfast, and often rose before everyone else. She rang for tea and some dry toast, and went to sit by the long window overlooking the stables. The sun was just peeking over the roof and its golden rays dressed everything with a delicate buttercup tint. Stable hands were moving about, bringing horses into the yard, and saddling them up. The beasts stomped and snorted impatiently, leaving trails of hot, curling breath poised in the crisp air. The morning was fresh and inviting, and she suddenly felt inclined to walk before breakfast.

Forgetting the letters that she was supposedly writing, she finished the delicate jasmine tea, and ran upstairs to find a light shawl, and ran down again, clutching a book under her arm. She had almost reached the foot of the stairs, when she cannoned into a hard, warm body whose arms held her firmly her before she could fall. A soft grunt, as the air was knocked out of him, made her feel both guilty and mortified. The scent of pine and cinnamon threatened to overtake her senses and she found herself shaking, not in fear at the thought of falling the last two steps, but in a most unladylike reaction to the gentleman, dressed in fine riding attire, whose flesh was so near to her own. His well-polished, black riding boots mesmerised her. She could not look up.

Collecting herself, she pulled her arm from his grasp less than gently, and stepped away, one stair below that which he was standing on. Then she made the mistake of looking up at him. His expression was one of mingled surprise and amusement. He towered over her and she felt even more keenly the embarrassment of her situation.

'Has no one ever taught you not to run on the stairs, Miss Milton?' He mocked her in chocolate tones, scolding her like a schoolgirl.

She coloured and said nothing, looking at her hands, which were bare, and her at book which had been knocked to the floor.

'Allow me.' He stepped past her to the hall floor, and retrieved her book.

She wordlessly held her hand out for it, but he was reading its title. A glint in his dark eye, he opened the book, and read a few lines, much to Charlotte's chagrin.

' *"The first was a fair maid, and Love her name; The second was Ambition, pale of cheek, ever watchful with fatigued eye"*. And are you the first maid, Miss Milton, or the second? You do look a trifle pale of cheek this morning. And you are certainly motivated by "ambition", even if it is just to avoid riding out with us this morning.'

He was openly laughing, and Charlotte snatched at the book, mortified that he thought she was avoiding the ride for any reason but that she gave last evening. But he was not finished with her. He held the book out of reach. 'So, you have a partiality for poetry, Miss Milton? You surprise me! But perhaps Mr Keats inspires your pen to write early morning letters? I hope you do not plan to write letters without paper and pen and ink? That would be quite difficult, indeed,' he observed in an amused voice. 'But perhaps you merely compose them in your head, to be written later? Although I hardly think that Keats would be the inspiration for a letter to your father, for he is too much engaged with the senses, to be rational. Unless you write, not to your father, but to an admirer?'

Charlotte hardly knew how to contain her anger. 'Indeed, I do not write to any other than my father and stepmother. As to admirers, I have none, Sir, and writing to them would be most unladylike,' she said indignantly. 'I was only going into the garden for air before I begin to write my father a letter. I beg that you will return my book,' she finished, again holding her hand out, looking very discomposed, and cross at herself for letting him know how discomposed she was.

He smiled but did not hand her the item, still thumbing through its pages. 'So, you have no admirers? I am all puzzlement, Miss Milton. But perhaps you turn them away with a sharp comment and a stern glare, and judge them wanting before they even open their poor mouths?'

He threw her a knowing, sardonic look which she interpreted immediately, and blushed with anger. She knew perfectly well to which incident he was referring. 'I only glare at people who treat other people with disdain, Sir, and who treat those below them in life, without the kindness they ought to receive. I do not — that is, I cannot — I do not judge unless I am certain I see clearly what is before my own eyes,' she finished, stumbling over her words as his eyes locked with her own.

'Perhaps you judge too quickly and see not as clearly as you imagine. I suggest you wait a little time before coming to conclusions and you might find one or two of your admirers might suit you after all,' he continued, a tiny smirk lifting his mouth. He was clearly unconcerned with her opinion of him and made no attempt to explain his business with the young lad she had seen him berate the previous day.

Charlotte decided that she would never ask him about the incident and would never be induced to reform her impression of him as the most odious man she had ever met! 'I find that my opinion, once formed, is seldom repealed, Sir Benedict. But I do not consider myself a hasty judge; rather, I fancy myself a discerning one.'

He chuckled, not being much intimated by her glare. 'You should take care, Miss Milton, for if you go about proclaiming yourself judge of others, you will be called nice, and over-fastidious, rather than discerning. You may give offence where you do not intend.'

'I do not intend rudeness. I simply and justly judge people by their actions, not by their words. I find people's actions far more telling than anything they can say. And I do not send away anyone who would wish my company, without first making sure that I am just in doing so. But I find that there are many people who would wish to know me, that I do not wish to know, on those grounds. I do not feel guilty Sir, for spurning the company of those of whom there is little good to say, or who treat others with unkindness and unfairness.' Her eyes blazed at him, their tawny depths sparkling with anger.

He tilted his head to one side and considered her, his eyes laughing. 'How do you get on at a ball then, Miss Milton? Do you not lack partners to stand up with? If you are so fastidious, you must find card parties and dances exceedingly dull!'

He was making sport of her and she resented it deeply. She knew not whether to be angry or chagrined at his response, so she remained silent.

He turned her book in his hands and closed it quietly. 'Well, I do not mind Keats myself, and but I do not think him a good choice for you, as he is too romantic for such a stern and serious young lady. He does not match your character at all, I think.' Holding the book back out to her, his face was serious, and his eyes seemed to look into her soul.

Charlotte snatched the book and then, feeling exposed and too open at his gaze, swallowed and dropped her eyes. She played with the edges of her book, tracing the outlines with a small finger. His eyes followed her finger for a moment, then seized on her downturned face. She was aware of his consideration of her, and felt the more exposed for it, as if she somehow should hide. But it was strange that she wanted to hide her face in his shoulder. 'You think such poetry is opposite to my character and therefore I would not enjoy it,' she said in a low voice. 'But you judge my character only from what you have seen in a few hours, Sir Benedict. If I judge, I try not to judge without cause. But you are correct. I *am* stern — with those who mock me, and who are unkind enough to point out my character flaws.'

He did not have the grace to look discomposed. 'If I offended you, then I am sorry for it,' he replied, blandly. 'I did not mean to imply that your character was flawed, merely that you judge too hastily, perhaps. Yes, I do think that is a flaw, Miss Milton, but perhaps not so very dreadful a one,' he added. 'I am sure your character is without fault in every other matter. But only time will tell,' he added, the glint in his eye taunting her once again, although she perceived it was not without a certain softness.

Charlotte stepped away from her host and backed toward the doorway. 'But I have many character flaws,' she said as lightly as she could manage, 'two of which you are familiar with — you have discovered that I run too fast down staircases and am prone to reading romantic poetry instead of attending to the things I ought to be doing. In these things, at least, I cannot defend myself.'

'Oh, I don't know if those constitute offences so very grave, Miss Milton; I shall turn a blind eye to both, provided you take care on my stairwells, as I cannot have you falling and breaking a limb!'

He was smiling, the way a devil smiles at an innocent, she thought. She pulled her shawl more tightly about her. 'If you will excuse me, I wish to get some air before breakfast. And — and write my letters.'

Sir Benedict bowed gravely. 'By all means, Miss Milton.'

Charlotte followed his tall, retreating figure with her eyes as he walked away, puzzled as to the odd sensation in her stomach, which was more like a soft fluttering than anger.

~~*~~

Conscience stricken, she decided against the garden after all, and spent the next hour upstairs in her room, pen, rather than book, in hand. Letters completed, and her mild guilt assuaged, she congratulated herself on doing her duty. She gave her letters to the footman, and decided to walk into the village for the fresh air and exercise. She went in search of Lavinia to see if she would accompany her, but found she was still out riding with her uncle.

Donning a spencer and bonnet, she set off, the morning sun flickering long trails of light and shadow behind her as she walked. After a few minutes, the exercise had rendered her cheeks a becoming rose, and brightened her eyes. She made good time to the village and slowed to enjoy the bustling scenes. It was not unlike her own dear little village at home and the thought gave her a sharp little pang of homesickness. Pushing it away, she paused to admire some bonnets in the window of a store.

As she did so she became conscious of raised voices. A very handsome young man of around five and twenty stood with what appeared to be his manservant and horse in the street beside her. The young man had been conversing with his manservant in an angry tone. Now he took something from the other man, which looked to Charlotte like a roll of pound notes. She was about to look away politely when the young man looked up and caught her eye. His look was most impertinent, and she felt indignant as he eyed her with open curiosity. Then, perhaps realising his impudence, he bowed slightly and turned away to his manservant again. Disturbed, and wishing to leave them to their private business, she started back on the road to the hall.

Passing some well-kept cottages, which she assumed were estate cottages for tenant farmers and workers, she walked a little more, enjoying the sun on her face. She bent to smell some flowers which lined the lane in a profusion of purple, then stood again. Two small figures rounded the curve of the little lane in front of her. As they came closer, Charlotte curiously noted the young lad, who was leading by the hand a small girl of about three or four years. Both children were ill-dressed, although clean. The little girl was clutching a flower.

'Good morning,' said Charlotte, and she stooped to smile at the little girl as she passed. She raised her eyes to the young man and startled slightly. 'Oh, Good morning!'

The lad stopped and nodded politely. 'G'morning, Miss,' he greeted her.

Charlotte smiled. 'I think I saw you yesterday. You were on the road which goes to the Delford estate, talking to a man. He seemed angry with you.' She hoped she had not offended the lad.

He nodded again. 'Yes, Miss.'

'I hope he — the man, was not too harsh?' she queried.

The boy looked sheepish. 'No Miss, I mean, I am sorry to anger the Master, Miss.'

'I am sure you could not have done anything too bad, for him to scold you in that manner?' queried Charlotte, hoping to find out a little more. She keenly wanted to justify her first impression of the man who put her so much out of ease, and felt certain that he was fault.

'I kilt one of his rabbits, off his property, what used to be our hunting land, Miss. He was right to give me what for, Miss. But my little sister was hungry and I thought it would be alright.

We dun always get enough food, Miss, what with the enclosures and all.'

Charlotte knew that many estates were now enclosing what used to be common land, where the village people and workers could hunt game to add to their limited food supplies. Such land was necessary for the welfare of the poor, and Charlotte felt her anger rise at Sir Benedict's apparent lack of concern for his own estate workers. She did not reveal her feelings on her face however, and hid her ire by bending to look more closely at the little girl.

'Is this your sister?' She bent to see the child better. The child was a little grubby and quite thin. The girl's large blue eyes looked at her silently. Charlotte straightened and addressed the boy again. 'What is your name?'

'James, Miss. James Wilcox. I live there,' he said, pointing to the cottages.

'I am Miss Milton. I am staying with my cousin, Miss Markham. At Delford. Do you know her? Maybe you have seen her with her uncle?'

'Yes, Miss, I seen her. She rides a brown mare, Miss, and she lives with Sir at the big house. Everyone notices when she goes by, on account of her being pretty an' all. Polly likes to watch her ride, dun you Polly?' he asked the little girl.

The child nodded solemnly and held out her flower. 'It my flower. I got a nice flower, see?' The child offered up the flower for inspection.

Charlotte bent over to examine the bloom and touched the petals gently. 'It's a very lovely flower, Polly.'

Standing upright, she saw the boy looking nervously toward the cottages. The bundle he carried was clutched tightly to his chest. It had an odd, heavy look, and she again felt all the difficulty of their sad situation. She refrained from comment on the bundle, so as not to embarrass the boy. 'Do you work for Sir Benedict?' asked Charlotte, trying to draw the boy out.

'Yes Miss. Our Pa died and my Mam is poorly, so she needs

me and my brother to look out for her and the baby. Not Polly, Miss, we have another sister. She's only six months old. I work on the estate Miss, cleaning the horses' stalls and such. And workin' in the fields when its hay time. My brother, Tom, he dun like me doin' work for the estate, but its good clean work Miss, and pays alright.'

Charlotte's heart went out to the mother who was looking after four children, who obviously did not get enough food. She determined to talk to Sir Benedict about them and see what might be done, but then she checked herself, feeling that he might not take interference in estate matters well, given that the boy was poaching illegally, however hungry he might be. But she would certainly try to do something for them while she was here. Opening her reticule, she handed the boy the few coins she had on her person. 'Please take these, James, and give them to your mother.'

The boy's eyes told Charlotte everything. 'Yes Miss. Thank'ee Miss.'

'Perhaps I will see you again. Goodbye, Polly!'

'Good day, Miss,' he said, nodding respectfully, and tugging at his sister's arm. 'Polly, look sharp. Mam is after us.'

They moved on up the lane towards the cottages and Charlotte saw a woman come out to meet them. Noting which cottage they went into, Charlotte turned down the lane and continued on, in deep thought. Once she reached the edges of Delford, Charlotte descended the hill into the estate grounds and walked to the hall via the pretty little path to one side of the house. Here, she found Elizabeth, sitting in the arbour with her sewing bag. She looked up at Charlotte's approach.

'Miss Milton! I hope you had a pleasant walk? You have missed breakfast, I'm afraid. Mrs. Ransom is very particular about having the breakfast cleared away so she can get on with her other tasks. We like to humour her, you know. She has been here for many years. But Lavinia and I always take luncheon when we are at home. I am sure you must be hungry.

Will you accompany me inside?'

Charlotte held her arm for the older woman to grasp. 'I did enjoy my walk, but I am sorry to be so late back. It is such a beautiful morning and I became diverted with the scenery. I do love to walk at this time of year! Have Sir Benedict and my cousin returned from their ride?'

Elizabeth responded in the affirmative, and Charlotte paused briefly, uncertain of how to broach the questions she wished to ask. 'I met young James Wilcox on the road coming back. And his sister.'

Elizabeth nodded and frowned. 'Yes, young James is a good boy. You may see him around the estate. Benedict employs the boy here, in the fields and stables. It is very sad about his father. Old Mr Wilcox has quite recently passed away, you know. His poor widow is left with the four of them to feed. I cannot go to visit Mrs Wilcox — it is too far for me to go alone, and Lavinia does not like to accompany me. I believe Mrs Wilcox is not well, and with three young ones to care for, I am afraid it is not a good outlook for them. My brother does what he can, I suppose,' she finished, shaking her head.

'But cannot they all be given work on the estate? Did Mr Wilcox work for your brother too?'

Elizabeth sighed. 'Indeed, my brother has been all too kind to the Wilcox family, but I believe there was some difference of opinion with the older son, and Tom Wilcox now refuses to take the employment offered by my brother. They are both determined at all costs to be stubborn and neither will back down. I don't know all of the particulars,' said Eliza, pausing, 'but I am sure my brother is right on his part, and it is his estate, so he may hire and fire whom he pleases.'

Charlotte quietly digested this information and refrained from questioning further, in case it would be considered bad manners by her host's sister. Rather, she changed the topic and shortly thereafter the two women went in to wait for luncheon to be served.

Seven

Charlotte found her cousin at the glass, and almost ready to go down for her meal.

'You ought to have come with us, you silly thing,' Lavinia admonished, adjusting the pins in her hair, 'but you must come next time. We cannot ride tomorrow, for my uncle says he cannot spare the groom to ride with us, but next week we will all ride together, and then I can show you all the best places to walk.'

'You know I am a nervous rider, Lavinia dearest. I prefer to walk, but please ride any day which suits you, and do not worry about me, for I am very content with my book for company.'

'I do think you have your head in a book more than is good for you, I declare! You will miss everything if you never lift your head from your silly books!'

Charlotte merely smiled at this and did not take Lavinia's mocking to heart. She knew her cousin was a keen rider and did not begrudge her the pleasure. Nor did she mind being taken to task for having "her head in a book", for as much as Lavinia was a keen horsewoman, Charlotte took much pleasure in her books, and admitted this frankly to anyone who might accuse her of the crime of reading!

She supposed her liking of books and dislike of riding was

due to her father's keeping no horses at home suitable for her to ride. Her papa had two horses for his carriage, and one for his rounds, which was of a size and girth unsuitable for ladies. Besides that, her mama had been a great reader and so Charlotte had been brought up on a steady diet of history, poetry, novels, and less to her liking, Fordyce's Sermons. But poetry became her favourite escape, although her Papa scolded her periodically for not reading rather more of the previously mentioned sermons, and fewer of what he called "frivolous" novels and poetry books.

Lavinia, who by her own admission had never had much inclination for the printed word, chose riding and being seen at every opportunity, over books, and could not understand why her cousin was indifferent to it. She turned from the glass and began to rummage about in a pretty jewel box. Pulling out a little necklace, she held it out for Charlotte to fasten for her.

'You will never marry if you read too much, Charlotte. Nobody shall want you if you are a bluestocking! I suppose you are so dull because you do not get to town! If you were in town you would have no time for books! There would be too many plays to attend, and the theatre, and opera! Oh, I do wish Uncle would let me have a season in town! I long for some fun!'

Charlotte, fastening the pretty gold cross in place for her cousin, raised her brows. 'Thank you for the advice but I think I prefer to keep my books and be called a bluestocking, and take my chances finding a husband,' she said drily. 'But I am sure Sir Benedict will take you to town soon, perhaps when you are seventeen? You must be given a come out, surely?'

'Oh, but I came out two years ago! I was just turned fifteen.'

'That is very young indeed,' said Charlotte, 'I would have thought—'

'Oh, don't fuss so, Charlotte. Mama thought I was ready and Papa, well, Papa did everything Mama told him to. Papa was to have given me a Season in town directly,' she added sadly, 'but then he died and I never got to London. I would have got into

Almacks and gone to Hyde Park and every good place! Papa said he would arrange it all. But it was not to be. All the gowns I could have worn! The gentlemen I would have danced with!'

Charlotte was grieved to think that her cousin appeared moved more by the loss of her Season, than by the loss which had made her an orphan, but she said nothing.

'Did you know, Charlotte,' continued Lavinia, 'that Uncle says I may not be married until I am eighteen! But I think that is old fashioned and silly. Why, my particular friend Mary Lawton was married at fifteen, and so are many other girls!'

Charlotte sighed as they made their way to the door. 'I am sure he is only trying to protect you from the wrong sort of suitors. You *are* an heiress, you know, and that could make you a target for unsavoury gentlemen. I am sure he knows what he is doing, dear.'

'But I shall never find a husband if I am not allowed into society. I don't want to wait another year! I shall be an old maid by that time, if Uncle had his way!'

Charlotte placed a placatory hand on her cousin's arm. 'You have the threefold advantage of beauty, youth and fortune; you need not fear being unmarried, dearest. You have your pick of young men, and your uncle, I am sure, is quite rational in his setting eighteen as the proper age for marriage. Surely you do not wish to rush into an engagement at a young age, then spend the rest of your life regretting an acceptance of the first man that came along? I think your uncle is extremely prudent, my dear.'

'Yes, Charlotte,' sighed her cousin. 'But still, it is very unfair.'

Charlotte murmured agreement with her cousin so as not to hurt her feelings, but she secretly thought Sir Benedict might be wise to keep his young charge from becoming known as a silly flirt if he was intending to find her a husband.

~~*~~

At four o'clock the tea things were brought in, and this event coincided with the entrance of the Misses Latham, their brother, and a Miss Anne Smart, a young lady of superior education and breeding, who was visiting the family and was included in their party. She had, Sophia told her in whispers, twenty thousand pounds, no relatives, and lived with an aunt. Miss Smart had an ingratiating manner when in conversation with others, Charlotte observed to herself, and a simpering quality that Charlotte did not much like.

The Latham and the Markham families were on such intimate terms as would make a visit at any time of day quite acceptable and the Misses Latham most unashamedly accepted Eliza's somewhat restrained invitation to take tea with them, in a manner which indicated an assumed familiarity, perhaps somewhat exaggerated in the presence of Charlotte.

The finely dressed older Miss Latham quickly enquired regarding the attendance of Sir Benedict, and upon discovering that he would not be making an appearance, she soon retreated to the window with her young protégée, leaving Sophia and Lavinia nibbling sweets on the sofa with Sir Frank Latham. The latter said very little of importance in Charlotte's hearing but gazed with such tender looks upon the visage of her cousin that Charlotte was forced to make mention of this startling behaviour to her hostess at the first opportunity they were alone.

'Ah, yes. I rather think that Sir Frank is more than a little charmed by your cousin,' Eliza told her, smiling at the thought. 'There has been, I think, a partiality on his part for some time, although it is hard to tell if your cousin returns his regard. You may know more of this than me! Lavinia does not share much of her heart with me, I think,' she added drily. 'As her aunt, I can have no share in the role of confidante. Familiarity as you know, breeds contempt. But I would not be surprised if an offer was made very soon.'

Charlotte raised her brows, puzzlement making her hazel

eyes more expressive than usual. 'The gentleman is very — ostentatious, is he not? But I dare say my cousin could make a worse choice. I wish them very happy. Still, she is full young to be in love. Does Sir Benedict approve?'

Eliza nodded. 'My brother would not be disappointed for Lavinia to marry Sir Frank. He wishes it. He considers Sir Frank stable and dependable, a good sort of character, and well-educated even if he is a little... over-enthusiastic.' She smiled. 'We both feel it is a good choice for your cousin. And she would live close to us, where I could advise her if she wished.'

Charlotte conceded that, for a young woman who only wished to enjoy herself, to be seen in the right circles, and to ride her beloved horses, her cousin might do worse. Not wishing to force a confidence, however, Charlotte determined to wait for her cousin to confide in her. She mentioned as much to Eliza and gratifyingly, was agreed with on that score, and the two women dropped the subject. The rest of the afternoon passed quietly. The Misses Latham and their brother eventually took their leave, and the three women went upstairs to dress for dinner.

~~*~~

Charlotte washed for dinner, grateful for the warm water her ewer had been filled with. Tonight, she was helped to dress by Mary, who had been appropriated from the kitchen earlier by Eliza, much to the disgust of cook. Charlotte, having sent Jane back home with the carriage and quite used to doing her own hair and dressing by herself at home, was coerced by good manners to concede to Eliza's insistence on a lady's maid for her guest. The young girl now helped her new mistress into a rather worn Prussian-blue silk, which Charlotte felt was still serviceable and quite acceptable, she thought, for a family dinner. Mary then took to Charlotte's hair with surprising dexterity and good taste, chatting quietly with Charlotte as she did so. Finally, the girl surveyed her handiwork with

45

satisfaction.

'There now, Miss, you do look pretty, if I may say so. Now just let me pop in this pretty pearl pin — see Miss, like that. Ah, yes, that's just the thing!' She held the mirror for Charlotte to see the back of her head.

Charlotte craned her head then nodded. 'Thank you, Mary, that will do nicely. It is only the family at dinner tonight, you know!'

'But you have such clear skin and glossy hair, that it would be a shame indeed not to show it up, Miss. Besides, there is the Master to notice,' she added, giggling.

'Now Mary,' began Charlotte sternly, 'none of that talk, if you please. There are no such thoughts in my head and neither ought they to be in yours!' She smiled in spite of herself. Sir Benedict look at Charlotte in that way? She would vouchsafe for them both that their mutual dislike for each other would prevent it!

'Yes, Miss. Sorry, Miss.' Mary looked chastised but for a moment. Then she brightened. 'Ah, but your cousin, Miss Lavinia, now that one is a beauty, indeed. And no beaus, although the servants say Sir Frank has his eye on her. La! He had best be quick or he'll miss out! One Season for Miss Lavinia in town and she will be snapped up! But don't you have a beau Miss?' Mary asked, ignoring Charlotte's warning look.

Charlotte, who did not have a beau, and found the conversation more than a little indelicate, declined to comment and steered the conversation toward Mary herself. 'Do you not have a sweetheart yourself, Mary?' she asked.

Mary ducked her head and smiled shyly. 'I do have a sort of a sweetheart Miss, although the Master's against it because of Tom's refusing to work for him here on the estate. They had a falling out and now the Master's against Tom courting me, but I do still see him sometimes, Miss, when he comes very early to see me, before the Master's out....'

She trailed off, as if she thought she had said too much, but

Charlotte smiled and nodded, beginning to understand. 'I would not dream of saying anything, Mary. And now I must go down. I am afraid I have kept dinner waiting already!'

She left Mary building up the fire and fixing her candle for later, and ventured to the drawing room where Lavinia, Eliza and Sir Benedict would be waiting to go in for dinner. She hoped she would not be called upon to speak more than half a dozen words to Sir Benedict, for Mary's sorry story had stirred her ire and she felt unwilling to look her host in the eye lest she give her feelings vent.

She schooled her face into composure and entered the drawing room. To her relief, Lavinia and Eliza at once informed her that Sir Benedict was not to be at dinner, having sent his apologies, and gone to dine with his bailiff, Walter Brock, at the Crown and Fox in the village. The three women enjoyed a quiet evening in their own company, Lavinia chattering in her lively way, and her aunt and Charlotte caught up in their own thoughts. Charlotte was glad when the maid brought their candles and they retired to bed.

The next day bought a little inclement weather and despite her shawl, Charlotte was glad of the fire in the breakfast room when she arrived there. Eliza was sipping tea and welcomed her with a warm smile, inviting her to make her fill of the various dishes cook had provided. She had just begun to eat when Sir Benedict appeared, closely followed by Lavinia. While Charlotte immediately lowered her eyes to avoid his penetrating gaze, Eliza rose to pour tea for her brother.

'Oh! How nice to see you at breakfast with us, Benedict. Do you not have your morning rounds to make? Or have you managed to complete them already?' she enquired, offering him a plate of rolls.

Sir Benedict accepted tea, declined bread, and sat down opposite Charlotte. His dark green jacket and cream breaches made his dark eyes look even darker. Charlotte carefully kept her head bowed and continued with her breakfast. She felt his eyes upon her.

'I have left my rounds for Walter. I shall be doing business in the library this morning and we will entertain a guest today. I have invited him to take an early dinner with us. Would you be so kind as to let cook know?'

Eliza affirmed this request with a raised eyebrow.

Lavinia rose from her seat to accept tea from her aunt. 'Whom is it, Uncle?' she asked eagerly, seating herself again. 'Is it someone from town? I do hope it will be someone from town, for then we shall have some interesting talk at table today! I do long to hear what the latest plays are, and the all the latest fashions!'

Charlotte for one moment felt gauche and out of place in her cousin's company and a pang of feeling crossed her face.

Sir Benedict raised one dark brow. 'If you make your cousin feel that she is not acceptable company Lavinia, she will go home.'

Charlotte raised her head and her eyes met her host's. How could he have known what she was feeling? But despite the solemn line of his mouth, his eyes were laughing at her, and she repressed annoyance at his ability to read her face so well.

'Oh, I did not mean to say that Charlotte is not enough company for me,' Lavinia explained, contrite in her uncle's presence. 'It's just that I long for news of the *ton* and Charlotte knows even less of the latest plays, fashion and people than I do! She always has her head in book, don't you, Cousin,' she added, her eyes mischievous.

'I must confess it is just as you say, Lavinia. I have not had a Season in town, nor would I wish to! I much prefer a quiet life, as you know. I am afraid I cannot help you with fashion, for my father does not go to town very often, and we attend few balls.'

Dark eyes turned to survey her thoughtfully, but their owner said nothing. She studied her tea and toast.

'I am afraid you will be disappointed in my guest, Lavinia, for being a man, and not much interested in such things, I doubt the Earl of Winchester will be able to give you much intelligence on the latest plays, or on fashion. Although you are correct to assume that he comes from town, but he has just taken Wythorpe for the summer.'

Lavinia clapped her hands in delight. 'Oh! An Earl! Think of that, Charlotte! We shall have an Earl as our neighbour! Lord

Winchester — how fine that sounds! Now that we have an Earl for a neighbour, that will put us in the way of other people of rank and situation. We *must* be invited to balls and dinners at Wythorpe, now that Uncle has made the connection!'

Charlotte frowned. 'Lavinia, you know my opinion on such matters. Please do not think that I condone making connections with those of rank simply to further one's social standing.' She felt Sir Benedict's eyes on her and studied her plate.

'Your cousin is right, Lavinia. I do not want you making unguarded remarks to our guest in that vein.'

'I won't, Uncle,' Lavinia promised. 'But it is still vastly agreeable to have an Earl in the neighbourhood!'

'And he has taken Wythorpe, you say?' asked Eliza. 'Well, I must say I am a little surprised, for while it boasts some lovely grounds, they are small, and the house itself has been empty for some time and would take some work to be fit for habitation again. It seems an odd choice for someone of his situation. But I dare say he sends his servants before him. Well, I am glad of its being occupied for summer. Did the new tenant call on you, Benedict? I did not hear anyone with you yesterday.'

'No, Eliza. Walter and I ran into him in the village. He is an agreeable sort of fellow and I invited him to dine with us. He returns to town tomorrow, early. You guessed correctly, Eliza. He was just here overseeing the servants that must make the place fit for living. He will take possession of Wythorpe the day after tomorrow I believe.'

'And where is his family situated? Did he mention it?'

'Lord Winchester has his seat in the north of this country, but he owns that his younger brother is more of a business man than himself and runs it in place of his older brother, I believe. Lord Winchester mostly sticks to town, he informed me, and all the advantages that town life might bring. In any case, he is here to hunt, and to enjoy the climate.'

'But can he not return to his own estate for summer? I declare, it is very strange, Benedict, his taking Wythorpe if he has land of his own in the north!' noted Eliza, puzzled.

Sir Benedict shook his head. 'I believe he wishes to be close to town, Eliza. For a gentleman such as Winchester, being too far from the society and diversions that town provides would make a very tiresome summer in the country for him. It would be very tedious for a lively young fellow such as Winchester not to have the continued diversions of town at hand. Besides, he professed a liking for hunting. You know that Wythorpe land adjoins my own on the western side. I offered him the run of the new lands there. I gave him leave to hunt my pheasants. I only hope he leaves some for me!'

'The newly enclosed land, Uncle?' asked Lavinia.

Charlotte looked up from her toast.

Sir Benedict inclined his head. 'Indeed. I have some fields which abut his. As you say, newly enclosed lands, so the work is done and he is most eager to make use of some new land for hunting. There is some very good game there now that Walter has released the pheasants ahead of the season. Plus of course, the deuced rabbits which always overrun the place.'

'Does he bring family, Benedict?' Eliza enquired. 'Ladies? A wife perhaps?'

'I believe he comes alone, but he says he will soon be joined by friends from town,' replied her brother gravely. 'He did not mention ladies.'

Lavinia was disappointed. 'I might have got news of town and the latest plays and things,' she lamented. 'I wonder if he attends many balls? But stay, he must have some friends of high rank who will visit him here! Did he say whom will accompany him, Uncle?' She jiggled about in her seat with renewed excitement.

'You may ask him yourself, Miss,' replied her uncle, smiling slightly and exchanging a look with his sister. Eliza put down her tea cup and put a hand on her niece's arm.

'Lavinia, stop jiggling in your seat, dear. Try to conduct yourself with more decorum. I am sure you will be able to ask our guest all the questions you want today at dinner.'

Lavinia's countenance conveyed her eagerness without the necessity of words. She looked excitedly at her cousin and Charlotte smiled, shaking her tawny head at Lavinia's enthusiasm for the fashion and amusements of which she herself knew so little and cared for even less.

However, she could not allow her own question to go unasked and ventured to look up at Sir Benedict. 'Excuse me Sir, but does not your enclosing of the land mean hardship for those poor living on the estate who cannot hunt on the common land as they have been used to doing? Are not those rabbits of which you speak, the food source for many of your poor workers?'

The room became silent. Sir Benedict placed his tea cup on its saucer. Charlotte half-expected anger, but his tone was mildly amused, if not a little nonplussed.

'I have always treated my employees with generosity, Miss Milton, and all estate workers choosing to avail themselves of my offer of more work, and extra pay to compensate, have done just so. Enclosure of the land is a necessary part of progress, of which women know little, and about which they should not concern themselves unless they have made reasonable attempts to grasp the subject.'

Charlotte's hazel green eyes flashed before she could help it. 'I hardly think that a female is any less able than a male, Sir, to grasp the concepts of farming, or the implications of progress.'

His eyes glinted but with anger or amusement, Charlotte could not tell.

'Really? You are very opinionated for one so inexperienced in farming practices. I understand your father is a physician, Miss Milton. What could you possibly know of farming?'

Charlotte's lips parted in indignation. 'I may not be a

farmer's daughter, Sir, but that does not stop me from reading! I do have two eyes, and a somewhat rational mind, I hope! As the daughter of a physician, I am not unacquainted with the idea of progress, for my father is always learning new methods and treatments in his field. I— I believe an informed mind is most important for a female. Although some men would not think so,' she added with sarcasm. 'Why should men only have the pleasure of stimulating and interesting conversation? Of improving and informing reading?'

'I do not believe that a female must not be informed, Miss Milton, I am just astonished at your knowing so much about farming!'

Charlotte contemplated hurling her cup across the table at him, but said mildly, 'I did not claim to know much, Sir. I merely wished to point out that progress for one, can cause suffering for another.'

'And what, Miss Milton, could you possibly know of farming practices? Please go on, I am most fascinated to hear your thoughts!'

She pursed her lips and suppressed her rising irritation. 'I have read some of Mr Goldsmith's essays, about your so-named "progress" and I understand that the word implies many things, but may be comfortably interchanged with "profit" on many occasions.'

Sir Benedict dabbed his mouth with his napkin and stood up, his eyes mocking her. 'As to the question of profits, I daresay that might be true, but as you are an enthusiast for reading, if you can bear to drag yourself away from Mr Keats, perhaps I can loan you some alternative material on the subject of agriculture? It may help you to gain a less... emotional understanding of the subject. You may even come to change your views, if you are able to sustain the shock of being contradicted.'

He was laughing openly at her now, and Charlotte did not know if she wanted to glare at him or leave the room and slam the door behind her. Aware of Elizabeth's curious looks first at her brother then at herself, she quickly stilled her breathing and turned back to her meal, refusing to meet his eyes. 'Thank you, Sir, but as the shock of being wrong may overwhelm me, I think I will stick to Keats, all the same.'

He chose to ignore her sarcasm, and went to the window.

She sipped her tea, schooling her face into a neutral countenance, although she could still feel her heart pounding, which she put down to residual anger. Sir Benedict gave his sister some instructions regarding dinner, while Charlotte seethed inwardly at his arrogance and open teasing. Just because she was a woman did not mean she did not have the right to ask questions, to improve upon her knowledge by closer reading and meditation on subjects some men might consider the intellectual property of themselves only! She bowed her head and pursed her lips, determined not to make eye contact with the infuriating man. Shortly, he left the room and the women were left to discuss the anticipated guest.

Nine

Dinnertime when it arrived, found the ladies eager to meet the new tenant of Wythorpe. Guests, apart from their neighbours, were rare and as Eliza explained to Charlotte, they also brought her brother in from his work which she felt was good for him. He tended to work rather too hard and would often forgo meals in order to carry on in the fields with his staff.

In this regard, Sir Benedict was a good master, and set the example for his workers. Charlotte begrudgingly allowed that her host had some redeeming features which made his tendency to harshness with others a little more tolerable. But, she meditated, he was too arrogant and ready to judge for her taste, and had they met socially, she would not be tempted to make an intimate acquaintance of him. And as for his opinion of women! She was determined not to limit her conversation for fear of offending her host with her so-called "unbalanced" views.

When Charlotte entered the drawing room to await the summons to the table, she found Sir Benedict, his guest and the two women already present, seated and talking animatedly. The stranger at once stood to meet her and her eyes widened. A look passed over his countenance, but he quickly regained his composure and smiled, coming towards her.

Sir Benedict introduced her. 'My niece's cousin on her mother's side, Miss Charlotte Milton,' he informed his guest.

Lord Winchester bowed deeply, and his eyes flickered upwards to meet her own, for a moment. Charlotte looked away in embarrassment, disposed to dislike the young man immediately on evidence of his earlier behaviour toward her the previous day in the village. Then she chided herself for pride and made a resolution to be polite to her host's guest, no matter what she thought of his earlier behaviour toward herself.

Lord Winchester's white teeth glinted from behind over-red lips. 'I believe I saw Miss Milton in town yesterday. I had stopped in the street and the lady walked by me. Please accept my apologies, Miss Milton, for I could not help staring at such a vision of loveliness. I did not intend to be impudent,' he finished smoothly, bowing again.

'Really, Sir, it is nothing,' she answered politely, a little disconcerted in front of Sir Benedict, who had not taken his eyes from the two of them. She hoped he did not think she had encouraged the man's attentions! But Lord Winchester was speaking.

'My man was being argumentative, and I had to put him down, teach him his place, as they say. You must have seen how he was insolent to me, Miss Milton.'

Something unreadable guttered across his features like a candle flame blown unexpectedly into life, then died again. He paused, as if waiting for confirmation of his words, but none was forthcoming from Charlotte, and he immediately became gay and changed the subject.

'But it is of no consequence now, and I dare say you had a very fine walk. I do adore the countryside here. I always say the Hertfordshire countryside is most delightful place to summer in. You have a very large estate here, Markham.'

Sir Benedict and Lord Winchester began to speak of estate

matters and the servant came to call them in to dine.

~~*~~

They sat to a plentiful repast of soup, hot and cold meats, vegetables, cheeses and pies, and fruits from the orchard, along with cook's excellent strawberry tarts and double cream. Wine was freely poured, and Sir Benedict engaged his guest in easy general conversation regarding Wythorpe and its grounds. Lord Winchester, who throughout the meal had four pairs of curious eyes upon him and yet, much to his credit, showed no discomfiture, appeared to Charlotte's powers of observation a gentleman with a pleasing address, good breeding, and an intelligent countenance.

He made himself very agreeable, both to his host and the three women before him. For herself, however, Charlotte thought he smiled a little *too* much and made himself *too* agreeable, for her taste. She found him slightly too eager to please and noted how he lent a little more attention to Lavinia than to any other of the party, although Lavinia, with her beauty and natural vivacity, would catch the eye of any young man with taste.

When their guest again ventured to begin a short conversation with herself, enquiring as to the walks she had taken and if she had any recommendations to make since he was an enthusiastic walker himself, Sir Benedict immediately inserted himself between them and made available his own, more knowledgeable advice, 'since Miss Milton had hardly been here three days, and would not be familiar with the best walks just yet'.

She was not much put out by Sir Benedict's high-handed officiousness since she did not seek to converse with Lord Winchester if it could be helped. But she sensed an odd attitude of antagonism toward herself, and puzzling a little, finally put this down to natural possessiveness of his estate and his not being in good spirits due to their earlier conversation.

Each time his eyes turned to her, she averted her gaze and tried to ignore the strange sensations in her belly and her limbs. She still smarted from his mocking words at breakfast. Perhaps her feelings of discomfort were due to that. And yet, his antagonism stirred her with a strange desire to be on better terms with him. At that thought, she chided herself for caring what he thought of her. His good opinion was not sought by her, just as he seemed not to seek her own good opinion of him! They were two people who would never find common ground, and as such, it would be best for her to try to avoid her host as much as possible in the coming days.

At any rate, it was not long before Lavinia had monopolised Lord Winchester's attention with her high spirits and lively conversation, the subject of which varied only between questions about plays he had attended, and with whom, and which riding habits and ball gowns were generally more in fashion this year. Although the subject was somewhat far from his direct experience, he made very wholehearted attempts to answer her from his general knowledge, and Charlotte thought he went out of his way to give Lavinia his undivided attention.

Eventually, the party rose from their seats and Sir Benedict conducted his guest back to the library for port and to discuss business. Before they had concluded however, Lavinia had secured their guest's promise to join their picnic party the following Monday, and to bring whomever of his friends he chose, to which Sir Benedict gave his added, although restrained, encouragement.

Lord Winchester gave his assurances that he would be delighted to join them, and they would of course 'do him a great honor by being his guests in turn at Wythorpe in the near future, whenever the day would be named by the ladies'.

Thus organised, the three women, gratified for the moment with the prospect of two social engagements to occupy them, wished their guest good afternoon and the ladies retired to the small family parlour to sew and chat companionably until teatime.

~~*~~

At supper, Sir Benedict announced his intention to be in town for the next three or four days where he had some matters of business, and Charlotte breathed a silent sigh of relief. Four days would give her time to get her feelings under control, and to be able to face her host with composure. Really, he had an astonishing way of discomposing her nerves! She was perplexed at how a single look from him could unsettle her emotions and cause such unladylike sensations in her. His character was beginning to be formed in her mind just as her cousin had described him; stern, unjust, and completely over-bearing!

Eliza enquired as to the date of his return and he prevaricated, but assured her he would send his man before him to let her know of his impending arrival. Charlotte perceived that Eliza took great pride in running her brother's house and planned all meals around his presence or absence. She was a devoted and loving sister who doted on her younger brother. He, in turn, treated her with great patience and kindness, was concerned when her health kept her to her room, and he took great pains to ensure that at these times, she was not disturbed. All this Charlotte noted with incredulity; not that he treated his sister with such care, but that he could be so overbearing and officious with everyone else!

Ten

Shortly after breakfast the following day, Sir Benedict left for town. Despite her relief at the news of his coming departure, Charlotte felt strangely out of sorts after he had bidden them farewell, and a kind of empty melancholy filled her heart. This she put down to a delayed homesickness, although she felt no marked inclination for home or her particular friends there.

A day or two passed, bringing no tidings of Sir Benedict, and Charlotte told herself that she was very glad to be able to relax, knowing a set of dark eyes was not on her constantly, discovering her secrets and inciting her emotions.

The ensuing days were peaceful, filled with quiet conversation with Eliza, or accompanying Lavinia on walks to the village to see if they might chance to meet Lord Winchester in the street. Lavinia was disappointed in her efforts, but Charlotte was secretly glad not to meet the man. They chanced instead upon James, while walking in the street one morning, and, asking after his sisters and mother, Charlotte gave the boy a few coins from her purse.

'Thankee Miss. My mam will be right grateful. Good day Miss. Good day Miss,' he nodded to both women and tipped his hat.

'Why are you wasting your money, Charlotte?' asked Lavinia as the boy trotted away. 'He has, likely as not, told his sorry story to ten others in the street and got as many silver coins in his grubby little pocket! Don't look at me like that! Besides, if you give to them, they come to expect it and won't work for their living. That boy works in my uncle's stables already. His older brother is a thief and a layabout.'

Charlotte's lips became a firm line. 'That is only hearsay, Lavinia. And besides, the mother is poorly and cannot work and they just lost their father. Your uncle, I am sure, has done his best for the family. But these are my coins to give, and I choose to help those in need where I can.'

Lavinia wisely changed the subject and they continued on, but Charlotte wished silently that her cousin would not say such outrageous things.

~~*~~

On the fourth morning of Sir Benedict's absence, Charlotte went down to the breakfast room again earlier than the rest of the family. Looking out the window, she idly watched the gardener move about the rose gardens which lined the sweeping front driveway, and waited for Lavinia to join her, since her cousin wished to plan the picnic party which was to take place early in the following week.

Charlotte's notions of a country picnic were largely unformed, having no experience of them, but she sincerely looked forward to what she imagined would be a pleasant day playing games and enjoying her cousin's company. If Lord Winchester and the Misses Latham and their brother were of the party, she did not feel she minded very much, as she would have Elizabeth and Lavinia to converse with, and if it was pleasant weather, she might take a solitary walk or convince her cousin to join her.

As she sipped her tea and enjoyed the charming view of the gardens with the mist of morning just lifting off them, she watched in startled amusement as a young man, roughly dressed, approached the house from the fields. Avoiding the driveway, he slipped somewhat furtively around the side of the house.

Intrigued, and somewhat alarmed, she slipped from the morning room into the garden, and peeped around the side of the house. The young man had entered the kitchen garden from the side gate and was staring at the back door, the one used the by the servants. At first, Charlotte frowned at the intruder, thinking he might have come to beg cook for scraps, or for work, but then she brightened and smiled knowingly.

Mary, the kitchen maid who doubled as her lady's maid, had run out to the gate. The two young people stood talking for a moment or two and the young maid bashfully looked down at the ground. The fellow produced a posy of wildflowers from behind his back and Charlotte smiled to herself. The young man, about to take his leave, spoke to the girl in a low voice and backed away.

Ashamed of herself for eavesdropping, Charlotte turned to retreat. Suddenly, however, she let out a little 'Oh!'. Sir Benedict had appeared as if from nowhere and was striding towards the couple from the opposite direction. Charlotte was both startled and disturbed that he had returned that very morning, and she felt a sudden fluttering sensation in her stomach. Sir Benedict was gesticulating with his arm. She could hear his voice, and the fluttering in her stomach increased.

The young maid backed away and lowered her head, waiting for Sir Benedict's fury. As the young man walked away, the girl endured a short but crisp censure from her master, nodded, bobbed a curtsey, and returned through the kitchen door. Sir Benedict strode away, in the direction of the stables, his feet crunching over the stones as he stomped off.

Incited to a moderate fervour by the injustice of the situation, Charlotte could not but help shaking her head. 'Really!' she said out loud. 'I am beginning to see Lavinia's point. He is a veritable grump!'

Incensed on behalf of the young lovers, Charlotte decided that Sir Benedict was only improving her impression of him as the most unjust, pig-headed, bad-tempered man she had ever had the misfortune to meet! She fumed at his treatment of what appeared to be the innocent courting of two young people. Being a romantic creature at heart, she determined to mention the scene to Sir Benedict at the first opportunity a private moment afforded and enquire as to his motives for interfering in an innocent courtship.

No longer hungry, and still churning inwardly at the unfairness of her host, she chose not to return to her tea, but decided, somewhat illogically, to sit in the garden. At two and twenty, Charlotte had enough sense to understand herself if she chose, but as any passionate young lady might, she did not always pause to examine her motives when she was much moved. Now, she was ready to speak, to fight passionately for those in need. When she ventured into the garden, if she half hoped to chance immediately upon Sir Benedict there, she did not admit it to herself, nor did she care to examine her motives for such a meeting. A little garden air would do her good! It was just the thing to give her an appetite for breakfast!

She had just rounded the corner into the shrubbery when she was gratified to see Sir Benedict striding over the neat, green lawn in her direction. The early morning sun framed his silhouette from behind and threw him into dark relief as he strode over the wet grass. His face was thunder itself. Charlotte turned on her heel, suddenly at a loss to speak her mind, but her host had reached her. She reluctantly turned to face him. He briefly halted his stride.

'Miss Milton. Good morning. I trust you are well?' he asked in a curt manner, as if consumed by other business and stopping only out of politeness.

Charlotte halted nervously and bobbed a curtsy. 'Good morning, Sir. I am very well, thank you. I– We did not expect you so early. I hope you had a pleasant ride home?'

He muttered a civility and made as if to leave, but Charlotte involuntarily moved her hand as if to stop him and he paused, waiting with raised brows.

'I hope you will pardon my interference,' she began, in a somewhat more agitated tone than she could help, 'but I could not help noticing from the window, when I was in the breakfast room earlier, a young man who seemed to be courting one of your employees.'

At this, Sir Benedict's countenance turned an even darker hue. 'What of the business?' he growled.

Charlotte stood her ground, allowing her anger at his curtness to fuel her courage. She did not bother to disguise her passion, and her hazel-green eyes flashed. Her voice trembled on the morning air.

'It seems to me that it is unjust to part two people who have done no wrong, and are in love. I was surprised, indeed, I was shocked Sir, to witness your grossly unfair interference in a matter which was innocent of anything immoral or in any way improper. I was concerned for the young people involved and determined to speak to you on the matter.'

'And what, Miss Milton, gives you the right to judge me regarding my dealings with my employees?' he asked, his tone icy. Charlotte winced but held his gaze.

'It is not my wish to interfere, Sir Benedict, but I felt obliged to make an inquiry. Here are two young people in love, and yet you appear to set yourself against the scheme! The young man seems to have honourable intentions and is doing no harm! I do not understand it at all!'

'Really, Miss Milton.' His voice dripped with sarcasm. 'I strongly advise you to keep your unformed and ill-equipped opinions to yourself in future, especially regarding how I run my estate. First last week, with your opinions on enclosure, and now this! You know nothing of *that* matter, and I perceive you certainly know nothing of love! Unless you suppose flirting with strangers in the street qualifies you to make such statements.'

She recalled immediately his suspicious looks when she'd met Lord Winchester at dinner earlier in the week. He made as if to dismiss her and turn away, but she could not allow it. Her feelings prevented her from it. She felt all the injustice of such an accusation, and yet was unable to find the words to defend her innocence. Instead, her feelings overcame her, and she flung out the words she felt in her heart. 'Just because you have been unlucky in love does not mean that you have the right to go around spoiling the chances of others!'

He stood very still. A *frisson* of emotion that might have been pain passed over his face for a second, and Charlotte immediately regretted her impetuous words.

'To what chances do you refer? Tom's chances with my kitchen maid, or your chance with Lord Winchester?' he ground out.

Charlotte's mouth dropped open. 'Of course I refer to that young man in the garden! I have heard that you have treated him unfairly, and his whole family suffers for it.'

'I think that you have said enough, Miss Milton,' he bit out coldly. 'You know nothing of the matter between that young man and myself. Perhaps your time would be better spent seeing to your own matters, than interfering in mine!'

He spun on his boot clad heel and was gone. The soft dewy grass, crushed under his retreating feet, bore the only evidence that he was ever there. Charlotte sat abruptly on the nearest bench seat with her book, and felt all the force of her vexation, fuelled by the keen injustice he had brought to bear upon her. That he thought she had been flirting with Lord Winchester! It was insupportable! The insolence, the arrogance of the man!

She sat for half an hour, composed her thoughts, and finally decided to take a walk. After returning to her room for a spencer and hat, she set off, this time over the hills towards a pretty little folly she had noticed, which stood by the lake in the distance. After several minutes of brisk walking, she felt more at ease within herself, and her vexation had abated as quickly as it had arisen. She was never one to remain in bad mood for long, and she was soon in better temper.

Upon approaching the folly, she found that she was not alone. A young man sat upon the steps, gazing moodily into the reflections shimmering on the lake's surface. He turned his head at the sound of her approach, and she uttered a startled 'Oh,' for he was the young man whom she had observed that morning with Mary.

She bobbed a polite curtsey and began to turn away when the man stood up and tipped his hat, just as startled to find his solitude encroached upon.

'Beg your pardon, Miss,' he began.

He made as if to walk away but Charlotte, who despised timidity, and felt that providence had heard her only an hour prior, seized her opportunity with both hands. 'Please, don't go away on my account! I was only passing. Do sit down again. I was going to continue my walk.' She smiled engagingly, and the young man paused. Charlotte hesitated. 'I saw you this morning, in the garden. I am staying as a guest of Sir Benedict and his sister. I am Miss Markham's cousin.'

The young man said nothing but looked away again, over the lake. His face was masked and still.

Charlotte tried again. 'If my seeing you this morning was inappropriate, I mean to say, I did not mean to spy. I was just looking out of the window at the time...' she trailed off, unsure of how to proceed, reluctant to be an intruder on the young man's misery. 'Forgive my intrusion,' she begged and turned away.

The young man shook his head. 'I'm sorry Miss. I did not mean to be rude. I should not even be here, on *his* property, that is. I'll be going now, Miss.' He tipped his hat and nodded to Charlotte.

Before he could walk away, she stepped forward. 'Please, is there anything I could do for you? That is, is there any...

message?'

The young man shook his head, understanding at once her meaning. 'No, thank'ee Miss. Me an' Mary had our talk this morning, before he came and put a stop to it, that is. No Miss, I'll talk to Mary when she gets herself to town, which she do occasionally.'

Charlotte smiled. 'Would you happen to be Tom?'

The youth raised an eyebrow and laughed. 'Now, how would Miss know that?' he asked.

'I think I met your brother James a few days ago, on the road from the village. You look just like him.'

Tom laughed again. 'Aye, we do look alike, so me mam says. So you've met Jamesy, have you? He's a good boy. He works for the Master. Whereas, I do not work for him, and not likely to either.'

Charlotte looked away, a little embarrassed and yet curious to understand. 'Mary told me a little about you. She said you and the Master had a falling out. Did you previously work on the estate?'

'Aye, that I did. Until he put a stop to me and Mary on account of him thinking I'm not good enough for the girl. Says I thieved from him, which I did not. Enclosed land it was, I took some pheasants off it, just as common law says us poor folks is entitled to, and it was ours afore he went and closed it and now my family must starve, or nearabouts. Well, I won't work for him,' Tom added defiantly, 'and what's more, I'll come back and collect Mary one day when I have us a good home to take her to. I work the Wythorpe estate now, for the new Master who's just taken it, Lord Winchester. I see Mary when I can, but only when himself is not around.' He shook his head, and fell silent, staring out over the lake.

Charlotte bit her lip, feeling the injustice of the situation, and her anger rose once again at Sir Benedict's cruel and unfeeling attitude toward his staff. 'I am sorry for your situation, Tom,' she said softly. 'I hope you can earn some money and come back for Mary soon.'

'Thank'ee Miss. You are very kind. Good day, Miss.'

Tom tipped his hat and nodded, then set off along the river bank. Charlotte watched him into the distance then turned back toward the house herself, her indignation at Sir Benedict's unfair treatment of his staff swelling her heart.

Lavinia met Charlotte upon her return, and Charlotte strove to subdue the tumult in her breast and find enjoyment and solace in her cousin's company for the remainder of the afternoon. Her aunt having given Lavinia full control over the details of the picnic outing, and having retired to her room for rest, the young lady was happy to plan and design all that the happy occasion would need to ensure the enjoyment of each member of the party.

Games planned, Mrs Ransom entreated and fussed over in order to procure all of the pies and sweets that Lavinia thought would be mandatory for a successful afternoon, and the stable hands and grooms all sent for, to instruct explicitly as to the carriages for the day after tomorrow, the two girls animatedly ran over the list of attendees. Both found it to their satisfaction, Lavinia because of one guest in particular, and Charlotte because of the number of guests in general. With a sizable party of people, she was not likely, she thought, to be in the uncomfortable situation of finding herself alone with Sir Benedict.

Lavinia was gleeful, with large hopes of claiming Lord Winchester to herself. 'He has quite some standing in society, Charlotte, and he is vastly rich! My maid says that her sister is housemaid at Wythorpe and *she* says he has thirty thousand a year! If he should pay his addresses to me, I would accept at once! The Countess of Winchester. How fine that sounds! How well we would live!' She laughed aloud and helped herself to a marzipan from a nearby box.

Charlotte frowned. 'Cousin, do not you think that your parents, were they still alive, would not wish you to be throwing yourself in such a way at a young man of whom we know so little? Yes, he is by all means a very handsome, and a very amiable gentleman, but we know so little yet of his character. I am sure your poor Mama would not wish it, if she were here?'

Lavinia snorted in a most unladylike manner and reached for another sweet. 'Well, Miss prim and proper Charlotte, she is *not* here! I am fully able to run my own life now, and I would thank you not to prate on about it.'

Charlotte was shocked into silence, the nearness of her own grief still weighing heavily on her heart. She knew it had been two years since her cousin had lost her parents, but to speak of her dead Mama in such a way! To demean by association, Charlotte's own feelings of grief and loss in such a manner! It was too much! She drew a shaky breath and endeavoured to remain composed although her emotions threatened to overtake her.

'If the death of your parents has left so little effect on you, I wonder at you, Lavinia. But for myself, who has lost one so dear to me, it pains me to hear such matters mentioned in such a frivolous way. I miss Mama so much—' Here she was distressed enough to be unable to finish her words.

Lavinia looked contrite for a moment. 'I am sorry Charlotte, I did not mean to belittle your own loss.' She looked away to the window, her face hidden from Charlotte's view. 'I do miss my parents. I just prefer not to dwell on it. Dwelling on it does not bring them back or make one feel better. I am not all heartless and unfeeling, you know! It is just my way. Mama always said a lady ought to hide her feelings, that it was our duty to be gay and happy on the outside, even if we were crying on the inside! Perhaps it would help if you did the same.'

She turned from the window, and Charlotte noted the unnatural brilliance of her eyes. Had she judged her cousin too harshly? She felt a pang of guilt and kissed her cousin tenderly on the cheek. 'You are right. It is perhaps best not to speak of these things. Now, what other games shall we play at the picnic? Do you think it advisable to take cricket?'

Lavinia seized the change of subject with enthusiasm, but Charlotte was privately warmed to find Lavinia had a heart after all, no matter how she chose to hide it.

~~*~~

Dinner that evening was a very quiet meal, for Eliza had retreated to her room with a headache, and Lavinia was unusually quiet. Charlotte too, was silent, for she had not the good temper tonight to hide misery and display gaiety. After their disagreement that morning, Charlotte felt unequal to feigning light-heartedness of any sort. That Sir Benedict thought her guilty of flirting with Lord Winchester! She did not know how to continue her meal, when she thought of it.

Her vexation, when she reflected on the matter, was yet quite unabated! She jabbed some meat onto her fork with quite unnecessary vigour when she thought of it. But then, when she did not think on it directly, her mood changed from angry to melancholy, and she felt herself unhappy to know that he did not think well of her. Then her food stuck in her throat and she could not swallow. She glanced over at him from time to time, during the meal, and caught his eye once, but she dropped her eyes again quickly, so that she could not tell if he was still angry with her.

But she must stop thinking on the matter at all, or she would never feel at ease again! She determined to clear her head and to master her vexation. Her mama had always said that Charlotte wore her heart on her sleeve, for all the world to know if she was feeling happy or miserable, and now, this thought came back to her. She resolved to cease to think about Sir Benedict's opinion, good or ill, and empty her mind of him! She would make Lavinia's habit of being gay and light-hearted on the outside, her own. She tried a smile at her cousin, who smiled faintly back. There, she had begun! It was strange however, that she while she thought Sir Benedict the most disagreeable man she had ever met, she could not prevent herself always thinking of him!

Dinner over, Charlotte hoped very much to retire to her room early, but the appearance of Eliza, recovered somewhat from her headache, and a very pleading wish from her cousin to stay, forced her into politeness for the sake of them both, and she withdrew into the drawing room with the others, to take coffee.

The women sat around the tall open window, for it was a warm evening, and looked out upon the charming night scene before them, while Sir Benedict stood first at one window, then at another, until his sister scolded him and bade him sit and relax. He settled at his desk and began to take out his writing quill and papers, his profile to the women so that Charlotte could not read his expression.

Soon, there began lively conversation among the women on general subjects, which then turned to domestic matters. Eliza needed advice on the plans for a new hen house, and applied to her brother for its best design and placement. Lavinia listened to all of this with little attention, but Charlotte, charmed by the idea of a poultry house, which her father had never kept since he relied on the butcher, listened with great interest and several questions, quite forgetting herself in her curiosity.

'And do you keep turkeys also, Ma'am? Do they go in with the hens?' she asked, amused at the idea of the large creatures and small together. 'Or must one build two houses, in that case?'

Eliza laughed at her guest's novice curiosity. 'Why, Miss Milton, I think it is you whom I ought to be teaching housekeeping, rather than your cousin! It is quite novel to me to have an attentive student!' She began to supply some answers but was smoothly interrupted by the chocolate tones of her brother.

'Hens, for all their small size, can be quite violent in defending their eggs from curious turkeys, Miss Milton. Small creatures are often feisty to compensate for stature. I rather think that is a human trait, too.' His mouth curved up in a slight smile.

Nonplussed, she did not answer immediately, but felt herself reproved by him. She knew to what he was referring. She pursed her lips and relied archly, 'I believe you are right, Sir. But it ought to be remembered that small creatures are often harassed by larger ones, especially the male of a species, for males always wish to assert their superiority over weaker creatures. It is only fair that the smaller ones have *some* defence!'

'And that, Miss Milton, is precisely why it is unwise to run hens and turkeys in the same house! The turkey is always sure to win the fight in the end!'

She gritted her teeth and looked away, determined not to be baited by him. There was so deep a blush on her face that Eliza and Lavinia might well have had a strong suspicion that the conversation was not at all about real turkeys and hens! But Lavinia, unmoved and apathetic when it came to domestic matters, was absorbed in a picture book, and Eliza had gone to the door to look for the delayed coffee things and missed the exchange.

Charlotte thought again on his words of only moments ago and laughed bitterly to herself. Yes, she thought, it is indeed unwise to house turkeys and hens in the same house, for the hen will certainly come off the worse for it. She began to think it would have been better if she had not come to Delford at all!

Twelve

Sunday morning brought with it light showers and nothing to improve Charlotte's mood. She shunned the breakfast room and rang for Mary, who brought her some tea and toast, and filled a bath with hot water for her. She enquired after Eliza and Lavinia, and was informed that Miss Lavinia was up and dressed, and that Mrs Granger was unwell and was keeping to her room. Charlotte asked Mary to convey her kindest wishes to Eliza and hoped her in better health soon. She privately wished she could also plead headache and stay home, but she knew that Sir Benedict would think she was deliberately avoiding him and did not want to endure a conversation on that subject!

Finally, her hot bath taken, and her tea drunk, she dressed for church in a deep lavender-and-white-sprigged muslin, and taking up a matching bonnet, dutifully went downstairs, reticule in one gloved hand, bonnet and shawl in the other, in search of her cousin. Lavinia was dressed delightfully in a beautiful white embroidered muslin with very fine lace trim, and a chaste straw bonnet of rose dressed with darker pink ribbon. She looked delicate and beautiful and for a moment, Charlotte wished she, too, could own such beauty. She did not realise that she had her own kind of delicacy, which was less obvious, but nonetheless arresting.

At that moment, framed in the window with the morning light behind her, her tawny gold hair glistened. Little damp strands, having escaped their confines, were now drifting down the slender curve of her neck. Her fine, lightly tanned skin glowed under the morning light. Although she was still thin, her figure was fine and well-proportioned under the soft lavender dress. Her gold-flecked hazel eyes, framed under the dark arches of her fine brows, were even more expressive than usual, tinged as they were with a pensive sadness. Her wide mouth, which seemed always about to break into a smile, was this morning as solemn as her mood.

She stood quietly before the window, haloed in light, as Sir Benedict came down the stairs toward the two women. Several emotions moved over his face in the course of a moment, which Charlotte could not read, and then his face was again impassive and bent toward the floor, as if to study his breeches and boots most carefully. She was sure he was still angry with her!

Lavinia greeted her uncle and Charlotte bobbed a small curtsey but said nothing, bowing her head to avoid his gaze. She felt his eyes on her several times, as if he could not but help staring, but she did not see anything but the parquet floor as they moved out of the hall and into the open barouche which was to take them into the village to the small church there. The servant handed the two girls into the vehicle.

Sir Benedict was silent during the short drive, and even Lavinia seemed lost in her own thoughts. After ten or so minutes, which Charlotte spent pointedly looking at the view to avoid conversation with her host, the driver delivered them, quaking and rattling over the rough lane, to the church door.

The Lathams were already seated in a near front family pew, both women looking extremely fine in their modestly bejewelled dresses and white gloves. Their brother sat with them, his ginger head twisted around on his neck at a very uncomfortable angle, Charlotte thought, looking expectantly at the door behind him, and then impatiently at the pastor, who stood blocking his view of the pews. Miss Smart sat beside Miss Latham, fanning her face gently and coyly peeking to the side of it from time to time to observe the other young ladies on her opposite side.

Sir Benedict led the way to the family box at the front of the church. It was well appointed and boasted a fine view of the pulpit. The two women followed and seated themselves quietly. Immediately, Sir Frank bowed and simpered at Lavinia, who all but ignored the poor fellow, and craned her neck instead to inspect the back pews. Charlotte observed her smiling very prettily at someone behind them, much to Frank Latham's consternation, but at this moment the pastor struck up the hymn, and all heads were, by force of propriety, returned to the front. Miss Annabelle Latham turned her head once or twice toward their box and glowered her disapproval, which Charlotte amusedly assumed was directed at herself, but she kept her face frontward and refused to acknowledge the interest of the other woman. The sermon, although uplifting and well read, dragged for an interminably long period, and it was with guilty relief that at last Charlotte quitted the box and followed Lavinia and Sir Benedict who had stepped outside. However, before she could leave the church, a sharp feminine voice at her ear at once made her startle.

'Good morning, Miss Milton. And how do you like our pastor's manner of preaching? Did it suit you? I suppose you are used to much less advantageous placement of boxes and fewer comforts at home? As a country physician, I suppose your father would not have the opportunity to enjoy such a box. How lovely that you could enjoy such unaccustomed comfort this morning.'

Miss Annabelle Latham smiled with her mouth, but not with her eyes. Charlotte curtsied coldly, her ire raised, but determined not to show that her pride had been touched.

'If the comfort or the position of the box were of greater importance to me than the sermon itself, then my father has not brought me up to be a good Christian, Miss Latham. But I was very pleased with the sermon. Mr Abbot has a fine speaking voice, does he not? I always think that a good sermon, where it is well delivered and makes what is heard often, seem entirely new, is a rare thing. Do you not agree?'

Miss Latham pressed her lips together as if to bite back a retort and then changed the subject. 'Sir Benedict must be very busy about estate matters these days. We see so little of him, of late. But I am sure we shall see him at Highview soon. His visits are invariably frequent and we have come to view him as one of our most — intimate — acquaintances.' Her eyes were shrewdly assessing Charlotte's reaction to this statement.

Charlotte remained silent, aware that those leaving the pews around her had almost deserted the church, and she was entirely at the mercy of Miss Latham. The lady spoke again in lower tones.

'I hope, Miss Milton, that you will forgive me if I speak frankly? It would be in your best interests not to not harbour any — aspirations, shall I say, toward Sir Benedict Markham. He is very much attached to *me*, if I may be so bold as to say so, and our family — indeed, there is an expectation that future events — well, need I go on? I think you understand the circumstances.'

Charlotte was shocked, but she gathered her composure after a moment. Her eyes flashed however, despite her calm demeanour. 'I rather think, Miss Latham, that unless any such event of the nature you have implied had been officially announced, it would be rather improper, and indelicate, for a lady to assume it as fact, much less announce it to the public. Perhaps the gentleman in question might be rather angry to hear of it?'

With these words, Charlotte turned on her delicate booted heel and walked angrily toward the church door. Behind her,

Miss Latham stood, her mouth opening and closing like a pike caught in a net and gasping for air. Shocked and angry, Charlotte stalked out of the church entrance, down the steps and went to stand beside Lavinia.

The latter was standing a short distance from the carriage, her attention engaged fully by Lord Winchester, who had his hand lightly on her arm and was speaking rather intimately into her ear. Acutely conscious of the impropriety her cousin was committing, in being party to such an improper address from the gentleman, and aware of how this must look to outsiders, she forgot for a moment her former anger. However, Miss Latham had now come to stand nearby, and was casting malicious looks at Charlotte.

Charlotte made to move away slightly and realised that Sir Benedict was looking speculatively at her, then at Miss Latham. Not wishing to draw attention to herself, she tried to look light-hearted, and deliberately moved between her cousin and Lord Winchester, who had politely noticed her presence and was addressing her regarding the sermon and its delivery. She gave some half-hearted answers and tried to pay attention, but her mind raced.

Sir Benedict and Miss Annabelle Latham? Perhaps what Lavinia had supposed was true! If the lady herself was so sure of the events that would take place, then there must be something to it. But the nerve of the woman! And to insinuate that Charlotte herself had designs on the gentleman! It was unspeakable. Nay, it was unthinkable!

Her distress over both the incident with Miss Latham and her worry regarding Lavinia made her anxious to get home, and it appeared that Sir Benedict was of a similar mind, curtly summoning the servant to bring around the barouche. But she could not go home in the barouche! She must have exercise, and time to think. She wished very much to walk a little.

Sir Benedict had just then signalled the manservant to open the barouche box door. Charlotte moved towards her host and kept her voice low. 'If you will forgive me, Sir Benedict, I prefer to walk. It is not a great distance, and I should like to walk a little.'

Sir Benedict again narrowed his eyes in thought, and his eyes darted to Miss Latham, who was following her sister into their own barouche. He nodded his assent thoughtfully. 'Very well, Miss Milton.'

Charlotte quickly told her cousin that she was walking, and Lavinia, who was saying good bye prettily to Lord Winchester, nodded distractedly and called out. 'Don't be late for luncheon, Charlotte, for we are to organise our card party afterward!' Laughing gaily, she allowed Lord Winchester to hand her into the carriage.

He waved his gloved hand and turned to mount his horse. He was soon gone at pace, and Sir Benedict's barouche followed sedately.

Charlotte waited a little while, then started toward home down the damp lane. A little rain from the night before had made the lane muddy, and the hem of her dress soon became damp and dirty. She did not heed it, for her head was occupied with her own thoughts. Deciding to walk over a small path which led down to the house, she opened a gate and began to walk along the hedgerow which ran parallel to the lane. Shortly, she came upon two or three sheep, and then rounding a hill, she stopped, for two figures were standing in the lane she had just left, although they had not observed her. One was a tall gentleman in a naval uniform, whom she did not recognise. The other was Lord Winchester!

Charlotte halted in her path, waiting in the convenient cover of the hedgerow. She felt very much an intruder, and she thought it impossible to continue on, for it was clearly a private meeting. She waited for Lord Winchester to mount his horse and move along. But the tall man in naval attire continued speaking in low tones to Lord Winchester, and after a few moments, handed him something.

Charlotte noticed with some surprise that Lord Winchester began to count pound notes, and finding the sum to be correct, he stuffed the notes into a pocket within his breeches, nodded curtly to his friend, mounted his horse and was gone. The tall gentleman mounted his own horse also and turned toward the village. Charlotte quickly dropped to the ground and retied her boot laces. Keeping her face averted, she waited long enough behind the hedgerow for the fellow to canter past, then stood and continued on her way. She felt guilty for having concealed her presence, and yet she felt that, had she intruded, the intrusion would have been unwelcome.

It occurred to her that Lord Winchester may have completed a business deal or was collecting on a win at the horses. And yet, there was something secretive about the way he had taken the money. Charlotte sighed. She tried to put everything from her mind, including her conversation with Miss Latham, and would wait for the quiet of her own room later that day to examine her thoughts and suspicions.

She was met in the hall by one of the servants who informed her that the family was waiting for her in the drawing room and refreshment would be served shortly. She quickly dropped her reticule and bonnet on her bed and ran downstairs again so as not to keep the family waiting.

All throughout the meal, Sir Benedict eyed her thoughtfully. She was more quiet than usual, and he was probably wondering what she and Miss Latham had been discussing inside the church, but despite her insinuation to Miss Latham, she would not mention it to her host, even if he enquired directly. It was too distressing to be accosted in such a manner by such a person, and she wished only to put the unfortunate incident behind her. If there was really some truth in Miss Latham's statements, then she could only wish them both very happy. But here she was again, thinking of the matter!

She smiled brightly at Lavinia and Eliza and enquired after Eliza's heath. Eliza assured Charlotte that she had quite recovered from her headache and suggested to Sir Benedict that they discuss the coming picnic party.

It was decided that an impromptu card party, to precede the picnic, was to be held that evening at Delford. Lavinia was animated at the prospect and lamented the short notice they would have to give others. However, Eliza offered to write some rushed invitations to be delivered that afternoon. These were directed only to the picnic guests: the Lathams, their guest Miss Smart and Lord Winchester. That was a party of nine, if all invited were to come, and Lavinia fussed over making a tenth, but Eliza assured her it did not signify much, for she herself would sit out of any games where an odd number made play difficult.

Invitations dashed off and sent with one of the servants to give to the footman to deliver, Lavinia went upstairs to decide upon her gown for the evening. Charlotte knew this concern was all for the benefit of one guest in particular, and wondered if she ought to speak to her cousin again. But then she remembered that Sir Benedict would be present, and would certainly curtail any impropriety himself. It was perhaps as well that they were giving this small gathering, Charlotte thought, since that this would allow Sir Benedict to observe closely his niece's behaviour and intervene if needed.

~~*~~

An hour before the party were to arrive, Charlotte put on a rather pretty embroidered calamine blue silk, the round neck of which was cut rather low, and her mother's pearl and silver cross. Mary came in to dress her hair, which she knotted in a pretty bun at Charlotte's nape, leaving a few loose curls to hang gently around her face. However, Charlotte would not allow Mary to add her mother's pearly hair adornments, since she wanted to stay as inconspicuous as possible this evening. The thought of Miss Annabelle Latham's jealous eyes on her made her long to plead headache and stay in her room, but she fortified herself on account of Eliza, since she wished not to let her hostess down. She thought she might easily avoid games, and sit in the corner with a book, if Eliza would stand in for her at the card table.

Lavinia met her at the top of the staircase looking lovely in a high-waisted white dress trimmed with coquelicot satin ribbon, and a rather striking hair pin in the form of a serpent, with rubies for eyes! Charlotte commented on its unusual appearance and Lavinia put her hand to her head self-consciously.

'It was Mama's, of course. I got all her jewellery when she died. She did have rather good taste! I shall wear them all more now that we are keeping *better* company... and I have someone to wear them for!' She ran eagerly down the stairs, leaving Charlotte to follow gravely in the wake of Lavinia's serpentine trailing ribbons and rose-water scented air.

They entered the salon just as Lord Winchester arrived, followed by the Latham party of four. The two Misses Latham looked around themselves in a disdainful manner and immediately retired to a window to talk in low tones, while Sir Frank bowed and bobbed and prattled to everyone in the room, except Lavinia who pointedly ignored him.

Charlotte saw with some amusement that Sir Frank had tonight applied his hair powder so liberally that every time he issued a bow, a little puff of powder fell from his ginger head. The effect was as if he was surrounded by a halo of white mist, giving him a somewhat saintly look that was so incongruent with his bobbing and prattling conversation that she did not know whether to feel sorry for him or raise her eyes heavenward. But, hiding her amusement, she was able to give him the satisfaction of engaging him in polite conversation for a few minutes, without so much as a smirk.

Sir Frank, she owned, was a kind-hearted, amiable man, and realising this, could not but excuse his vanity and empty conversation. He managed to say a few half-sensible things, before he politely excused himself from Charlotte, and disappeared in another puff of powder towards his real object of interest.

The poor man hovered attentively around a cold-hearted Lavinia for another few minutes, making little headway with her, until Lord Winchester, having made his solicitations to Eliza, inserted himself smoothly between them. He took Lavinia by the arm, whisking her off to a private corner by the window.

'I say, well! Gracious! Yes, very good, very good,' said Sir Frank, and bowing to no one in particular, took himself off to the side of Miss Smart. He proceeded to strike up a conversation with that lady, who coloured with practiced blushes, and smiled decorously behind her fan.

Charlotte was somewhat relieved to note the entry of Sir Benedict, whom she supposed would intervene in any improper *tête-à-tête* between Lavinia and Lord Winchester. He looked very handsome in a fine brown jacket and cream cravat, and she dropped her gaze before he could notice her looking at him. Heaven forbid that he should think she was staring! However, although he kept an eye on his niece, he made no attempt either to join the conversation in the corner, nor to address herself and Eliza on the sofa. Presently, he sat at the card table where he was immediately and most eagerly joined by the Misses Latham and Miss Smart.

Cake was served, and little tarts, in addition to madeira, and cordial, and soon the party was happily making conversation and arguing which card game was superior, Vingt-et-Un, or Whist. Miss Annabelle Latham loudly declared herself a sharp at Vingt-et-un, but Frank Latham very much wished to play Whist, and immediately invited Lavinia to be his partner. Lord Winchester immediately sided with Miss Annabelle Latham and the decision was made, much to Sir Frank's disgust, which he hid unsuccessfully by looking very keenly into his glass of madeira and not speaking for several minutes. A second table was formed by Lord Winchester, Lavinia, Eliza, and a very discomposed Sir Frank. Eliza smiled and cajoled Sir Frank and soon had him in good spirits again, while Charlotte amused herself in watching the two groups from her private corner, and idly reading her book.

After two or three hands, Charlotte was politely entreated by Sir Frank to join them, and Eliza encouraged to take a small rest in front of the fire, but Eliza took one look at Charlotte's face, and declared herself fit for at least one, nay, perhaps two more hands. Sir Benedict eyed her once or twice, but observing that she was deeply engrossed in a novel of Miss Burney's, he did not direct any address her way. They played on and thus another hour went by pleasantly. Charlotte noted that Lord Winchester behaved decidedly well, despite his high-spirited mood, and noted nothing untoward in his behaviour toward her cousin. Miss Annabelle Latham's hostile glance was more than once levelled at the corner of the room also, but Charlotte kept her head down and this way, enjoyed relative calmness in her breast for most of the evening.

At last the hour became late, and the party dispersed, with promises of seeing each other on the morrow, and many happy good-nights. Charlotte watched Lavinia walk arm-in-arm with Lord Winchester from the house and into the darkness outside, and she followed them anxiously into the cool night air. In the dark of the evening, the two figures stood to one side in the shadows and Charlotte was reasonably sure she saw Lord Winchester bend to kiss Lavinia's hand, and then lean in closely to her head. Furthermore, Miss Annabelle Latham and her brother, standing in the doorway, had witnessed the scene and Miss Latham uttered some remark to her brother with a smirk on her face. Shocked, Charlotte withdrew quickly and her eyes sought Sir Benedict's. He was immediately at her side.

'What is it, Miss Milton? Have you seen a ghost?'

'Please, Sir, you may wish to speak with Lavinia,' she told him in a voice tinged with distress.

'And why is that?'

'Because she is making a spectacle of herself, Sir.'

Disbelief creasing his forehead, he stepped outside and was gone. The Lathams and Miss Smart were now making their way outside also, their carriages having been called around. Lord Winchester and Lavinia were now walking side by side on the gravel driveway, bathed in moonlight, toward Lord Winchester's carriage. They were accompanied by Sir Benedict. Nothing appeared amiss with either party, and Charlotte felt puzzled and vexed. If Lavinia wanted to throw herself at this young man and Sir Benedict saw nothing indecorous in the behaviour of the two young people, she hoped sincerely that Lavinia knew what she was about, and that the Lathams would not gossip at home about her cousin's obvious flirtation with the gentleman.

The carriages departed. Eliza had already gone to her bed,

having smiled a goodnight at Charlotte in the hallway. Lavinia followed her uncle indoors with a secretive smirk on her lips, and wishing Charlotte and Sir Benedict goodnight also, went upstairs with the maid who had come with a candle for her.

Finally, Charlotte was alone with Sir Benedict, and keeping her voice low, she took the opportunity to inquire as to how he had got on outside?

His countenance did not flicker, but his eyes mocked her. 'You seem much concerned for your cousin, Miss Milton. But please calm yourself. I have seen nothing amiss. I understand your fears regarding your cousin, but I can assure you, Lord Winchester is a fine young man, and a gentleman of good breeding by all accounts. I think you have nothing to fear.'

'But, Sir, I observed Lord Winchester — that is — I believe I saw them...' she trailed off, unable to proceed further.

'What do you suspect them of? Did you observe some indecorous behaviour, a... kiss, perhaps?' asked Sir Benedict, his lips curving in patronising disbelief.

She blushed furiously as he uttered the word. 'Do not you think that her behaviour is putting her reputation at risk? That the gentleman's own behaviour is putting her at risk?'

Sir Benedict shook his head. 'I doubt you saw what you think you did. Winchester is a gentleman and would never put my niece's reputation in danger. I believe you have been misled, by your own eyes, and even, perhaps, by that ability you have to jump to conclusions, Miss Milton. Yes,' he added, holding his hand up as she started to reply, 'I concede that my niece is highly strung, and perhaps a little silly at times, but I have not yet observed in her conduct anything very much amiss. She seems to be forming a strong attachment to Winchester and I am not against the match.'

'But,' cried Charlotte in distressed tones, 'even aside from her conduct, Sir, we know nothing of this young man, as much as his connections might be rumoured to be good. My cousin appears to be forming an excessively hasty attachment to Lord

Winchester, and he for her. Do not you yourself, as her guardian, have some apprehensions for her?'

Sir Benedict smiled slightly and shook his head. 'I take my role as Lavinia's guardian very seriously, Miss Milton, and I would never allow someone whom I thought was a fortune hunter or someone of ill-repute, someone *not* a gentleman, to pay his addresses to your cousin. Lord Winchester is a gentleman of rank, and reputedly a man of wealth and property. I did think perhaps that Frank Latham — well, it is obvious that she has formed an attachment to Lord Winchester, and I am not unhappy for her to regard him as a serious contender. Perhaps it would be best to trust me, rather than your own weak understanding of such matters.'

Charlotte bit back a retort and schooled her vexation. 'Sir, my cousin has always been a high-spirited girl. Even I, as her cousin, and who regard her with affection, can see that she is throwing herself at this man. She has violated every commonplace notion of propriety with Lord Winchester! People are noticing her behaviour. If she is not careful, the whole neighbourhood will come to regard her as the silliest flirt in the county! Her reputation will be ruined, even before she is married!'

Sir Benedict smiled patronisingly down at her. 'By "people", I presume you are referring to the Lathams. As usual, your enthusiasm for interfering in matters not relevant to you is undaunted. You seem to take delight in trying to run my estate, my staff, and my guardianship of your cousin! As a woman, you know nothing of these matters. Your concern for your cousin, while gratifying, is wholly misguided. Please drop the matter. Goodnight, Miss Milton.'

He strode up the staircase, leaving a stunned Charlotte standing at in the hall, with Stokes, who had just come to lock up and blow out the candles.

'Will you be wanting a candle Miss?' the servant politely inquired. 'The drawing room fire is still lit if you wish to sit there, Miss.'

Charlotte declined politely, wished good night to Stokes, and made her way upstairs. Well, she had tried to warn Sir Benedict! But apparently, she knew "nothing" of these matters! The arrogance of the man! Was Lord Winchester sincere in his attentions to her cousin? Sir Benedict seemed to think so. Perhaps he was correct, and yet, she felt something was amiss. There was something secretive about Lord Winchester, something too keen about him. And yet, as Sir Benedict pointed out, he could not be a fortune hunter, for he was a man of rank and wealth. She undressed for bed in deep thought, and when she laid her head on the pillow, it was some while before sleep overtook her.

Fourteen

A sound sleep and a hearty early breakfast found Charlotte's mood almost fully repaired and ready for the day. It was now only ten days from midsummer, and the weather, charmingly compliant with the wishes of everyone, stayed cloyingly warm and clear; flowers bloomed with vigour, and trees decked themselves with prodigious greenery to shade the overheated souls who walked about beneath them.

The first freshness of the morning of the picnic gave way to brilliant sunshine, and the awaited party of guests. Frank Latham's carriage drew up at the middle of the great sweeping driveway, from which issued Sir Frank, and then his sisters, Miss Anne Smart, and from the open seat, a greying gentleman of near fifty years, Mr Weatherby, friend of Sir Frank Latham and a man of the church.

Lavinia was anxious. 'Oh, I *do* hope Lord Winchester is coming! He did not send any servant to say he was not coming, did he Uncle? Oh, I *do* hope he will not bring *ladies* with him!'

Charlotte did her best to console her, and her cousin was content once more, when shortly after ten o'clock, a figure on horseback appeared alone. Lord Winchester, for it was he, was immediately claimed by Lavinia, who gazed adoringly up at him and excluded all others from her conversation.

As they collected around the driveway, waiting on the carriages, Charlotte managed to position herself near the younger Miss Latham and Miss Smart and exchanged some lacklustre comments on the weather and the undoubted probability of happiness for the outing. In this way, she managed to avoid any direct conversation with Sir Benedict, and it was only his mocking gaze which followed Charlotte wherever she went. Between the two well-dressed women, Charlotte again felt drab, with only her rather plain white-on-white muslin and a pretty straw bonnet trimmed with azure ribbon to do her justice, while the other ladies were in fine cloth and the latest designs from London.

Miss Sophia was more animated than usual and seemed in such a good mood as to find conversation with Charlotte quite acceptable as a diversion while they waited for the servants to organise their things. However, Charlotte felt Sir Benedict's eyes upon her frequently, and could hardly concentrate on the conversation at hand. Servants ran around in a flurry, stocking the two carriages with a variety of dishes and boxes of fruits and wines. Blankets and cushions were added, and at last the carriages were ready.

Then there was the urgent problem of whom ought to travel with whom. Sir Benedict was to ride, along with Lord Winchester. Miss Annabelle Latham loudly lamented the absence of Sir Benedict in their own carriage, and implored him to leave his horse and travel with them, for safety 'in case the carriage should overturn or some dreadful accident should befall them', but Sir Benedict assured her that riding alongside would do well enough for safety and if they overturned, he would endeavour to return immediately for the women without delay, after saving his horses. Lavinia tittered at this, and Sophia Latham smiled unkindly at her sister's obvious pique at this rebuff. Annabelle Latham sniffed, and vowed she would not find anything amusing in Sir Benedict's teasing and he was too, too unkind!

Snorting and tossing her head, she condescended to allow him to hand her into the carriage. This was followed by some vigorous discussion as to who ought to accompany them, but it was eventually decided that Frank Latham, his younger sister, and Miss Smart would occupy their own carriage, and that Lavinia, Eliza, Charlotte, and Mr Weatherby would occupy Sir Benedict's carriage. Sir Benedict and Lord Winchester would follow behind them. The party set off, accompanied by three servants bringing up the rear, and after a five-and-twenty minutes' ramble through lanes, across fields and up a hill, the lake which was their destination appeared below. The party of excited picnickers gathered themselves up and allowed the servants to set up blankets beneath a large oak tree, at not too great a distance from the lake.

Again, seating was to be arranged with the greatest of urgency from Miss Annabelle Latham, who did an admirable job of attempting to arrange everyone as artfully as a vase of flowers, Charlotte thought to herself, placing whom with *whom*, with all the subtlety of a charging horse.

'My Lord,' said she, addressing a surprised Lord Winchester, 'would not you sit here, next to my sister? Sophia, sit down at once! Do not be jiggling about like that, you will upset the fruits by your feet... Oh, you stupid creature, look what you have done!'

It was obvious to Charlotte that Miss Latham, her own suit in the interest of Sir Benedict fulfilled in her heart, if not quite yet solid in physical fact, had suddenly decided to try the idea of luring Lord Winchester away from Lavinia, for her sister Sophia instead. That young lady, however, was lunging about rescuing the upset apples, a glint of hostility in her pale blue eyes when she glanced at her sister. Wisely however, nothing was remarked upon by either Lord Winchester nor the lady at his feet, and the apples were returned to the basket by means of them both.

Lord Winchester then very uncooperatively rose from the

blanket and, after noting where Lavinia had seated herself, casually arranged his own arrival at the vacant spot next to her, and plopped himself down neatly, half lying at her side in an attitude of nonchalance. Lavinia simpered down at him and placed her fan over her mouth. Frank Latham, not yet quite given up on securing Lavinia for himself, seemed much put out by this artful manoeuvring and positioned himself as near as possible to Lavinia and her admirer.

All this Charlotte noted with an amused eye, but she was content to seat herself next to Mr Weatherby with nothing but a basket of peaches for company on her other side. Sir Benedict strode about, attending with much quiet authority to the servants, and the unloading of their picnic.

Miss Annabelle Latham had placed a cushion next to her person, and had reserved it with her parasol. She seemed to be willing Sir Benedict to sit beside her, so intent upon him were her eyes. Her powers of hypnotism were sadly lacking, for, after a moment, Sir Benedict walked over to the basket of peaches next to Charlotte, moved it behind them, and dropped down onto the blanket next to a very surprised, and disconcerted, Charlotte.

Much startled, and quite out of sorts, she turned quickly to her neighbour to hide her consternation. When she had gone to so much trouble to avoid him! What could he be about? He disliked her as much as she disliked him. Really, he must wish to deliberately make her uneasy, or perhaps he wished to be nearby the carriage where the servants were unpacking. She engaged Mr Weatherby in conversation almost urgently, by immediately asking him about his parish in the neighbouring town, and was gratified to receive some rational and detailed answers which allowed her to expand on the conversation and turn her back almost fully to her host while regaining her composure.

Sir Benedict did not at first address her, but rather ignored her and undertook to pour some madeira and water for his sister opposite. For some time, he remained engaged in conversation with Eliza and Miss Latham, who was looking alternately all sweetness for Sir Benedict and daggers at Charlotte.

Miss Latham petulantly began to complain of the heat, so early in the day, and could there not be some refreshment served immediately? Really, the servants were very slow! The servants hastened to be more immediate in their attentions, and hurried to lay out the cold collations, fruits, madeira and water, and plates of little cakes and tarts. Soon everyone was much about the business of eating, drinking, and becoming as merry a party as possible.

Charlotte was conscious of her host's presence to the point of being unable to eat. The masculine scent of him filled her senses and her appetite disappeared. Mr Weatherby did little to distract her, being now equally engaged to his right-hand side partner, Lavinia. Poor Mr Weatherby attempted to intervene twice in the conversation between Lavinia and Lord Winchester, but apart from some polite acknowledgements, Lavinia's attentions were all to her right side, not to her left.

All this Charlotte watched with some increasing concern. Lord Winchester had made his attraction very clear from the outset, and now held nothing back, in increasing his smiles, his flattery, and his whole attention to the young lady. His address was polite, not lacking in finesse or gentlemanly behaviour, and yet, Charlotte felt wary of the speed of the attachment. She had not forgotten the stolen kiss in the shadows! There was something amiss, but she could not describe it. It was a feeling within her that could not be explained.

She shook her head. Her host's choice of seating had simply unnerved her, and she owned she was still vexed after their conversation the previous evening. Awareness of his body only a slight distance from her own disconcerted her, even though he addressed those opposite her and never glanced her way once. And yet, her nerves tingled with awareness, and she was careful to keep her head turned away from his figure. The object of her attention had then, perforce, become Mr Weatherby, who had given up trying to address Miss Markham, and had resigned himself to destroying as many tarts and pies as possible and making occasionally desultory remarks about the weather to Charlotte. Charlotte nodded and smiled gravely, picking at her peach, but not able to eat.

'Do you often play with your food, Miss Milton, or have you no appetite today?'

Startled, she turned to face Sir Benedict, who had apparently abandoned his conversation with his amorous partner and was nodding at Charlotte's uneaten peach. Annabelle Latham darted a hostile look her way and stood up to yawn loudly and suggest a walk to no one in particular. Sir Benedict was still looking quizzically at Charlotte, awaiting a reply.

'Why I — I am not very hungry, Sir. The day is rather warm — that is, perhaps my appetite...' She could not think of anything to say and hoped the panic in her heart, did not show in her eyes.

Sir Benedict smiled, his eyes glinting. Helping himself to a rose-coloured peach from the basket behind him, he bit into it with great relish, and Charlotte watched in increasing alarm as his jaw, sprinkled with a day's growth of stubble, moved up and down smoothly, and juice ran over his long, brown fingers. She was unable to take her eyes from his mouth. Sir Benedict licked the juices from his fingers casually, and spoke again.

'May I enquire as to how your reading is progressing? I have seen you devour Keats, one of Miss Burney's novels, and you boast of having read several agricultural tracts. You have a varied taste in literature, very admirable for such a young lady. Pray, what is your preference, novels or poetry, or agricultural tracts?' His mouth was a firm line, but his eyes were sparkling.

'You are teasing me again, Sir Benedict. If I answer, you will no doubt find me at fault, no matter how I choose. Therefore,

I give no reply.' She folded her arms, not sure if she ought to be laughing or annoyed with him. She glanced up and saw that he was smiling.

He shook his head in mock seriousness. 'Ah, now I have upset you. I am sorry for it, but I had a mind to discuss literature, even though I may not converse so readily upon it as you do, for I do not understand the poets as well as you. But agriculture now, I think I can have a share in the conversation and say something not so small on the subject. But perhaps you can instruct *me*?'

'Now you openly mock me Sir. You are quite aware that I know little on that subject.'

'But you are so much more well-read on progressive techniques in farming than I! It is one thing to practice agriculture, to farm one's land, but quite another to be a scholar of the subject. I would be a most attentive student, I assure you.'

His eyes were laughing at her although his countenance was serious to anyone looking on. Miss Latham watched them from across the circle of picnickers, her eyes little ovals of sharp resentment.

Charlotte pursed her lips, as irritation rose momentarily to be so observed. 'I think you are making a fool of me, Sir Benedict. I never meant — that is, I am interested, but I do not pretend to know more than yourself on such a subject,' she responded warmly. 'I have only read some tracts by Mr Crabbe on the subject of enclosure. I am eager to learn and to read on many subjects, to learn about the world around me.'

Sir Benedict remained silent, his brows raised slightly, and she continued, nervous but eager to correct his low opinion of her.

'I do not shrink from reading and learning anything at all which concerns the world that I live in, although I do not partake of that world the same way a man does. I seek to learn, only that I might converse with intelligence on a subject dear to the hearts of many where I live. I have been on familiar terms with many of the poorest families in my own neighbourhood. The problems of enclosure are near to hearts of many in our little village, proof of which I see daily, I am afraid. Poverty is a sad thing, Sir Benedict, and it shames me to think that those of us who have it in their power to provide income and sustenance to the less fortunate sometimes do not, where the lure of progress, and profit, are to be enjoyed.' She stopped, not wishing to anger him as she had the previous day.

'I see.' He looked grave. 'And you have judged me wanting in this regard, have you? Progress is not all bad, you know. But you are such an eager student of farming practices, that I have no doubt you will come to a conclusion in its favour in time,' he noted, with a smile. 'But tell me, Miss Milton, do your studies also include the arts of love? For you seem particularly well versed in *that* topic, too! Or are your opinions the result of reading too much poetry? Is Mr Keats to blame for your passionate opinions on that subject?'

His eyes laughed at her and the colour rose in her face, but before she could find a retort, he laughed aloud. 'Ah, but come now, let us not quarrel, for it is a pleasant day in pleasant company, is it not? I think it is unwise to argue in this heat, or your appetite might decrease further and if you were to faint, I would quite certainly carry the blame for it. No indeed! We shall not quarrel today. Let us shake hands and be friends today, for I divine that I will be much safer from your tongue as your friend than your enemy, I think,' he added, chuckling. He tossed his wet peach stone into the nearby grass. 'Truce, Miss Milton?' He held out his hand.

Aware of the eyes of Miss Latham boring holes in her back, Charlotte nervously nodded and briefly shook hands with him. His hand was warm and firm, and again she felt a sudden awareness of her own femininity as his masculine hand held her small, feminine one, and she withdrew her hand quickly and began to tidy up her plate and glass.

Fifteen

Miss Latham had begun to organise a walking expedition, but the party was divided as to the object of it. One side, of which Miss Latham had clearly become the organiser, wished to walk to the top of the hill to admire the view, while Lord Winchester, Lavinia and Mr Weatherby wished to walk down the hill to the lane and glean what nuts or berries they might find in the hedgerow. They were informed by Sir Benedict that it was not the season for nuts but the berries were plentiful and that both parties were welcome to divide and take exercise as they pleased. For himself, he would choose to gather berries as he was fond of berries straight from the bush.

At this, Miss Annabelle Latham looked as if she would like to stamp her pretty foot, and then thought better of it. 'Why, that is a true statement! There is no finer thing to be eaten on a hot day than berries from the bush! What a pleasant thing it is to do, to gather berries like gypsies, to eat the wild produce of nature while in nature ourselves! Come, Sophie dearest, I believe Sir Benedict has hit upon the thing!' She animatedly began to gather the baskets which the servants had found for the party, and took it upon herself to distribute them.

Lavinia sidled up to Charlotte, having torn herself from Lord Winchester for a few moments. 'Why, I do believe Miss Latham is jealous of you, Charlotte! When she saw you and my uncle deep in conversation, she looked quite in a panic! No, no, do not bother denying it,' she added, laughing, 'you have quite put her out of sorts and now she is in "mode du recuperation" as they say.'

Charlotte laughed mirthlessly. 'I do not know why she regards me as competition. To tell the truth, Cousin, your uncle and I disagree on so many subjects that it is difficult to have a friendly conversation. According to him, I am all sharp tongue and unformed opinions, and I think he is overbearing and unfair,' she said tartly. 'Miss Latham has nothing to worry about, and I would assure the lady of that myself, if given the chance,' she added with a wry smile. 'But Lavinia, I would caution you to be careful. I know we have spoken of this before, but we know nothing of Lord Winchester, although he seems to be a very agreeable young man. You are making your preference for him so very clear, and I am afraid it looks a little—unladylike—to show such a strong preference after so short an acquaintance.'

'Oh Charlotte, there you go again, being a spoil-sport. Why should I not show my preference? Should I show less of my feelings, as if I am not interested? Then he will go away, and look at Miss Smart or Sophia instead! No, indeed, I shall have him! He is a most agreeable young man, and he is an Earl! If he shows an inclination for me, then I shall do my best to encourage it. His status in life means that I would be able to enjoy the finest circles of society and be seen at the best theatres, and in the best of company!' she added excitedly.

'But we know nothing of his connections, his friends. He could be a fortune hunter!'

'Don't be silly Charlotte, he is not at all interested in my fortune. He has his own wealth! Besides, he has asked me nothing about it; I think he cannot know! But I must go at once, for now it has all changed and we are to walk up the hill with Frank Latham, Miss Smart and Mr Weatherby, who is so entirely dull I think I shall kick him down the hill again if he makes any more comments on the weather!' she finished dramatically, and danced away to her companions.

Baskets having been officiously handed out by Miss Annabelle Latham herself, those walking to collect berries began to trail off down the hill. Sir Benedict was of that party and was to be found beside his sister, who leaned heavily on his arm while he walked slowly for her comfort. Miss Latham quickly abandoned her sister and attached herself to his other arm. Charlotte was not able to see Sir Benedict's reaction to this manoeuvring, but he amiably offered his arm, and poor Sophia was left to walk along behind them.

Charlotte paused, unwilling to join the berry-picking party, but too hot to walk up the hill with her cousin and, she conceded, the very dull Mr Weatherby. She decided to walk a little with Sophia, and then to veer off around the hill to explore a wooded area she had noticed. Joining Sophia, she was gladdened to receive a grateful smile and the two women followed their party down the hill.

Watching Sir Benedict and Miss Latham together, Charlotte felt a little pang in her stomach, and her fine brows knitted together with puzzlement for a moment. She did not even like the man! Why should she be disconcerted to see them walk side by side, so intimately in conversation as they seemed to be? Why, it must be that she did not think Miss Latham very suited to Sir Benedict after all! She owned that she did not like the lady, and her apparent lack of *finesse* when it came to pursuing a man seemed unsuited to his gentleman-like manner. She decided it would be a very odd match indeed if he did choose to marry her. And yet the lady seemed so sure of his attachment!

They rounded a little wooded area and the berry pickers moved forward to hunt for wild berries. Sophia offered to share her basket with Charlotte, but the latter declined, and pleading a need for shade, she made her way into the cool of the woods and idly strolled there for a time, enjoying the peace and quiet under the leafy boughs of the great green and silver beech and oak trees which formed the principle part of the little wood.

After a time, she sat upon a fallen log and her thoughts turned to her father, and then to her poor dear mama. She rarely allowed herself to dwell on the past, but something in the beauty of the natural scene before her made sad thoughts rise up more readily and a moment more found her cheeks wet. Surprised at herself, she used the back of her hand to wipe her face, silently admonishing herself for allowing sombre thoughts to cast a pall over a lovely day. As she did so, a movement out of the corner of her eye made her turn her head in alarm. A dark figure stood under a tree not far from her.

'Forgive me, I did not mean to intrude.' Sir Benedict came forward and, noting her red eyes, he frowned. 'Miss Milton, are you ill? Can I assist you in any way? Perhaps the heat has made you unwell?' he said, concern deepening the rich tones of his voice.

Charlotte shook her head, acutely self-conscious. 'Please, Sir, it is nothing at all. I was feeling a little melancholy. That is all. The result of being overcome with the natural beauty of this place, I think.' She glanced around at the quiet forest scene before her. 'It is just the place where one might dwell on more melancholy thoughts, although I ought not to encourage that in myself,' she added, half smiling, half hiding her head in shame.

Sir Benedict was silent for a moment, then came to stand in front of her. 'Perhaps it would help if you tell me your troubles?'

His voice was unusually gentle, and she resisted the surprising urge to unburden her cares upon him. He was silent a moment more. 'You have recently lost your mother, I believe?' he asked quietly.

She could not answer, astonished and dismayed that he had

so readily guessed her thoughts. She was very conscious of his nearness.

He continued quietly. 'When my brother and his wife died two years ago, Lavinia came to live at Delford. For a time, she was very low in spirits. It grieved me to see my niece unhappy. But after a short period of time, she became gay and happy once more. You *will* rally, Miss Milton, although I know it does not feel like it now.'

Charlotte could not help feeling a rush of emotion at the sudden change of attitude of her host and remembered their agreed truce only an hour beforehand. She felt herself at once overcome with his unexpected kind words and bent her head to hide a fresh flow of tears. At length, she lifted her eyes and dabbed softly at her cheeks with her skirt.

'I am sorry. I do try not to dwell on it. But it is not just that... I do miss my poor mama, but—' Here she halted, unable to explain herself further, and afraid he would think her complaining or ungrateful.

Sir Benedict sat beside her on the fallen tree, and she felt his sudden nearness as if a spark of lightning had passed between them. Her acute awareness of his presence caused her hand to tremble as he offered her his own clean kerchief. She took the item with gratitude.

'I think I can penetrate what you must be feeling,' he offered in a low voice as she clung to the soft linen of his handkerchief. 'Your cousin tells me that your father has remarried somewhat sooner than is expected in polite society? And perhaps there is some problem with your new stepmother?'

She nodded, head down, surprised at his clever guess and ashamed of her ungrateful attitude toward Mariah.

His voice held tones of amusement, but it was not unkind. 'Well then! Let me guess. Hmmm... it is a very tragic story indeed. You are struggling to accept your new step-mama, who is unkind and makes you clean the fireplaces and work in the kitchen like a slave. Moreover, she is plotting to remove you from your father's house by some canny trick, in order that she can install her own daughter, who is exceptionally ugly by the by, in your place, and thus cast you from your father forever!'

Charlotte lifted her eyes to stare up at him in unaffected astonishment, only to find him smiling at her in a way that was most unnerving. She was startled out of her melancholy and laughed despite herself. 'If I was feeling sorry for myself, I am cured of self-pity now, for that story is much worse than the one I had in mind, and besides, I do not have a half-sister,' she smiled. 'But, in my defence, I am not usually prone to bouts of self-pity and I am much embarrassed that you have caught me at it.'

Sir Benedict chuckled and shook his head. 'That makes three faults I have discovered in your character then, Miss Milton. Running on the stairs, a desire to interfere in anything and everything not your business, and a tendency to self-pity.'

This was uttered without any malicious overtone, but Charlotte coloured slightly, reminded of their encounter the first morning of her stay.

Regarding her gravely he said, 'I should not be unkind and tease you. I apologise for it. But pray, do not feel uncomfortable that I have seen you give way to melancholy. Everyone must be allowed a little self-indulgence from time to time. You have been through a trying time. It is natural, I think, to feel a little lowness of spirits. You have lost a parent only recently. It is natural that you must suffer a longer period of mourning when your circumstances at home are a reminder of what you have lost.'

'I would not wish a long period of mourning, or any pain, when it is real and true pain, on anyone,' she rejoined earnestly. 'I would wish it much lessened, or to do as Lavinia does, and force gaiety until it becomes natural.'

Sir Benedict cast her a look which she could not interpret, but seemed full of feeling, and her heart fluttered under his study of her face. After a short pause, he bent to pick up a stick from the ground and idly began to peel the bark from its stem while he spoke. He seemed deeply affected by her words.

After a moment, he spoke again, his voice full of emotion. 'I myself am no stranger to loss, and to "real and true pain", Miss Milton. When you, a few days ago, reminded me that I had been unlucky in love you were correct. I assume my niece has spoken to you on the subject, although I do not thank her for it. Do not ask me for details, but,' and here he flung his stick into the woods, 'I can assure you that it is true that the passage of time heals all wounds. In time, you will have memories without the pain, and gaiety will be natural, rather than forced.'

She looked up at him, wide-eyed, remembering her conversation with Lavinia the first day she had arrived, and her words of anger the morning that she had confronted him about Tom Wilcox. That she had brought up a private subject, and used it to hurt him! She felt shame and was sorry she had flung such sentiments at him. To be jilted by someone you love! She sensed that he had suffered a great loss and felt a sudden deep connection with the man who stood before her. The sensation shocked her, and she looked away to hide the feelings that passed across her countenance.

Feeling unaccountably safe to confide in him, she dropped all her reserve and became as frank as he himself had been with her. 'My father's hasty remarriage did indeed grieve me for a time. But mostly I think of Mama. I do not — that is, I try not to hold feelings of resentment in my heart, for I am glad that my father is not alone at this time of his life. But sometimes it is difficult to remember how things were, and my father seems to have moved on quickly, while I — I cannot forget the happy times I had with Mama, especially now that Mariah has come to live with us! It is not that she is unpleasant, but perhaps not as warm as I would have liked her to be.' Her voice trembled.

He was quiet, as if in sympathy for her unexpected admission. 'Perhaps,' he offered gently, 'if you will accept my advice, you might give your new stepmother more time to adjust. It must be a great change for her, too.'

She felt the gentle reproof, and yet strangely, she did not mind it, at all. 'I concede,' she replied after a moment, 'you are right. I have been behaving as if all the difficulty of our changed circumstances was entirely on my own side. Of course, I am not a fairy tale character — I am no Cinderella,' she added with a smile, 'and I must try harder to make a friend of my stepmother. I am determined, as you see, Sir Benedict, to make the best of my situation,' she finished with a smile. 'Your words have produced a cure in me — thank you! It was adequate and quite efficacious. I am back to my old self once again!'

Sir Benedict contemplated her thoughtfully, and her heart gave a little jump as his eyes met hers.

'I did not mean to wholly dismiss your discomfort, you know,' he explained. 'It must be difficult to accept a new parent, so very soon after the loss of the other. My advice for now is to try to enjoy your time with us, here at Delford, and do not feel that you cannot confide in my sister, or even in your cousin, who must be able to enter in to your loss, with the experience of her own.'

Charlotte played idly with the handkerchief in her hands. 'I have not had the solace of sharing my feelings until today, with you. It has been a relief to speak of it. Because of my father's rather quick recovery from his loss, there have been few people in whom I could confide, even among my most intimate friends at home. I did think that I might confide in my cousin, but she is wise to wish not to speak of it. She has made a speedier recovery from her loss, than I have from my own! I have made the mistake of dwelling on my circumstances too much, I think. I should not like to become maudlin! Lavinia is right not to mention the subject, I think, for I would only feel self-pity, and that I do not wish to encourage in myself,' she explained with a rueful look.

Sir Benedict nodded thoughtfully. 'What you say is true, and I admit that my niece lacks some sensitivity, considering her own loss. For yourself, it has only been, what, less than one year, has it not? But do not distress yourself, Miss Milton. Your cousin does not mean any ill will by her indifference, I think. She is too young to know better, although her aunt tries daily to instil some sense into her head. As you know yourself, her head is full of fashion and the latest news from the *ton*. But her heart is, I am certain, in the right place.'

Charlotte allowed herself to study his form in the shady light of the great oak above them and wondered to herself. There was something about the way he held his head, a certain look in his eyes, and something about the way he had comforted her in her melancholy. He might be sometimes harsh and unyielding, but there was a hidden softness and a deep insight into other people, which warmed her to him. She perceived in herself, not without some surprise, a newfound respect and compassion for the man. Underneath that rough exterior was unexpected kindness. His sensitivity to her situation, his astute perception regarding her anxiety relating to her father's remarriage, she confessed she found pleasant. She felt a perceptible lifting of the sadness which had burdened her heart for so long. She found herself wishing to extend their conversation and began to speak again.

At this moment however, they were interrupted by female voices, one shrill and one placating, and a few moments more gave way to two figures approaching in the pale light of the afternoon. Charlotte realised that she still held Sir Benedict's handkerchief in her hands, and pushed the item into her pocket, without rational thought.

Miss Latham and her sister came into view. They were arguing about something, and when they noticed Sir Benedict and Charlotte sitting companionably together, Annabelle Latham shot Charlotte a look of malevolence before changing the tone of her voice to one much softer than that she was using for her sister. 'Why, here you are, Sir Benedict! And Miss Milton, you sly creature! Keeping Sir Benedict all to yourself! Why, we were ever so perplexed as to where you might have gone! You could have fallen down a bank or into a quarry and we wouldn't have known,' she added in silky tones.

Charlotte could well imagine that were such ill luck to befall her, Miss Latham would be the last person to notice, let alone come to her rescue! She remained silent at the other woman's malicious insinuations and let her continue.

'How lucky we found you! I am monstrous tired from gleaning berries! What a full basket we were able to collect! La, but I'm tired! Perhaps I might sit a while?' and she gestured at the rough woodland seat on which Charlotte sat.

Sir Benedict smoothly interjected. 'I happened upon Miss Milton, and remained with her while she rested. She is somewhat fatigued after her walk, and there are gypsies nearby. One can never be too careful,' he added blandly.

At his words, Charlotte sprang up, the pleasant companionship of the previous moments now a memory. Mumbling that she was quite rested, she became most interested in a nearby flower, and Miss Latham took her place on the log beside Sir Benedict with a gloating smile. Sophia Latham looked much put out at her sister's forward behaviour, and Sir Benedict at once offered his own seat to that lady, whereupon her sister exclaimed that Sophia did not need a seat, for her sister was an excellent walker and could not possibly be fatigued after so little exercise. Perhaps Sir Benedict might wait a little while with them and accompany them both back to the others in a short time?

The slight to Charlotte was not lost on Sir Benedict. Glancing amusedly at Charlotte, he bowed his assent. 'If Miss Milton and the Miss Lathams will remain a little longer, it would be my pleasure to escort all *three* ladies back to the main party in a few minutes.'

Charlotte noted the poisonous look that Miss Annabelle Latham sent her and she shook her head. 'I am quite rested, and if you will excuse me, I will find my cousin. She must be wondering where I am.'

Immediately, Miss Latham pounced on her opportunity. 'But Sophia, you must not wait for me! Do return with Miss Milton to the others, and tell them I shall be along presently, once I have recovered my strength. No, Sophia dearest, I will be quite alright with Sir Benedict to look after me. No gypsies will dare to pounce whilst I am under *his* protection!'

Annabelle smirked up at Sir Benedict, and her sister, having been dismissed, snatched her reprieve before it could be revoked, and linked arms with Charlotte. 'Come, Miss Milton, let us find my brother and Miss Markham. They are sure to be playing games by now and we do not want to miss cup and ball! I am very partial to cup and ball!'

Sofia Latham chattered on and Charlotte remained quietly lost in her thoughts as they made their way back to the group. Charlotte wondered at the scene they were leaving behind, and rather thought Sir Benedict looked less than besotted with his intended, but his countenance was all pleasantness as they departed. Charlotte thought that Sir Benedict would not be likely to linger long, since he was the outing's host.

Sixteen

The others had regrouped and were playing Bilbocatch. Lavinia and Lord Winchester were the principle leaders of this endeavour and the former was laughing delightedly as Lord Winchester tried repeatedly to catch his ball and failed. Looking abashed, Winchester handed the cup and ball first to Frank Latham, who refused it curtly, and then to Miss Smart, who simpered up at him and flailed about with the toy until Sophia Latham offered to improve her technique by showing her how it was to be done. Charlotte went to Eliza, who was seated upon some cushions in the shade with her fan.

'How glum Sir Frank looks,' Eliza noted as Charlotte sat down. 'I collect he is vastly disheartened at your cousin's obvious preference for Lord Winchester. Observe how cast down and out of sorts he is! I do hope they will put him out of his misery quickly and announce an engagement soon.'

Charlotte was taken aback. 'Oh, do not you think it quite soon for that? After all, they have known each other barely a week!'

'Where you young people are concerned, a week is often enough to secure hearts, and presume, with all the cheerful blindness of youth, one's future happiness,' laughed Eliza. 'Besides, it is better not to know one's intended too well, for then, nobody would ever marry! I am convinced the shorter the courting period, the greater the chance for success!'

Charlotte could not help smiling a little at this statement, since it was so opposite to what she herself felt was necessary before matrimony, but it made her think immediately of her father and Mariah, and she acknowledged that in some circumstances, Eliza may well be right!

Sir Benedict and Miss Latham strolled into view, and shortly they joined the others, who had now got up a game of charades. Mr Weatherby begged to be excused from such frivolity, such as did not become a man of his calling, to which Miss Smart and Sophia exclaimed that as it was only riddles, it would not signify at all, and if the church viewed riddles as subversive then why, they felt monstrous sorry for clergymen in general! However, despite this sincere outpouring, Mr Weatherby remained firm and declined to join in. Eliza pleaded tiredness and joined Mr Weatherby in observing the game.

Lavinia caught at Charlotte's hand and made her join the circle. She obligingly sat on an overturned basket and tried to summon her wits. The others sat on cushions, waiting expectantly. Sir Benedict stood to one side, opposite Charlotte. She could not make out the meaning of the expression on his face, but his eyes were very dark and thoughtful, and she dropped her head, wondering if she were the object of his thoughts. It gave her no ease to sit under his scrutiny and she wished he would not stare so!

Lavinia opened the round, seated on a cushion and, unlike her cousin, seemed quite content to be the object of everyone's attentions. Lavinia began:

> '*My first, tho' water, cures no thirst.*
> *My next alone has soul,*
> *And when he lives upon my first,*
> *Then he is called my whole.*'

She finished the charade triumphantly, and assured the whole party that they would 'never guess it.'

'Why, Lavinia, dearest, that is easy!' exclaimed Miss Annabelle Latham, 'for it can only signify "seaman". She laughed delightedly, looking very pleased with her own wit, and continued. 'Now it is my turn. I dare say I shall come up with something very droll for I have heard enough of them from my brother, have I not, Frank? Riddles are so much in your favour, we are always being asked to hear you! But you must not answer this round, for you know the one I am about to repeat.'

Frank inclined his head and assured his sister that he would not dream of revealing the answer before the others had had their chance to solve it.

Annabelle began. ' "*I wound the heart, and please the eye. Tell me what I am, by and by*". Why, Sir Benedict, can you not guess my riddle?' she added, smiling engagingly up at him. She adopted an attitude that was popular with very young ladies, posing with her hand framing her chin, in such a way as would draw attention to her face.

Charlotte looked away, unsure whether to be amused or embarrassed for the lady. If Miss Annabelle Latham was so sure of Sir Benedict's affection, she was certainly trying very hard to keep it!

'Why, that is not difficult, Miss Latham,' began Lord Winchester, looking meaningfully at Lavinia. 'It is something not all women possess, but those who do have great power over a man.'

Lavinia smiled her prettiest smile at him and giggled into her fan. Sir Benedict glanced at Charlotte, then at Miss Latham, who was holding her pose and simpering up at him.

'I agree, Winchester. The answer to your charade, Miss Latham, is "Beauty".'

Annabelle looked like that cat that had got the cream, thought Charlotte.

Sir Benedict continued. 'But it is wisely noted by the same riddle that beauty wounds; therefore, beware the woman that uses her outward beauty to entrap a man! For a *wounded* heart may no longer see the beauty it once observed.'

Miss Latham at once dropped her pose and coloured slightly. She laughed carelessly. 'Why Sir Benedict, you are almost poetical today!' she drawled. 'Perhaps Miss Milton has influenced you with her keen interest in the poets. I always find that too much poetry is not good for the mind and puts one in a gloomy mood. I am not at all fond of poetry. My friends say I have a great deal of good taste in literature — and for myself, I much prefer history and novels to poetry. La, it is so very warm this afternoon. So very warm. Shall we not walk again, Sir Benedict?'

At this moment, a servant approached Sir Benedict and a brief interchange took place, the servant reminding him politely of the time and that the carriages were at his disposal to take them all home again. Their host was obliged to agree with his man, and the young fellow was forced to endure the cross looks of a disgruntled Miss Latham while the picnic things were packed up.

The party waited while the servants bustled about, collecting up baskets and cushions, and the berries that the ladies had gathered, and took their places in the carriages or upon horseback as they had arrived. Charlotte took her place beside Lavinia with a strange fluttering in her stomach, but she remembered that she had eaten little at lunch and thought that some tea, when they arrived home, would revive her.

Lavinia chattered excitedly with Eliza, ignored Mr Weatherby, and did not attend Charlotte's subdued mood until they arrived back at Delford. Charlotte went gratefully upstairs after the party departed, ordered tea to be sent to her room, and then lay on her bed. She put a hand into her pocket, and pulled from it the handkerchief which Sir Benedict had loaned her earlier. She opened it up, and traced the 'B' with her finger, lost in thought.

Tuesday and Wednesday, although warm, bought rain and kept the women indoors most of the day. Sir Benedict, as always, was out on the estate with his bailiff; rain would not keep him from his duty and besides, he told Eliza one evening at dinner, animals and fields did not stop being animals and fields when it rained. He was, Charlotte decided begrudgingly, to be admired for his work ethic, being willing to get his hands dirty alongside his workers, unlike so many gentleman farmers, whose incomes were so sufficient as to free them from the necessity of manual labour and which fact they boasted loudly.

Sir Benedict however, appeared to take a great pride in being out on his estate with his manager for long hours, in all weathers. Charlotte found she admired her host more as she came to understand him, and yet, she could neither understand nor forgive him for his unrelenting attitude toward young Tom Wilcox. She felt very sorry for Mary, who bore the separation from her intended well, but often looked downcast and solemn when she was at her duties.

Charlotte felt in her heart that it was unfair to separate two people who loved each other. She puzzled but could not understand the conflicting sides of Sir Benedict's personality. On the one hand, on the day of the picnic party, he had revealed a warmth, a sensitivity, a deep insight into human suffering, which did him great credit. His unexpected kindness towards herself moved Charlotte greatly. However, experiencing this unexpected side to his nature had puzzled her exceedingly; it was so different to the harsh attitudes and actions she had seen him display previously. Despite suffering a painful loss of his own, he would brook no discussion upon the subject of Tom Wilcox and Mary, and remained stubbornly against allowing the match. This bewildered Charlotte and she pondered it often. She wished keenly to make out his character further.

Mulling over these matters on Wednesday morning, her thoughts turned to Tom Wilcox's mother and her sick infant. The few coins she had given young James had probably not gone far. Charlotte wished very much to do something more for the Wilcox family, and made her mind up to walk to the Wilcox cottage when the rain eased.

First, a morning call from the inhabitants of Highview was to be endured, which, upon Miss Latham's discovery that Sir Benedict was not in, was announced to be 'a short call, to see our dear friends at Delford, before we walk into the village,' much to Charlotte's quiet relief. She did not find the company of the Miss Lathams and their guest to be so relished that she would gladly be drawn from her books, or her beloved walks. She wishfully eyed her volume of Keats on the low table near her seat, and politely sat as the other five ladies talked over the picnic, fondly proclaiming its delights, and the Miss Lathams venturing vague promises to give their own picnic party very soon, before the summer was over.

Sir Frank, not yet absolutely discouraged in his suit to Miss Markham, was delighted to find that his rival was not in attendance, and paid much attention to Lavinia, while she repaid his efforts with all the politeness of an ice maiden. She avoided all conversation with him, preferring to gossip with the Miss Lathams and Miss Smart, and poor Sir Frank was forced to appear as if this was all going exactly as planned.

Only ten minutes had passed in this manner, when a knock at the door was followed by the entrance of Sir Frank's aforesaid rival and all of Sir Frank's hopes for a monopoly upon his favourite's attention were destroyed in a moment's work.

Lord Winchester entered the room with éclat and a distinct air of confidence, and immediately sat as near to Lavinia as he could do with decorum, and another several minutes was spent once again reminiscing over the picnic party of the previous day. After this subject was exhausted, Lord Winchester turned to Lavinia and after a few moments of private discussion, Lavinia uttered a loud exclamation and clapped her hands in excitement.

'Oh! A puppy? But how delightful! Where is the little creature? Oh, how I long for a puppy!'

Lord Winchester revealed that his man was waiting outside the door with the animal, and a moment later the servant presented the puppy to Lord Winchester at the door, who then presented it to Lavinia.

Charlotte was shocked. She held back from saying so, but she could see from the glances that Miss Latham and her sister were exchanging, that Lavinia was doing herself no service by accepting the gift, and Charlotte's expression was grim as Lavinia took the wriggling little black and white spaniel pup in her arms. Lavinia, unaware or uncaring of the impropriety of such a gift, lifted the pup, kissed it, and fussed over it for a few moments and then set it down, whereupon it ran all over the parlour, and made a wet patch in the corner.

Eliza frowned, but whether because of her niece's behaviour or the puddle on the floor, Charlotte could not tell. 'Lavinia my love, perhaps you had better give the animal to Stokes who can set it up in the kitchen and feed it. No, don't chase it my dear; there, it has knocked over a vase already! Stokes? Please take the pup and see that it is looked after.'

The servant took the pup, after Lavinia had kissed it once

again, and departed with the struggling animal in his arms. Lavinia laughed and clapped her hands again. 'Oh, how adorable, Lord Winchester. How did you know I longed for a puppy? But you are so clever to have known! I shall call her Belle!'

Lord Winchester's lips curled smilingly over his exceedingly white teeth. 'A puppy is never a bad gift for a young lady, since it can entertain even while becoming useful. She is one of a litter from my favourite bitch, you know. You will have to get one of the servants to train her. And I hope very much,' he added, looking meaningfully into Lavinia's eyes, 'that when you cannot be in the company of those who are — fond — of you, that her company will suffice.'

Lavinia glowed and hid her eyes, demurely casting her gaze at the floor then back up at him momentarily. 'I shall think of you, my Lord, whenever she is in the room.'

Sir Frank uttered a strained cough into his kerchief and seemed to choke a little. Miss Annabelle Latham smiled archly and glanced sideways at her sister who returned her look with a knowing smirk.

Charlotte wished she was not witness to such obvious flattery and flirtation between Lord Winchester and her cousin, and looked away to cover her distress. Although she was no supporter of Sir Frank, she owned that he must be feeling rather ill-used by this time. A few moments later, Lord Winchester turned the conversation back to the picnic and then quickly became the most popular person in the room with most of the ladies, even if not with Sir Frank. Lord Winchester proposed to give a ball next Saturday evening, and wished to invite them all!

The happy news of the ball sent five of the ladies into paroxysms of delight, while Charlotte remained quiet, observing from her seat at the window, all the physical and intellectual manoeuvrings of Lord Winchester, and thought that nothing good would come out of a ball given on his own territory and so obviously meant to allow him more access to her cousin. However, she remained silent on the point and indulgently nodded her assent when asked by Lavinia if it were not the happiest occasion in the world! After a few minutes more, their guests left, and Lavinia rushed upstairs, new puppy forgotten, to look over her gowns, declaring that she must have a new one made, as everyone had seen her best ones already!

~~*~~

Later that afternoon, when the rain had eased to a dull grey sky, Charlotte went downstairs to the kitchen to speak with Mary. Then, after finding Lavinia lounging in her little parlour, eating sugared almonds and playing with her new puppy, she put on a plain bonnet, found a warm shawl, and put on a pair of Mary's pattens, who had been happy to loan them. She went to the glass to see the effect, then smiled at herself. How Lavinia would laugh and chastise her for being so old-fashioned! Lavinia would not be seen in pattens! But at home, Charlotte often wore pattens to walk about the countryside, and was not ashamed to do so now. It did not signify what she wore to a worker's cottage to visit the poor and sickly, and she wished to keep the hem of her dress clean so that Mary's job would be easier.

She left by the back entrance, much to the amused smiles of the servants in the kitchen, taking with her the loaf and the fresh-churned butter which Mrs Ransom had slyly passed her. She smiled her thanks at Mary, for it was likely she who had tipped off the cook, and set off at a brisk pace with her basket. The air was fresh but not cold, and the sky a pale blue strip beneath long streaks of silvery cloud. She was very glad of the pattens, for the roads were excessively wet and muddy and the hem of her dress was hardly as soiled as it would have been without them!

She went by way of the village, and was a little stared at by one or two passing ladies, for she made a quite a ridiculous picture in the unfashionable footwear, but since she was used to wearing them at home, she did not mind the amused looks she received, until, leaving the village, she chanced upon the Misses Latham and Miss Smart coming towards her!

There was nothing to do but keep walking, but she wished excessively that she did not have to pass them! When the three women spied her walking towards them, they slowed to give her a polite, if cold, acknowledgement, casting smirking glances at her feet, and tittering rudely amongst themselves after she had passed. Charlotte lifted her chin and shrugged to herself. If they had servants enough to clean their dirty hems, and did not care to lighten the workload below stairs, that was their business. She cared not for their opinions and would rather save the servants from extra work and her father's money for the new boots she would need after walking in the mud!

She stomped along, jumping stiles, and trudging down the dirty lane, and presently came to the workers' cottages. Remembering which cottage James and his little sister had disappeared into, she walked to the gate and called out. The door was closed, but presently, it opened slightly and then wider when the inhabitant saw her at the gate. A thin, dark-headed woman in a torn apron and a clean but torn dress nodded at her and beckoned her in.

Charlotte shut the gate carefully and greeted Polly, who had now come barrelling out, gleefully calling out, 'The lady, my lady come 'ere, Ma! 'Ello lady! Look Ma, it my lady!'

Polly's grubby little hand took Charlotte's and Charlotte was pulled inside. She smiled and nodded to Mrs Wilcox and was returned a shy smile and curtsey in return.

'Please come in, Miss. I'm sorry there ain't no clean place to sit,' the woman said, brushing the only chair furiously with her hand, 'but here Miss, please do have a seat, if you would be so kind.'

Charlotte shook her head and sat on the side of a bed which

was in the corner and placed her basket on the floor. Polly immediately hopped up on her knee and began to play with Charlotte's reticule.

'Please, Mrs Wilcox, you take the chair, and rest your feet. I won't stay long, but I've wished to make your acquaintance since I met Polly and James in the road last week. I'm Miss Milton. I'm staying at Delford, as a guest of my cousin, Miss Markham.'

'How d'you do, Miss Milton? It were very good of you to come. James and Polly tol' me they met you. Thank'ee Miss for the coins. You were very kind to help us. Since Thomas, senior that is, died, it's been very hard. Polly, mind your manners and don't play with the lady's reticule. Leave it alone, girl!'

'I am not anxious, Mrs Wilcox. She is doing no harm.' Charlotte smiled at Polly who hid her face in Charlotte's dress.

Mrs Wilcox sighed and got up. She limped to the corner and fussed over something, and Charlotte realised there was a baby asleep in a box in the shadows. 'How is the baby doing, Mrs Wilcox? James told me she was poorly? Is she improved now?'

The woman nodded. 'Aye, the baby is doin' much better. Would you like to see her Miss? She's asleep but you can look at her.'

She held up the box and Charlotte crept over to view the infant. She was a tiny little thing for a six-month-old baby and her heart went out to the mother.

'She's beautiful,' Charlotte smiled. 'Oh, I almost forgot. Mary and Cook sent this basket for you — bread, and some fresh butter, and I think there is some cream and a little mutton in the bottom — oh yes, there is. Good. Here you are.'

Polly's eyes were wide. 'Butter Mama, want butter!'

Charlotte handed the basket to the woman who was shaking her head.

'Thank'ee, Miss. That be very kind. Aye, Polly, you can have some later, girl. Please thank Mary and Cook for me, Miss. Mary always brings me a little something when she comes to visit, but she don't often get away now,' added the woman sadly. 'Our Tom and that girl, well he's heartbroke over her he is, but they'll figure somethin' out. Tom's working very hard over at Wythorpe and he's got his plans, he has. But I've probably said too much Miss. It ain't your mess, Miss, sorry for speakin' of it!'

The woman bent to cover the baby more thoroughly, and Charlotte jogged a giggling Polly on her knee. 'I know a little of the story, Mrs Wilcox. I am so sorry for poor Tom. But perhaps Sir Benedict will relent and allow him to marry Mary once he establishes himself? It must be very hard on the two of them.'

'Aye, that it is, that it is. My Tom is a good boy, and he niver stole nothin' in his life. Sir at the manor was very good to my Thomas until he died, but all this enclosure business, it ain't right for us poor folk. We had fresh meat from the pickin's of the fields, but now! Nothin' for us 'cept what the boys can earn. Young James stays on up there at the manor, and God knows we need what he brings home, and Tom gives us everything he can, but I myself cannot work with the baby to care for. Aye, tis very hard times Miss, very hard.'

Charlotte nodded, determined to give the woman some coins from her reticule before she left. 'And you, Mrs Wilcox, how are you keeping? James said you were poorly yourself?'

'Aye Miss, I have the rheumy in my bones, and movin' about is hard. But I get myself to the gate for milk every day when I can, for the little one, and Polly. I can walk about Miss, but it's the pain what gets me after a bit. But if I rest up enough, it's alright. I is in better state than some I knows! I thank the good Lord in heaven I can still walk about! It's not so bad, really it ain't Miss. Thank'ee kindly for askin.'

At this moment, the door opened again and Tom strode in. His bobbed his head and raised his brows in surprise when he saw Charlotte. 'Good day to ye Miss.' He strode to the hearth and bent to look at the baby. Polly ran to him and he brought her up to his face for a kiss.

'Good day, Tom.' Charlotte was pleased to see that Polly was fond of her big brother.

Mrs Wilcox sat heavily in the chair again. 'Miss Milton brought us somethin' from up at the big house, Tom. Butter, and mutton! But what are you doin' home so early, boy? Git ye off to your work, lad, or the boss will cane ye!'

Tom shook his head and threw his hat on the hearth. 'Nay, Ma. I'm droppin' by on my way to the village. I called in to give ye something,' He paused, looking sideways at Charlotte. 'It's out front. I need to take the bag with me.'

Charlotte took her cue and rose, gently extracting her hand from Polly's tight fist. 'I will take my leave, Mrs Wilcox and let you tend to your work.' She opened her reticule and took out two coins, and handed them to Polly, whose eyes became round as plates. 'Polly, please give these to your mama,' she smiled.

Mrs Wilcox shook her head and allowed Polly to place them in her hand, reverently. 'You are very kind, Miss.'

Charlotte donned the pattens once more, waved her farewell at Polly and smiled at Mrs Wilcox who was still seated inside, and opened the gate. She did not look directly at the brown hessian bag at the door step. As she stepped through the door, avoiding the worst of the mud, Tom followed her outside to close the gate behind her and she turned to face him.

'Tom, do you know of anyone in the town who is a naval gentleman? Someone with dark hair? Perhaps a captain or a lieutenant?'

'Aye, Miss. Lord Winchester has a naval gentleman friend who visited at Wythorpe a few days back. A Captain Williams. Perhaps it is he you are thinking of, Miss?'

'Perhaps, Tom. Thank you! Good day to you!'

Charlotte began to trudge back down the lane, lost in thought. It had begun, again, to rain a little, and she did not notice the figure on horseback in the field next to the road.

Then, unaccountably, her skin prickled as if she were being observed, and she stopped and looked up. Sir Benedict sat on his horse, and had seen her. Even at this distance, Charlotte could see that his face was clouded with anger. She stared him down, unwilling to feel guilty. The rain ran in defiant little streams down his jacket. They locked gazes, neither of them speaking. After a moment, he turned in the direction of the village and was gone.

Lavinia was adamant she should have a new gown made for the ball. She insisted that Charlotte should accompany her to the linen-draper in the town the next morning and Charlotte acquiesced, for she wished to walk and did not mind accompanying her cousin. For herself, she thought one of the gowns she had brought with her would suffice, for she had nobody to impress, and her gowns were quite adequate, if not truly what was deemed "fashionable" in the eyes of the Misses Latham.

Lavinia had hoped to assail her uncle at dinner the previous night to request him to procure a dressmaker from London to bring cloth and patterns and have the dress made on the spot, but her uncle, being irritatingly uncompliant by his absence at dinner, could not offer his permission, and so she had to make do with a visit to the nearer, but not nearly as well-stocked, village shop.

The two young women set off for the village, Lavinia having received her aunt's permission to charge the dress to her uncle's account.

'And you must have a new dress, too, Charlotte, for your old gowns are not very stylish, you know, and you might pick yourself up a husband if you take some care with your appearance!'

Charlotte laughed, unoffended. 'My dear cousin, my ambition to "pick myself up a husband", to use such a vulgar expression, is much less keen than yours, and if someone who can excite my esteem is willing to take me, unstylish gowns and all, then I shall be perfectly satisfied. I shall wear my best white muslin and that shall be an end of it!'

But Charlotte was not to have her way, for, upon entering the dressmaker's shop, she was accosted by Miss Anne Smart and Miss Sophia Latham, who, Charlotte realised, was far more agreeable and friendly to Charlotte when her sister was not present!

The two women were making much ado over the latest bolts of fabrics which had just arrived that day from London. Charlotte and Lavinia were immediately dragged into the fray and forced to browse the fabrics and assist the two young ladies to choose which they would have made up into a gown for Saturday. The linen-draper and his assistant looked on, astonished at having so many ladies in their shop all at once, and looked rather worried as to how so many dresses were to be completed within two days.

Sophia Latham chose an emerald silk which set off her pale red hair very well, while Miss Anne Smart made loud exclamations against all the fabrics that Sophia held up against her. She could not *possibly* do justice to such and such a silk, or she thought herself unfit to wear *this* one with the grace it deserved, until Lavinia suggested a very plain cotton muslin. At this, Miss Smart finally seemed to give in with the greatest ease, as if all her exclamations had never been uttered, and allowed a very fine puce silk to be chosen for her by her friend. These purchases made secure, the two ladies then insisted that Charlotte stand still while they held up various fabrics against her face and compared colours, while Charlotte shook her head, and laughingly but quite vigorously voiced her intention not to have a new gown at all.

Alas! To suppose a young girl of twenty-two can hold her ground for longer than five minutes in a linen-draper's shop, when the latest fabrics are just arrived from London, is too much to expect! Even the most modest of misses would be a saint indeed not to allow her thoughts to form an image of herself wearing a beautiful dress. It is too much to expect that such a temptation would not wreak havoc with her modesty and her frugal intentions, and cause such a young woman to give way to the making of such an exciting purchase.

Charlotte, for all her modesty and good intentions of keeping her expenditure low and saving her father's money, was a normal young woman nonetheless, and it was only a few minutes before she, too, had fallen under the spell of the fine fabrics. With the enticing picture in her mind of herself in a gossamer gown trimmed in the latest mode, she found her former determination weakening. Charlotte made laughing rebuttals of the other women's entreaties, but when a delightful pale lemon silk shot with silver thread was spotted, even Charlotte herself fell in love with it, and succumbed to its purchase along with Lavinia's.

She promised to pay her cousin back immediately, for at home she had the present of five pounds in her purse, which her father had given her, with five more should she write and ask for it. She felt equal to the purchase, and yet she was not used to wearing such fine gowns. She hoped her papa would not think her extravagant, but she had bought little else since being at Delford.

Lavinia was ecstatic about her own purchase of a white chiffon, sheer and gauzy, trimmed with rose-red ribbons and rather elaborate beading in a new style, which the assistant cleverly illustrated with drawings. The poor linen-draper, charged with having to get the dresses ready within a short time, assured the ladies that the hiring of an extra seamstress or two would expedite the process, and received assurances that any additional costs would not be minded, if only they could have the dresses by Saturday. Purchases completed, the young ladies went upon their way, chattering excitedly about their gowns, and even Charlotte was incapable of not being caught up in the excitement of the coming ball, however hesitant she was about Lord Winchester's attentions to her cousin.

~~*~~

Upon their arrival home, the two girls went in to tea with Eliza, each quite satisfied with their purchases, and in good spirits. Eliza mentioned that a letter had come for Charlotte, and at once the letter was brought and opened, with Eliza's encouragement. It was from her father, and was brief, only mentioning their current address and that the newlyweds were both well. Dr Milton listed a number of places they had been, names which were unknown to her, or of which she knew little but yearned to know more, and of where they were to go next, but the overall air of the letter was one of distraction, and the fulfilment of duty, rather than a real and genuine caring for its recipient. Nothing but a passing enquiry was made as to Charlotte's health or happiness in Hertfordshire. No note from her stepmother was cheerfully attached at the end of the letter.

She felt a little melancholy upon finishing the letter and folded it away again. It was not that she missed her papa so much as she had thought she might, but she felt, in some strange way, that her last, tenuous connection to the dear parent who had given her so much, and who was now in heaven, was through her remaining parent, and his lack of attentiveness to her in the letter caused a loneliness in her breast, which she tried to put aside. It was not that she was lonely at Delford, for she had good company in her cousin and Eliza, and she did not crave the society that her cousin did. But she still missed her Mama, and there were times when all the company and good society in the world would not fill the empty rooms in her heart, where once her mother walked.

Her father was, of course, distracted by his new wife and the bustle of visiting and taking in new places, and she hoped that later perhaps, he might write to her in more detail, and ask more attentively after her health and happiness. It was only their first correspondence, and she would no doubt receive more detailed correspondence as they traveled.

Much heartened at these thoughts, Charlotte settled upon answering her letter after lunch and went to her room directly upon leaving the table, to write a rather longer account of her stay at Delford, including some details regarding Lord Winchester's ball and the purchase of her dress, and a humorous drawing of local characters which she hoped would amuse her papa and Mariah.

Her letter completed and sealed, she decided to walk to the village and went to find Lavinia to see if she would walk with her. Not finding her within her room, she enquired of Stokes and was informed that Miss Markham had gone riding, and had insisted upon being unaccompanied. Charlotte raised her brows in surprise since her cousin knew her uncle had forbidden her to ride alone. When he could not accompany her, the head groom always stepped in. Charlotte shrugged her shoulders. Her cousin had shown a strong-willed nature since leaving the cradle, and Charlotte was not surprised that Lavinia would not blush to break her uncle's rules. Charlotte would walk to the village alone and enjoy her solitude.

She rambled in the lane, jumped stiles, and found pleasure in the day generally. After a few minutes, she came to a vantage point where Wythorpe was visible beyond the trees in the foreground, and Charlotte paused to consider its pretty appearance. Although it was smaller than Delford, and did not boast the large parklike setting of that estate, Wythorpe was a pleasing residence, with a handsome prospect over its own smallish lake, and was very picturesque when viewed from a distance. She wondered about the interior of the house, and her natural curiosity led her thoughts immediately to dwell on how she would find it, when entering it two nights hence. She had not heard Lord Winchester boast of his house, or its pretty garden, although she was sure it was fitted out in good enough taste to satisfy any discerning gentleman, and she could only imagine Lavinia's excitement at the prospect of viewing, on the night of the ball, what she may come to call one of her future homes.

Just as she was having these thoughts, she noticed a figure on horseback approach the distant house. She could not make out the rider, but it was most definitely a woman, dressed in a scarlet riding habit with a tall hat covering her hair. The figure was met by another, who walked from the house, this time a male, whom Charlotte decided must be Lord Winchester. The two figures talked together for a few moments, and then Lord Winchester kissed the hand of the woman, lingering over the action. The groom aided the figure in red to mount her horse again, and a moment later the rider was gone.

Charlotte was alarmed exceedingly, and felt that it did not bode well for her cousin. The kiss was so obviously a sign of deep and familiar affection. Unless it was a sister, Lord Winchester was doing no service to her cousin. She reflected seriously for some time as to whom this female guest could possibly be, but after a while she put the problem aside, since it was Lord Winchester's business alone, and she did not wish to pry, even in her own thoughts. She continued on toward the village. She was resolved to make enquiries, for she did not wish to alarm Lavinia, and did not feel equal to another conversation with Sir Benedict on the subject.

Rounding a now familiar hill, she paused to admire some trees and then gasped. The object of her most recent thoughts was suddenly before her, as if she had conjured him up. He was on horseback, passing along under the trees. She stopped, but he had seen her. He halted and dismounted immediately, tethered his horse, and strode toward her. Gathering her composure, she waited patiently.

'Good day Miss Milton.' He bowed curtly. His face was leaden.

'Good day, Sir. As you see, I am just on my way to the village.' She gave him a bright smile. She could guess at the cause of his anger, but she would not give him the satisfaction of knowing it. When he remained silent, she made as if to walk on.

'I wished to see you.' His voice was commanding. 'I was told you had gone to the village and I followed you. I must speak with you.'

She was silent and waited for him to continue.

When he did, his voice was low and deep, full of angry feeling and accusation. 'I have been very patient, Miss Milton. I have endured your interference into my affairs, the running of my estate, the interests of my employees, and the discharge of my duty toward your cousin. I now find that you are visiting the cottage of my ex-employee.' He gestured with his riding crop, toward her. 'Yes, Miss Milton, do not try to deny your dealings with that family, for I saw it with my own eyes yesterday.'

Her irritation rising, she turned her face from him. His accusations produced in Charlotte a confusion of painful and agitated sensations. She took a breath and lifted flashing eyes to meet his. She endeavoured to speak calmly. But she could not hold back from expressing the feelings that were in her heart.

'I neither attempt to deny it, nor do I deny taking an interest in that family, Sir. I understand that you have treated the young man with contempt, tarnishing his name with the unfair label of "thief" and obstructing his future happiness. His family, Sir, depend upon the income that those young men bring in. In participating in the enclosure of the lands that they once used to support themselves, you have affected their family directly. Mrs Wilcox is in ill-health, and she has two infants to care for.

The older child is thin and undernourished, Sir, and the baby must suffer the same fate. I do not deny that I called there, to offer what comfort and assistance I could. It is a travesty of justice that they live on your estate and yet you do not feel yourself called upon to make reparation to a family whom you have severely wounded.' She finished defiantly, her eyes flashing and meeting his own dark ones courageously. Her heart pounded and yet she could not look away, for she was mesmerised by the intensity of his own stare. His eyes betrayed anger, and something else she could not name.

He held her gaze for a moment, then flung his crop at the ground and uttered a curse. Striding toward his horse, he stopped abruptly, and returned to face her. 'If you are so ready to believe ill of me, then I have not the means in my power to change your opinion. Nothing I say will alter your bad opinion of me. However, my own sense of justice demands that I explain myself, whether or not you choose to believe me.'

Charlotte waited to hear him out, although she was confident that she was sufficiently appraised of the circumstances attending, and quite just in her accusations. She schooled her face into calm and waited for him to continue.

'In relation to your first accusation, that I have called Tom Wilcox a thief, I do not deny this charge. But allow me, if you will, to inform you of the full facts as they stand, from my own dealings with him. The crime of which you charge me, Miss Milton, of enclosing my land, I plead guilty. I have indeed enclosed some common lands which border my own, and which I have a right to enclose under common law. I do no worse than my fellow gentleman farmers do, for the object of making my estate a more profitable business. However, to enclose lands surrounding my own is to increase my need for staff to work those lands, to make them into good pasture, and to care for the animals from which I procure my profit. You see, enclosure of common land may also benefit workers who can no longer hunt on enclosed fields, Miss Milton.'

She acknowledged this mocking reprimand with only a frosty glare. She was provoked beyond anything to receive such a set-down from such a man, and yet, she could find no immediate rejoinder, so she remained in place, fixing him with her icy glare.

He continued, unabashed by her ill-temper, and determined, it seemed, to give explanation, although she could hardly imagine what he might say that would change her mind about him.

'When I, six months ago, saw fit to enclose this land, Tom Wilcox was not in my employ. He was in the employ of a blacksmith in the village. He and his younger brother had been hunting on the land and using it to feed their family since the death of their father, my former employee. I regarded old Thomas Wilcox with the highest esteem and upon his death I immediately offered his oldest son work on my estate, at a rate of pay which was considerably higher than he would have received at the blacksmith. I dealt fairly with him, because he was his father's son, and because his family had been affected by the enclosure and subsequent hunting bans rightfully imposed in such a situation.

'However, because the boy harboured ill-feeling toward me, regarding my refusal to give him permission to court one of my staff, his own pride stood in the way of his acceptance of my offer to make reparation to his family. It was, Miss Milton, a matter of great pride to me that I made this reparation. However, Tom Wilcox chose to refuse my help and remain in the employ of the blacksmith. After this, I caught him on several occasions poaching on my land. For this, I do indeed accuse him of thievery; poaching is a crime, Miss Milton, and I stand by my accusations. After this, he was laid off from the blacksmith, in shame. Out of my regard for his father, I offered him employment once again, but he refused, again. It is his pride that harms his mother and siblings, nothing more.'

Charlotte was indignant. 'But – but to obstruct two people

who clearly wish to marry! I do not understand it! It is wrong to separate two people who are in love, unless there is good reason. It is unjust, nay, it is cruelty of the sort I have struggled to understand!' she cried, incredulous. 'You, who have in the past, suffered in love, might understand the pain of being separated, might wish to spare the hearts of two people who rely upon you solely for their happiness!'

Sir Benedict looked mortified, became red in the face, and uttered a curse. 'Once again, Miss Milton, you know nothing of the matter of which you charge me. I have never considered Tom Wilcox to be suitable for my housemaid, and it is precisely because I know her family, and her father, that I wish to protect her. The family are against the match in every regard. Tom Wilcox is reported to be a philanderer, and his attentions to Mary cannot be trusted. I prevented a courtship not to cause pain, but to protect the girl.'

Charlotte gaped in disbelief. Every sentiment she had felt, every idea of young Tom Wilcox would not submit to such a character reference. She could not believe it. She stood silent, unable to refute such a claim, but knowing her intuition about Tom was not misplaced.

Sir Benedict continued in a softer tone. 'Forgive me if I have distressed you. I do not taint the reputation of Tom Wilcox with such accusations without good reason. You know nothing of his character; you are kind-hearted, Miss Milton, and wish to see the good in all people, but you are naïve and wanting sense. You are unable to believe ill of someone who has all the appearance of innocence, and yet, you are eager to believe ill of me, to whose character you have been intimately exposed for some weeks now. Surely you do not think that I, who know Tom Wilcox and his family, would willingly accuse him unless I perceived that my accusations were just? I suggest that in future, you reserve your judgement, and your interference, although meant well, for matters which are solely a woman's, and for people and circumstances with which you are intimately acquainted.'

Charlotte's colour rose with the snub to her sex, and a haughty look passed over her features. 'If Tom Wilcox has misplaced pride, Sir, I can only sympathise with his decision to decline your offer of employment. But regarding your second accusation, I cannot believe it. There must be some mistake, some misapprehension. He loves Mary, of that I am sure.'

Sir Benedict bent to pick up his riding crop, and sighed. 'Perhaps. I doubt it, however. But I have detained you long enough. Please continue your walk. Good day to you, Miss Milton.' He gave her another curt bow, mounted his beast, and cantered away, leaving Charlotte gaping, and chagrined. Her feelings were in tumult, one minute angry, the next puzzled. She walked on slowly, allowing the breeze to cool her flushed cheeks. Her feelings in disorder, she tried to make sense of the confusion she felt.

Why did he make such a point of explaining himself when she knew he did not care what she thought on the matter? Had she been so misguided in her opinion of his treatment of Tom Wilcox? Was he telling the truth about his offer of employment and Tom's refusal based on pride? This made some sense to her, when she recalled what Mary had told her the previous week while doing her hair. But to think Tom was a philanderer, was not in keeping with what she had sensed from her own conversations with him. He loved Mary, there was no doubt, and if he had been rather wayward earlier in his youth, she was sure he was reformed in his character now, and steady in his affections for the girl. She was determined to discover more, and resolved to ask Mary, if she would be willing to confide in Charlotte. This course of action determined upon, and her feelings somewhat soothed, she made her way back to Delford, the mystery of the woman in red temporarily forgotten.

As she approached the house, she noted the groom was leading her cousin's horse to the stable around the back, and she went inside herself to find Lavinia. In the foyer, she went to the bottom of the stairs and then froze in place. A flash of scarlet fabric was disappearing up the stairs, and she was just in time to see her cousin slip into her room.

Nineteen

'Oh Lavinia, you careless girl! What are you doing?' she exclaimed aloud to herself. Had anyone but Charlotte seen her at Wythorpe, alone and unchaperoned, her reputation would be tarnished. Stupid, blind fool of a girl! To put her reputation in such danger! She must speak to Sir Benedict! But nay, she acknowledged, he would not listen. He had made himself very clear on that subject! He held that she knew nothing, could know nothing, of love, and perhaps he was right, given her inexperience with that subject. Her own heart had, at the age of two and twenty, remained as yet untouched, and she had been careful not to allow her feelings to become attached to any man who paid her his attentions.

But for all her inexperience, she was sure her cousin was sincerely attached, as much as she could be with her fickle heart and flirtatious ways, to Lord Winchester. But as for *his* attachment to Lavinia, she felt in her heart that it was not true, that it was not sincere. She suspected him of she knew not what, and yet, she could not approach Sir Benedict. He had made it clear that he would brook no interference in his affairs, including the management of her cousin.

Perhaps, but she knew impropriety when she saw it. She had no doubts that Lord Winchester was encouraging her cousin's bad behaviour, and did not care for her reputation at all. If he did, he would never allow her to visit his house, even to be outside, to meet him, to linger over a kiss on her hand! And in clear sight of the servants! Unless, thought Charlotte suddenly, they were engaged, and the engagement was a secret? Even so, it was impropriety indeed to visit his house without a chaperone. It put her cousin's reputation at risk, whether she cared or not.

Charlotte attempted to collect herself. Approaching Lavinia would only anger her cousin. And yet, she must find out if they were engaged. Perhaps he had advanced his suit to her in a letter and she had gone to give her reply in person? Yes, that must be it! That would explain the familiarity with which Lord Winchester acted. Charlotte sighed and decided that to force Lavinia's confidence was not likely to improve relations between them. No doubt they would announce their engagement at the ball. She would wait until the ball, and all confusion would be cleared up. She rang for Mary as soon as she was in the privacy of her room and asked her to enquire of the footman if a letter had come in the mail that morning for Miss Markham. Mary obliged her, and a few moments later confirmed that it was so.

Feeling relieved on that score at least, and having the proof of her suspicion made solid, Charlotte changed for dinner alone, having sent Mary away. Her thoughts still dwelt on the events of the day. She was anxious as to how she was to face her host, after their quarrel earlier. She was still angry and humiliated that he thought her naïve and feebleminded. It would be a tense meal, and she wished she could simply avoid it, but if she remained in her room, he would think he had succeeded in intimating her! Nay, she would appear at dinner, outwardly composed and serene; she would not let him think he had affected her!

Dinner was a quiet affair, for Lavinia seemed lost in thought, and although Charlotte thought she knew why, she said nothing. Sir Benedict seemed lost in thought also, saying very little and avoiding Charlotte's eyes as much as she avoided his. Eliza suffered one of her headaches and went directly to her room after dinner, so that only the three of them remained in the drawing room. Sir Benedict took port, which was declined by the two women. Charlotte took up a small volume of Keats, one of her favourites, which she had discovered in the library earlier in the week, and Lavinia had Belle brought in to her.

Lavinia played half-heartedly with the creature and nibbled sweetmeats, while her uncle wrote letters in the corner at the writing desk. Charlotte could hear the hushed scratching of his quill against the dry paper, and wanted to look up and watch him while he was not aware of her gaze, but then she chided herself for silliness. It did not signify what his opinion of her was, either now or in the future. She cared not for his moods, his arrogance, and his insufferable conceit, thinking himself the only person capable of making judgements or understanding. That he thought she was a scatterbrain, too young and inexperienced to know anything, and too *female* to have any sound judgement, was clear. Why did she feel melancholy then, when she thought he did not care for her? That he disliked her? She resolved to put it from her mind, but when she took up her favourite poet, and began an unusually solemn stanza, she felt such strong feelings overtake her that she paused her reading. "*Forlorn! The very word is like a bell, to toll me back from thee to my sole self!*"

She could not go on, for the words caused in her a pain, a sense of loss, of which she could make no sense. Attributing her sudden, similarly forlorn mood to general anxiety on account of her cousin, and a certain loneliness that had crept upon her during the day, she put aside the book with the private thought that such verses ought not to be read unless one were in a rational frame of mind, and excused herself to go to bed.

The three women called at Highview the next day, Eliza insisting that she was well able to walk the short distance with Charlotte's and Lavinia's arm on either side of her. They were all received with sincere warmth by Sir Frank, and Charlotte with cold politeness by the older Miss Latham. Eliza was at once ushered to a chair by a solicitous Sir Frank, she having walked further than she ought, he exclaimed kindly, without the aid of a gentleman's arm.

Aside from his attentions to Lavinia's aunt, Charlotte noted that Sir Frank seemed quiet, and not his usual self. This she put down to his being a failed suitor of her cousin. Although he was quite a fop, she felt sorry for him, for she admitted he had been ill-used by Lavinia, who had encouraged his addresses and flirted with him until a higher-ranking suitor had supplanted him.

A young man generally values his pride as equal to his heart. Once, twice rejected, he may not have the heart to try again. Many times rebuffed, Frank Latham did not again try to engage Lavinia in conversation, at which Lavinia looked sulky and put out, but, thought Charlotte, her cousin could not have everything. She must not expect attention from Sir Frank when she had made her choice clear.

Lavinia sat with Annabelle Latham in the corner of the room and talked in lowered tones of the ball, the dresses each should wear, and snippets of conversation that Charlotte could only just overhear. Miss Latham cast dark looks at Charlotte from her position across the room with Lavinia, and never addressed her directly, which Charlotte did not much mind. She made light conversation with Miss Anne Smart, who was still with the Lathams as their particular guest, and would remain so for a week or a fortnight more. She would then remove first to an aunt in London, and then on to Bath, she informed Charlotte, where she would remain for the autumn and winter.

'Such a cold, dreary place, Bath, but of course there are many diversions… and many young men, if I may be so bold as to say a such a thing,' she added, simpering behind her fan.

Charlotte smiled and sipped her tea while Miss Smart continued her train of thought.

'It is always advantageous to a young woman to be situated in a town where there are many young men passing in and out, for with so many dance partners, a young woman can never be sitting long at a ball! And a young lady of good fortune can be most sure to receive at least one marriage proposal if one spends enough time in Bath,' she tittered. 'But Miss Milton, do you dance? I believe you must, for you cannot have bought a new gown simply to sit about at the ball and be a wall-flower! Ah, but perhaps you wish to catch the eye of a young man, yourself?' she smirked, and cast a quick glance in the direction of Annabelle Latham. 'Are you engaged for any of the dances? Has Sir Benedict engaged you for the first two, perhaps?'

She cast a sly look again at Miss Latham, and Charlotte at once ascertained that Miss Latham had urged her protégé to dig about for information. She smiled politely and put down her tea cup.

'If I were engaged to dance with any person, Miss Smart, it would be impolitic to admit it to my competition. A young lady of *your* beauty and style cannot be insensible of the disservice she may do to other young ladies simply by being present in the room! You, yourself, may catch the eye of the young man with whom I had been engaged to dance, and do all in your power to steal my dance partner! No, Miss Smart,' said Charlotte, laughing good naturedly, 'I shall not admit to anyone in this room with whom I may or may not be engaged to dance, for fear of never having any dances at all, for the rest of the evening!'

This she uttered loud enough for Miss Latham to hear, and hoped it would deliver an effective set down! Heaven knew, she would not want the sly Miss Smart spreading a silly fudge about her and Sir Benedict; if such nonsense got back to him, she would never be able to face him again!

Miss Latham had indeed heard Charlotte, and cast her a look of such evil that Charlotte immediately guessed that Annabelle had taken her comments as an affirmative that she was engaged to dance with Sir Benedict! Heaven help the thought! Charlotte smiled to herself, and surmised that if only Annabelle Latham knew the animosity between herself and Sir Benedict, she would fret no more on the subject. Sir Benedict, she was sure, would no more wish to stand up with Charlotte at a ball than he would wish to take tea with the town simpleton. She smiled at the thought and finished her tea.

Miss Smart was smiling and hiding coyly behind her fan at Charlotte's compliments and had dropped her head in mock humility. 'Why, Miss Milton, you are very kind but you exaggerate, I am sure! I am not so *very* handsome, you know, not next to such beauties as dear Annabelle. Although I *do* have my fortune... but I must be careful as to *that*! I may not give *my* heart so quickly as your—'

Here she stopped before she could give offence, although Charlotte knew full well to what, and to whom, she was referring. Eliza, who had been talking quietly and seriously to a morose Sir Frank, stood with Sir Frank's assistance, to indicate to the two girls that their fifteen minutes had long passed.

Miss Smart put her arm in Charlotte's and accompanied her to the door. 'I am all eagerness for Saturday night, Miss Milton, and I do hope we shall sit together and go down the dance together with our partners. I am vastly curious as to who you will dance with, you sly thing!'

Charlotte smiled slightly and extracted her arm. She added her goodbyes along with Lavinia's fond farewells, and the three women walked slowly back to Delford, Eliza leaning a little on Charlotte's arm, each lost in their own thoughts and none of them particularly pleased with the visit.

~~*~~

Later that afternoon, when Eliza had excused herself to lie down, and Lavinia, too, had pleaded a headache and gone to her room, Charlotte put on a bonnet, took up the wriggling Belle under her arm, and went out on what she intended to be a long walk to clear her mind. Sir Benedict, was, as customary, about the estate tending to matters of his business. Charlotte chose a path that she thought would take her away from his vicinity, which crossed the estate and meandered toward the workers' cottages. This path had a particularly fine view of the hills beyond.

She set off, a slight figure in her white muslin, and blue trimmed straw bonnet, and climbed toward the lane. The little puppy gambolled about, making Charlotte laugh. Approaching the lane near the cottages, where she would jump the stiles and carry on up the hill, she saw Tom Wilcox, and young James lugging firewood behind him.

She hailed them kindly, and waited to greet them. Tom and James both nodded politely. 'Afternoon, Miss,' Tom greeted her. Belle nosed about, and allowed James to pet her.

'How are you, Tom? How are you James? How are your mother and the baby, Tom?' she asked, eager to hear good tidings. She was rewarded with a nod and smile.

'Aye, mother is doing as good as she can, and the little ones

148

too, thank'ee Miss.'

Tom bent to speak to James in a low voice and James nodded good day to Charlotte and carried on up the hill with his firewood. She watched him go then turned back to Tom, her eyes curious.

'Miss, I have something I would speak with you on,' began Tom seriously. 'I wouldn't want to interfere, but I cannot speak to the Master on it, and you be the next best person, seeing as you and Miss Markham are cousins, Miss.'

Charlotte became even more intrigued. 'Tom, what do you know? Does it concern Miss Markham?'

Tom studied the ground as he weighed his words. 'It may do, Miss. As you know, I work for Lord Winchester, over at Wythorpe, since he took it a few weeks ago. Well, Miss, there's talk amongst the servants. He mostly hired local, Miss, but he brought some of his own, an' word's been gettin' about that he has not the money he says he has.'

He looked at Charlotte, who nodded anxiously. 'Go on, Tom.'

'Well, Miss, his own manservant told the stable master privately that there's no money left. They say he's a gambler, and he lost his fortune. Gambled away half his estate in Norfolk, too, they say.'

Charlotte's heart dropped. 'But, Tom! Lord Winchester has taken Wythorpe. He employs servants. Why, he is giving a ball in two days. Surely he cannot be so much in debt? There must be some mistake?'

Tom shook his head. 'I don't know, Miss, but I thought to warn you. I know a fellow who knows a fellow who works on the estate in Norfolk. I'll make enquiries on the quiet, if you'll forgive my impertinence, and when I find out anything more, I'll tell you Miss.'

'Thank you, Tom. You are very kind.'

She watched him make his way toward the cottages, and she climbed the second stile, deep in thought. Surely there would be more open talk if Lord Winchester had indeed lost his fortune? And he had undertaken to give a ball! Surely the man could not be so in debt as his manservant surmised? The memory of her seeing Lord Winchester receive money from a tall naval officer, in the lane after church last weekend, rose to her mind. Was that indeed his friend, Captain Williams? Would his friend loan him money when he knew Lord Winchester was in debt? Surely not! There must be some mistake, for he would not be able to afford his carriage, his horses, his servants, if he had so few means left to him.

And yet, she still sensed that Lord Winchester was not sincere in his attentions to her cousin. Was he, after all, so wicked? Was he hoping to make an advantageous marriage to settle his debts, or worse, to fund his gambling? She felt most anxious, most disturbed, that Lavinia may be on the point of announcing an engagement to the man. But, if he was so bad, Sir Benedict would surely discover it after an engagement had been announced, for people would come forward with the truth if it were common knowledge that he was marrying an heiress.

But then, many men did marry for money alone, thought Charlotte sadly. Her own father had been tempted by Mariah's money, she suspected, more than by her character. And yet, that in itself did not make a man evil. It was often necessary. A young man must have means, and often those means came from an advantageous marriage. If Lavinia married Lord Winchester, she might be exchanging her fortune for rank, but she herself had declared that she cared only for rank, and did not care to marry for love. Whether Lavinia was sincerely attached to Lord Winchester, or not, she was obviously happy with the arrangement if she was on the verge of announcing her engagement. If Lord Winchester was so wicked, or so much in debt, Sir Benedict would have time to make enquiries, before the marriage took place, and stop it if he felt the situation warranted such an action.

Her mind more at ease, she continued her walk, spending a long time seated on the grass at the top of the hill and playing with Belle, who, poor creature, seemed somewhat neglected by her owner. As the sun went down over the hills, she sighed, and puppy under her arm again, made her way thoughtfully towards home. Some of those thoughts were on her cousin, and some of them dwelt on a pair of dark eyes which seemed to see through her and cause her the most unladylike sensations.

Twenty One

Charlotte dressed for dinner in her best calamine blue silk, feeling in need of the confidence a pretty gown could bring. She put on her mother's silver and pearl cross, and asked Mary to put up her hair. Mary, happy to be playing lady's maid, took her time over Charlotte's hair and seemed disposed to chat. Charlotte saw her opportunity.

'Have you gone into the village lately Mary? Have you seen Tom?'

'Why yes, Miss, he waited for me behind Blackie's yesterday, when I went in to get loaves for cook, and gave me ever so pretty a bunch of wild flowers, Miss!' She curled and pinned Charlotte's hair and began to hunt for a pretty pin to finish her work.

Charlotte thought she might try her question. 'Forgive me if this distresses you, but there is some talk, about Tom, I mean. Sir Benedict mentioned something. And I wondered. I thought it could not likely be true, but...'

'Oh, Miss, that my Tom is a philanderer? My father says he is a bad fellow, for before me, he used to go on with the Miller girl and led her a merry dance he did, with his unsettled ways. The Master shouldn't listen to my father, Miss. But all the rest of what they say, that he is a bad fellow, that's not my Tom,

Miss. He loves me now, and I don't care what he did when he was a young fellow. No, it's all idle talk that finds its way into people's heads, and the ones that want to believe bad of my Tom, I can't stop them. But I know he's a good man, and he has never done no girl wrong, despite what anyone says.'

Charlotte smiled her relief. 'I know he is, Mary. I never believed the talk for a moment, but I wondered if it bothered you and if it was true in part. No, not that pin, it hurts my head. That one, yes, thank you, Mary.'

'There, Miss, you look a treat as usual. I hope to have the honour of dressing you tomorrow night, Miss? How well you will look in your gown! Although you are still a little thin. But your face has plumped up a little in the last week. Your cheeks are quite rosy!'

Charlotte laughed rather self-consciously and sent the housemaid-turned-lady's maid downstairs again to help serve dinner. She made her own way downstairs, pausing outside Lavinia's room. She knocked and entered, and found Lavinia on the floor, knee deep in gowns. Her trunk lay open and empty on the floor beside her, and into this, Lavinia was stuffing a gown and some shoes.

She jumped, startled at Charlotte's entry, and then laughed nervously. 'I am just storing some of my unwanted gowns, for my closet is too crowded for all these. How silly it is to have so many pairs of shoes! I must get my maid to help me tomorrow, for my new gown will never fit in my closet if I do not store some of these first.' She indicated the dresses which she had heaped on the floor, creasing them badly.

Charlotte's expressive eyebrows rose in genuine surprise. Usually her cousin treated her gowns like children. She would never throw them on the floor!

'Why Lavinia dear, call for Rose now and have her fold them neatly away if you are not going to wear them for a while. But stay, is not this your best white muslin? Surely you will not store this one? Nor this one, for you wear it every week! It is your favourite,' she added, puzzled, fingering a soft pale pink muslin.

Lavinia uttered a high-pitched laugh and shook her head. 'Silly me! I have gotten them all mixed up! I will call Rose and she can tidy them up during dinner.' She went to the bell cord and yanked hard, then went to the glass and fingered her hair. 'I will be down soon. I shall just give Rose instructions first, when she comes.' She smiled widely at Charlotte. 'Lord, I am monstrous famished! I shall be there directly.'

Charlotte kissed her cousin and left her fussing over the gowns. Downstairs, Eliza and Sir Benedict waited in the drawing room, Eliza on the chaise and Sir Benedict at the window. They were talking, but he turned when Charlotte entered the room, and advanced to her, bowing briefly. 'Good evening, Miss Milton.'

She curtsied politely, and went to Eliza, to ask after her health. Lavinia entered the room at this moment, and she, too, went to join her aunt and cousin on the chaise.

Sir Benedict approached the women and addressed Charlotte. 'Miss Milton, may I enquire as to whether you intend to dance at the ball tomorrow night?'

Charlotte was taken aback and her brows rose slightly. 'Why, I did not... yes Sir, if I am asked.'

Lavinia broke in. 'Oh Uncle, she despises dancing and will carry her book in her reticule to overcome boredom! Charlotte looks down on most of her prospective dance partners. She told me so herself! Why, I am sorry for every one of them, after she has declined their offer to dance!'

Charlotte smiled good humouredly at her cousin's teasing. 'Do not believe everything my cousin tells you, Sir,' she responded. 'I do not despise dancing and take every opportunity to do so, when there are suitable partners to be had. I do not refuse anyone unless I have it on good authority that they will stand on my toes, or refuse to converse with me! There is nothing so dull as dancing without interesting conversation!'

Sir Benedict smiled. 'I am at a disadvantage then, Miss Milton. I wish to engage you for the first two dances, but I cannot promise you either good conversation, nor to spare your feet. I dance so little that I cannot recommend myself as a good partner. On consideration of my lack of ability to meet your requirements, I should then, expect a refusal of my request. But nonetheless, I put my request before you, and leave my happiness in receiving a positive answer, in your power.'

On hearing Sir Benedict's request, Charlotte's colour increased, the more so with her realisation that both Eliza and Lavinia were looking at her expectantly. She had a moment of painful confusion. Would not he dance the first two with Miss Latham? Perhaps he meant to make his intended jealous? But surely he was not that unkind! Her emotions were in tumult. Why did he wish to dance with her? Did he not regard her as interfering and uninformed? Did he think it a joke? Did he make sport with her? And yet his request was so polite, so gentlemanlike. She felt puzzled and yet her puzzlement was tempered with a sudden gladness that he was not wholly against her, that he did not think as ill of her as she had suspected after their talk yesterday.

She could think of no polite way to refuse, or of a good reason to accept! And yet her lips made her reply almost before she could be sensible of it. 'I would be happy to dance the first two dances with you, Sir.' After a short pause, she added lightly, 'I dance so little myself, that perhaps you will be in danger of my standing on *your* toes!'

He raised dark brows. 'Unlike your cousin, you do not eat a great many sweets, and therefore, it is unlikely to signify if you happen to stand on my toes. In any case, I do not think you capable of such a thing, since you are, in general terms, so light on your feet,' he replied imperturbably.

With this remark, which left her cousin spluttering

indignantly, and Charlotte unsure if she should feel complimented or confused, he gave a brief bow and returned to his position at the window, where he remained until dinner was announced.

Over dinner, Charlotte was left to contemplate the wisdom of allowing herself to dance at the ball with him, when she would bear all the force of Miss Latham's anger, and all the sly amusement of Miss Smart. She pondered why, too, he should wish to dance with her at all, when she was sure that his opinion of her must forbid it in every respect! She was so wrapped up in these thoughts that she scarcely paid attention to Lavinia who was just as distracted as her cousin, and when Charlotte noticed finally that little of Lavinia's desert had been touched, she put it down to nerves over the coming announcement of her engagement, and did not question her cousin. Charlotte had also failed to notice the speculating gaze of Eliza on both herself and Sir Benedict, during the course of dinner.

Twenty Two

The following morning was the day of the ball. The early arrival of the gowns the girls had ordered preceded a flurry of activity in trying them on, and many happy exclamations which followed. Charlotte was very happy with hers, which had a diaphanous quality and suited her expressive hazel green eyes.

'Oh Miss, you look a picture,' exclaimed Mary who was helping her try on the gown.

Charlotte surveyed the picture in the glass, and sighed. It *was* charming, she acknowledged. The pale lemon silk suited her colouring, the fabric shot with silver thread which would sparkle in the candle light later that evening. The style was simple, high waisted with pretty detail in the bunched short sleeves, but sheer and elegant and showed off her fine figure. She wished she had plumped out a little more to better fill the bodice of the dress, but then she smiled at her own vanity and shrugged away the thought. She would never have Lavinia's great beauty and pretty plump form, and she was happy enough with what God had graced her with. She would wear her mother's pearls with the dress, and have Mary put up her hair with her mother's ornaments. She imagined herself dancing with Sir Benedict, and wondered if he would think her pretty.

'Don't be ridiculous!' she admonished herself out loud. What did it signify what he thought!

'Pardon, Miss?' asked Mary.

'Oh, I was just deciding which shoes I shall wear tonight, Mary. Can you please fetch me those silver ones? Thank you. What do you think? Or do you think the white?'

They were interrupted by Eliza wishing to see the dress, and Lavinia, who had flounced down the hall to Charlotte's room to show off her own gown, her lady's maid running behind her carrying ribbons. Both girls were very pleased with their purchases, and the day passed quickly in chatter, needlework, and two meal times, until it was time to get ready.

Charlotte had not forgotten Tom Wilcox's warning, and she pondered the problem of how to ascertain Lord Winchester's true motives for attaching himself so quickly to her cousin. As she dressed, she determined to look for any symptoms of sincere attachment toward her cousin, which might put her mind at ease. She also pondered the possibility of meeting Captain Williams there, who was by Tom's account a particular friend of Lord Winchester, and of perhaps being introduced to him and being able to find out more about his friend.

But all Charlotte's suspicion was speculation until she had more proof. Her feelings only were what guided her, her intuition that something was amiss. She dared not go to Sir Benedict with Tom's warning unless she had something solid to present him with. She did not think she could bear him to think any more badly of her than he now did!

At seven o'clock, all of the women were assembled in the drawing room, awaiting the carriage which would take them to Wythorpe. Lavinia, face framed by soft curls, was ethereal in white and deep rose, with a beaded bodice and fine diaphanous short sleeves. The detail was exquisite, and all was set off by the soft curvature of her bosom and figure. In short, she looked like radiant bride, and Charlotte wondered if her cousin was not fully aware of the fact, given what she suspected.

Belle came running into the room as one of the servants entered, and jumped up at Lavinia who screamed as if she was being murdered! 'Get down, you wretched animal! You will spoil my gown! Stokes, take the animal this instant!'

Stokes immediately appeared from the shadows of the room where he always seemed to conveniently hover, and seized the puppy who was growing larger and more vigorous by the day.

Eliza frowned. 'She did not mean to hurt your gown, my dear. There, it is unharmed, there is nothing out of place! Stokes, give Rose the creature to look after. That will be all, thank you.'

Stokes left, puppy carefully under his arm, and was immediately succeeded by Sir Benedict who strode into the room, looking quite fine in white and dark green. His stockings and black shoes were of the finest quality, without being overdone, thought Charlotte, and his hair was glossy. He did not, she noted, make much use of pomade or powder, as was the fashion among men, but looked as if he presented himself just as he was, with no embellishments and no apology for it. It was an attitude she rather admired, she thought to herself. She infinitely preferred the look of nature than that of artifice, such as Sir Frank and his sisters practiced.

Sir Benedict complimented her cousin immediately, noted to Eliza that the carriage was ready, and turned to Charlotte. He paused, taking in the picture she presented in the soft candlelight of the drawing room, silver threads glittering as brightly as her eyes. She smiled uncertainly, and Eliza spoke.

'Does not Miss Milton look wonderful, Benedict? And Lavinia is a divine picture in her new gown. Neither will want for partners tonight, I am sure!'

Sir Benedict made no reply, apart from a brief bow of acknowledgment to Charlotte, and to hasten the women to the carriage which was waiting in the driveway. Charlotte did not know whether to be offended or relieved that he had no comment to make upon her appearance, and then laughed at herself again for her vanity.

~~*~~

When Charlotte entered the ballroom at Wythorpe, she was a little overwhelmed at the number of guests already crowding the supper room and hallways. Lavinia clutched her arm in alarm as three gentlemen pushed past rather roughly. Charlotte wondered if they were all particular friends of Lord Winchester, and marvelled at the number of acquaintances he could boast!

Sir Benedict had left them to find a seat for Eliza, who could not stand for long. After a moment, his head was sighted, bobbing taller than most of the other guests, and he led them all to the ballroom, where many chairs had been set out. Handing his sister onto a comfortable chaise with a great deal of solicitation and concern, he then went away with an apology, to speak to a gentleman with whom he had business.

The two girls sat next to Eliza and looked around them with interest at the other women, their gowns, and the overall decoration which Lord Winchester had provided. The room had been decked delightfully with summer flowers, and traditional peasant garlands of St John's wort, roses, and verbena hung on the walls and festooned the windows. Numerous candles were lit and the room glowed gold and pale pink. The musicians were already tuning up for the first dance. Lavinia immediately exclaimed over Lord Winchester's fine taste, the beauty of the decorations and the quality of the gowns around her, while Charlotte was distracted by her own thoughts.

She was not sure if she felt nervous or glad that she would dance very soon with Sir Benedict. No sooner had she thought this, than she noticed the Lathams entering the room, and her feelings were so excited that she immediately decided nervousness was the dominant emotion! She did not wish to incite the wrath of Miss Annabelle Latham, and yet she inexplicably wished to dance with Sir Benedict. Why her feelings would urge her to do so, when her rational mind so very decidedly urged her otherwise, she knew not!

But the Lathams and Miss Smart were now approaching. Following close behind them was Lord Winchester, who cut rather awkwardly in front of Sir Frank to immediately take the gloved hand which was offered to him by Lavinia. Loud enough for Sir Frank to overhear, he formally requested the pleasure of the first two dances.

Lavinia, coyly smiling behind her fan again, was only too happy to oblige him. She ignored Sir Frank and looked away as he approached. Sir Frank knew when he had been outwitted. He turned away, a look of thorough disappointment obvious on his countenance, and accosted three ladies who were standing nearby, asking the prettiest one for the honour of the first dance if she was not otherwise engaged. This display was lost on Lavinia, who had not paid the merest attention to him, and was now simpering at Lord Winchester as he spoke to her. Charlotte again felt a pang of distress for Sir Frank, for although he was all great pomposity and mean understanding, his feelings were sincere.

The Latham sisters stood nearby, having come to pay their respects to Eliza. Miss Smart was with them, looking around her with interest. They were dressed in their finest gowns, and even plain Sophia looked rather pretty in her emerald silk with her fine red hair. Annabelle Latham was finely dressed also, in a deep taupe silk in a new French style, which she knew did justice to her skin tone and fine dark eyes. She made a polite, if cold, acknowledgement of Charlotte, curtsied more warmly to Lavinia, Lord Winchester, and Eliza, and seemed to search about the room with her eyes, anxious for the sight of someone. That someone, thought Charlotte with irritation, could only be Sir Benedict.

As the object of both women's thoughts suddenly

appeared, the music began for the first dance, and couples began to move toward the centre of the room. Sir Benedict bowed politely to the Latham party, and Annabelle Latham made a little expectant gesture with her hand, ready to be led out to the first dance.

However, Sir Benedict delivered a second, short bow to the Latham sisters, and turned to Charlotte. 'Miss Milton.' He held out his hand.

Charlotte stood nervously and placed her gloved hand into his own warm one. Their eyes met for a moment. Something moved between them, like distant music or light from a yet unrisen moon. Charlotte could not take her eyes from his. Her lips parted, but no sound came forth. A promise of something she did not understand hid in the darkness of his eyes. Sound grew quiet. She stopped breathing. She fell gently, slowly, into a place she did not know, in which his soul met hers, took her hand, and asked her to dance. Distant music lifted her into the depths of his gaze, and she settled there, unwilling to leave.

Then his eyes released her, and he was escorting her down the dance. The lights from the candelabras cast a pale golden glow on her face, blinding her a little. The musicians struck up the first bars and she looked around, bemused at the sudden noise of it all. She became suddenly aware of the open-mouthed horror of Miss Latham behind her, and the knowing look of Miss Smart. Oh dear! It must look to them both as if, when Miss Smart had enquired regarding her being engaged to dance, she had known she was to dance with Sir Benedict after all! She did not want to appear cunning, and yet it had all the appearance of it! So nervous was she, that she felt unable to look at her dance partner directly, and was unwilling to look out upon the crowd, in case she should catch the eye of Miss Latham and Miss Smart.

Therefore, the first few moments of the dance she kept her head down and tried only to concentrate on the rhythm of the music and the placement of her feet, which she hoped would not connect with those of her partner! The dancers wove in and out, and she was at once painfully aware of him, at first approaching her, only to retreat again. Their hands briefly met, then released. She stumbled once, her nervousness overcoming her for a moment. However, after a minute or so passed, in which she grew more comfortable, she allowed herself a glance at his face, to find his eyes glittering with something she could not read. His mouth curved with the hint of a smile. She felt the familiar twist of vexation in her stomach.

'I am glad you find me an amusing dance partner, Sir, if not a competent one,' she noted archly. Her awareness of him had never been so heightened. She wondered at herself to be so at odds with her own will. Did she not dislike Sir Benedict? Why, oh why had she not declined to dance with him? But without being found rude, she could not, and she must be resigned.

He smiled his reply, but then added, 'It is true I find I am disappointed somewhat in my partner, for you boasted of being so little accomplished at dancing that you promised to stand on my toes! But I find that you mislead me entirely, Miss Milton. You are an accomplished dancer, and it prevails upon me to match your skill, and try not to stand on *your* toes, for fear of being shown up.'

Charlotte laughed, despite herself. 'If you remember, Sir Benedict, it was you who threatened both to stand on my toes, and to deny me any good conversation! But it seems it is you who have reneged on your promise, for you have spared my feet thus far, and have engaged me in tolerable conversation.' They danced a little more in silence, Charlotte painfully aware of his nearness, her arm tingling a little each time his fingers brushed hers.

Sir Benedict addressed her again. 'May I enquire after your reading? Do you confine yourself solely to Mr Keats, who seems to be favourite with you, or have you increased your knowledge of farming practices, so as to tax me with opinions and interfere with my business? I ask not,' he added, 'to vex you, so do not look so sternly at me! No, I ask only that I might prepare myself for war at dinner this week.'

His eyes glinted with humour and she felt herself become more comfortable. 'I think "war" is rather a strong word, Sir Benedict. But it is true that I think for myself. My mother brought me up to have an inquiring mind, and I was educated in subjects considered unwomanly. My mother said I ought to be useful, and to think for myself, rather than let a man tell me what to think. I have always valued her attitude, although it has sometimes made me unpopular! I suppose it is not considered womanly to argue on undomestic subjects, and yet, I think it is in my nature, I am afraid,' she admitted ruefully.

'Your education has certainly been a most unusual one then, but I do not think it a bad one, all in all. It does have the effect, however, of making you most argumentative!'

They were at this moment forced apart, being directed by the steps of the dance to move down the set and meet again at the foot of the line. They passed Miss Latham, who had managed to join the dance after all. She darted Charlotte a look of pure hatred as she passed. Charlotte looked away quickly, and got up her courage to address her partner once more. 'I was surprised, Sir, that you had not engaged Miss Latham for the first two dances. She seemed to expect that you were to partner her.' She immediately felt that she should not have made such an impetuous observation, for fear he would think her prying into his affairs, but he seemed not to mind.

He guided her up the dance, his hand very warm over hers, and then replied drily, 'What Miss Latham expects is sometimes not what Miss Latham gets.'

Charlotte was silent a moment. She withdrew her hand. 'Forgive me, but I was informed that there was an — understanding — between the lady and yourself. I would not wish to be the cause of distress to anyone. That is, I feel that Miss Latham night construe your dancing the first two dances with me as inappropriate, considering that she — that you and she—' Here Charlotte stopped. Warmth rushed into her cheeks and gave her a becoming colour. Sir Benedict's eyes pierced her own and she felt open and exposed. She could not hide.

Sir Benedict raised a brow. 'Ah, I see. The lady herself has been forthcoming, has she? This is the source of your information, I suppose. And do you believe everything you hear, Miss Milton? But you must, for your opinion is fixed on many subjects, based only on the hearsay of others.'

Charlotte felt a flush of annoyance, and opened her mouth to protest, but the dancers moved down the dance and she was momentarily removed from his presence. When they came together again, she was more composed, and Sir Benedict continued.

'As to the impropriety of engaging a woman other than one with whom I have an "understanding" as you put it, I must disagree with you as usual, as much as it pains me to do so. It is not at all inappropriate to dance with the cousin of my niece. I would dance with my sister too, if she were inclined to dance. Miss Latham has a strong mind, and I am sure it will do her no harm to be solicited by other partners than myself. And if it consoles your sense of propriety, I intend to dance with both the Misses Latham later in the evening.'

With this comment, the dance came to a conclusion, and there was a short pause before the second began. Charlotte's thoughts tangled in a knot of confusion. So, his engaging her to dance was intended to make Miss Latham jealous, then? It seemed that this must indeed be the case. He did not deny that there was an understanding between them, so it must be true! Charlotte felt a confusion of feelings, and the dejection of spirits that had assailed her the previous week returned with force. So, she was a pawn in his game! But she would not allow herself to be used in such a way! She thought that he had asked her to dance because he had revised his opinion of her. But it had all the appearance of the opposite, for if his opinion of her had improved, surely he would not use her simply as a pawn to make Miss Latham jealous!

She closed her eyes, feeling suddenly closed in by the dancers and the warm air. Sir Benedict moved forward to her. 'Miss Milton Are you ill? Perhaps you wish to sit down?'

Charlotte nodded. 'I feel a little faint. It is very warm. Perhaps you will excuse me if I sit down?' He escorted her to the seat next to Eliza, and immediately left them to fetch refreshment. The air was cold where he had stood only moments before. She shivered and pulled her shawl around her.

Eliza was concerned. 'Miss Milton, are you well? I think my brother has tired you out! Please, rest here until you feel refreshed. Ah, here he comes again, with some punch.'

She took the punch from Sir Benedict's hand unwillingly, and sipped a little, and Eliza bid him away to leave Charlotte to rest. Sir Benedict took his leave, and Charlotte was able to compose her thoughts quietly. If his asking her to dance was merely a manoeuvre to secure Miss Latham's affections, or to demonstrate his authority, then she would avoid him for the evening, for she did not like to be used! And if his thought was to manipulate a woman into loving him, then they were both as bad as the other.

She watched the couples moving down the dance and miserably wished herself far away, but after a few minutes, she began to enjoy watching the couples, and began to feel better in herself. She found herself looking to see if she could ascertain Sir Benedict's whereabouts, but he had left the room, or she could not see him. How puzzling had been their first moments of the dance! She almost felt she had been dreaming! It must be that her nerves had been overwrought by all the activity. And now to find that he had merely been using her, was somehow more bitter to her than she felt she had a stomach for. She put this thought from her, for it puzzled her, and she did not feel equal to an examination of her heart or mind so soon after dancing with him, feeling him guide her down the dance floor, and feeling so — so at peace!

She looked for Lavinia, and soon discovered her cousin in the dancing couples. Lavinia had been claimed by Lord Winchester, as she had been for the first dance also. Charlotte took this as a sign of his intention to announce their engagement, since it was now apparent to the whole world that they were courting openly. Miss Anne Smart danced with an anonymous gentleman, but cast her a sly look as she sailed past. Charlotte looked away, exasperated.

After a few minutes, she observed Annabelle Latham alone, gliding across the room toward her. She rose quickly, intending to find Lavinia, but Miss Latham was already approaching, with an expression of cold fury upon her face. She hissed at Charlotte in a low voice.

'What is the meaning of your attempt to capture Sir Benedict's attention? Did you not mark my words last Sunday in church? Do you suppose that he could have any real interest in *you*, you who have no money, no connections, who do not move in the first circles of society? You are trying to captivate him with your pretty manners and false modesty! You may think you have won his affection, Miss, but do not be mistaken. Sir Benedict may have stood up with you to dance, but he has merely taken pity on you as Miss Markham's relation, as a favour to her. I wish you to assure me that you will no longer try to engage his pity nor his attention. It makes you look desperate and ridiculous in the eyes of his friends!'

To this astounding speech, Charlotte could find no immediate reply. The shock Charlotte felt on hearing the woman's astounding accusation, that she was trying to captivate Sir Benedict, was surpassed only by the ridiculous assumption by Miss Latham that Sir Benedict had any real affection for her! If only Miss Latham knew Sir Benedict's opinion of her, she would be at ease!

Charlotte flashed angry eyes at the older woman. 'I do not willingly give offence to anyone,' she began warmly, 'but the matters which you mentioned tonight do not merit a polite reply. You have insulted me and my family, by thus addressing me. I have done nothing to deliberately captivate Sir Benedict, and I assure you that that gentleman holds as little interest for me, as I do for him. I deny that I have attempted to engage either his pity or his attention. Believe what you wish, Miss Latham, but I must insist you do not address me again tonight! As for looking ridiculous, I might advise you to use a looking glass!'

She walked quickly toward the doors of the ballroom, seething with anger. She knew Sir Benedict was only using her, but she had not considered the possibility that he had danced with her out of pity. She was no pauper, but she had not the means nor the opportunity to attend many balls at home, and seldom danced or came into society. He was aware of this for she had confessed it soon after her arrival. She allowed that if his motive was pity, there was perhaps kindness behind it, but she was still convinced that his prime motive for dancing with her had been to make Miss Latham jealous.

His tactical manoeuvrings had succeeded, for the lady was incensed, and Charlotte had borne the brunt of that jealousy! She thanked him not for it, but felt better once she had ascertained his motives in her mind. She would avoid him for the remainder of the evening, and stick close to Eliza when not dancing. Composed but pale, she made her way back to Eliza, and if she was rather subdued, the older woman was kind enough not to comment upon it.

Miss Latham was all smiles by the beginning of the next dance, and darted victorious looks at Charlotte as Sir Benedict went down the dance on Miss Latham's arm. These were lost on Charlotte however, because her attention was taken up by another person.

Mr Weatherby, a late arrival, had approached herself and Eliza and greeted them both warmly. After several minutes of general conversation with them both, Mr Weatherby sat next to Eliza, and the two conversed for some time in lowered tones, Eliza appearing quite animated in his company. Charlotte wondered that Eliza did not appear to find Mr Weatherby's conversation as tedious as Lavinia did, but her thoughts were diverted by the appearance of another gentleman, dressed in naval attire, accompanied by Lord Winchester and Lavinia. Her eyes widened and she waited to see how the naval gentleman would be introduced, although she thought she could guess.

Lavinia dropped into a seat beside Charlotte, complaining of the warmth of the room and a monstrous thirst. Lord Winchester wished to fetch Lavinia some punch immediately, but hoped she would excuse him first, to introduce to them all his friend, Captain Williams, of the HMS Formidable, and recently returned from representing British interests in India.

Captain Williams bowed, and sat for a few minutes, answering Eliza's questions politely, and conversing with them all in a generally charming manner. He lived with his sister in Plymouth, and had returned from the war several years ago, having made a modest fortune. He was, Charlotte owned, a pleasant gentleman, but like his friend, there was something sly in his quick looks at Lavinia. Perhaps, like all men, he was enchanted with her ethereal beauty, but Charlotte thought there was something more, something calculating.

At this moment, the orchestra struck up again, and Captain Williams rose. He turned to Charlotte. 'Would Miss Milton do me the honour of being my partner for the next dance?'

Charlotte did not particularly wish to dance, but thinking she might have the opportunity to ask some questions about his friend, she accepted his hand and they took their places in the set. Sir Benedict stood opposite, two rows up, with a new partner in Miss Sophia Latham. His eyes narrowed when he saw her standing up with Captain Williams.

The music began and the couples performed graceful figures. Charlotte made a fine image in her diaphanous lemon and silver gown, but was oblivious to the effect that she was having on her partner, and some other of the curious and admiring gentlemen and ladies who were watching. Lavinia might have her very fair skin and blue eyes, but Charlotte was not without her own beauty, which was accentuated under candlelight, and shone from her expressive eyes when she laughed or smiled. Now she was determined to make the most of her opportunity to quiz the friend of Lord Winchester.

'How long are you staying in the county, Sir?' she began.

'I shall remain for a month or two longer, I collect I am very much at my friend's service, for as long as he wishes me to remain at Wythorpe. Do you know the county well, Miss Milton?'

'Why, not at all, Sir. My home is Sussex, where my father resides. He is a physician there. We do not travel much at all—

it is three or four years since I have been in this district.'

'And how do you find Hertfordshire? Is it to your liking?'

'Very much,' smiled Charlotte. 'Your friend, Lord Winchester, has a family seat in Norfolk, I believe?'

'Yes, his father had a large estate there, but my friend does not find running an estate much to his taste, and his younger brother runs it. Winchester prefers the town, and its varied attractions, to country life. I myself was pleased he took Wythorpe. Town is so hot and stuffy in the summer; do you not agree?'

'Why, I cannot say – I have not had the pleasure of being in town during the summer. I am afraid my father's work keeps him at home all year round. But tell me, will Lord Winchester return to Norfolk at the end of summer, or does he remain here?'

Captain Williams hesitated a little. 'He will return to his house there in a few months, I believe, when the weather is cooler. How well you dance, Miss Milton! What a charming dance partner you make.'

Charlotte smiled but continued her train of thought. 'Lord Winchester is fortunate to have his brother to run the estate. I understand that it generally falls to the lot of the younger brother to enter the church, or take up law.'

Captain Williams separated from her to move down the dance, then continued. 'I believe that his brother studied law, but he is such a good fellow that he agreed to keep an eye on estate matters. There is a very competent manager, I understand.'

'And is it a very large estate, Sir?' she asked with curiosity.

Her partner paused a moment, and Charlotte discerned some unease pass over his countenance, but this was masked in a moment, and he readily answered to the affirmative.

'Aye, it is tolerably large enough, I suppose, for all the uses a man like Winchester can put it to. It brings in a fine income from tenants, and boasts some fine birds in hunting season. I myself hunt there every season when I am ashore.'

Charlotte thought a moment. 'And you, Captain, do you visit Lord Winchester in Norfolk frequently?'

'Why, yes. I am on good terms with both Winchester and his brother. How very pretty your cousin is! I have not had the pleasure of dancing with her but she seems a very charming partner, too. How fine they look together!' he noted, nodding at Lavinia who was going down the dance away from them, Lord Winchester beside her.

Charlotte refrained from comment, and was relieved to briefly separate from her partner once again. She went down the dance shortly after, and took her place at the end, opposite the Captain.

Out of the corner of her eye she noticed Sir Benedict watching her, and thought he looked displeased, although she could not guess why. If he was displeased with her, it was not a new development! She attempted to look happy and carefree, and infused her dancing with some vigour while she addressed her partner again.

'And have you known Lord Winchester long, Sir?'

'I went to school with him, and we have remained friends. What a charming dancer, you are Miss Milton. How light on your feet!' he exclaimed politely.

Charlotte remained quiet for a few moments, absorbing what little she had gleaned. They made some more polite conversation when Charlotte asked him about the East Indies, and whether he had been at Trafalgar, and the dance finished. Captain Williams escorted her to her seat beside Eliza and retreated with a bow. Eliza had, by this time, been left by Mr Weatherby and joined by another lady, an intimate acquaintance of long standing, Eliza explained.

Leaving them after a moment to their private conversation, Charlotte looked around and wondered if she might soon suggest to Eliza that they go into the supper room for some refreshment. At this moment, however, Sir Benedict approached her, and once having enquired after Eliza's comfort, turned to Charlotte, and took the liberty of seating himself next to her!

Charlotte was painfully aware of the possibility of Miss Latham's seeing them together, and yet she could not bring herself to deliberately snub her host, and therefore felt obligated to reply to his questions.

'You seem fully recovered from your fainting spell, Miss Milton. I hope it was not too severe?' he taunted her, his eyes very dark in the warm light of the ballroom.

Charlotte raised her brows. 'You are trying to provoke me, Sir Benedict, and I will not allow myself to be drawn in. You know full well that I was in no danger of fainting. I was a little fatigued, that is all.'

'I observed you dancing with such vigour, only fifteen minutes ago, that I thought you might well honour your partner with the privilege which you denied me—that of standing on his feet!'

She laughed. 'I was rather afraid of that myself, Sir.'

'But perhaps it was the company of your partner which induced such spirited dancing? How did you find Captain Williams as a dance partner?'

'Captain Williams is a perfectly adequate dance partner Sir. I can neither complain, nor boast, of his dancing.'

'And did you have tolerable conversation? Did he amuse you?' enquired Sir Benedict, in a colder tone.

She made no immediate reply, puzzled as to his motives for asking such questions. It arose in her mind suddenly that he was jealous of her dancing with Captain Williams, but surely, she was mistaken. She tried again. 'Captain Williams is the friend of Lord Winchester. He has recently returned from India. He was most entertaining on the subject.'

'I am glad you found so verbose a partner. It was, after all, your wish to have good conversation while dancing. I am sorry that you did not manage to stand on his feet, however,' he added.

She glanced at him to find him half smiling at his own joke. She sighed, unable to understand his changing moods, and wished he would leave her, for he puzzled her exceedingly and made her uncomfortable by his presence. Annabelle Latham had not seen him sitting by her yet, but surely there would be more distress for her when she did.

She turned to Eliza to ask if she would take refreshment with her in the supper room, seeing this as her best opportunity to move away.

Sir Benedict rose and held his arm out. 'Allow me to escort you both.'

Eliza thanked her brother and Charlotte was obliged to take his other arm and allow him to escort her to supper. Her senses reeled at the scent of pine, and her arm tingled under his touch. She remembered the puzzling moment of his escorting her to the first set, and she released his arm as soon as was polite, for his touch disquieted her very much. When they had both been seated and served with some cold cuts and cake, Sir Benedict hovered close by, not seeming to have any purpose but to put Charlotte ill-at-ease, knowing he was watching her!

Eliza spoke in lowered tones to Charlotte. 'I wonder where Lavinia and Lord Winchester are? I must confess I have every expectation of a certain event being announced this evening, Miss Milton. It now seems very clear that Lord Winchester intends to have her. My friend, Mrs Waring, believes I am correct. She tells me all the room is talking of it! I must say, it will be a relief to have her married,' she sighed. 'I think she has made a sensible choice.'

Charlotte put down her fork. 'Do you really think so Ma'am?'

'Why, yes, my dear. Lord Winchester will be able to indulge her taste for fashion and society, but I believe he will keep a firm hand on her. He has a certain sharp look about him. But has she said anything to you at all, my dear?'

Charlotte shook her head. 'Do not suppose that my cousin confides in me any more than she confides in you. But I must confess, I am of the same expectation.'

Shortly, they were joined by Lavinia and Lord Winchester. Her aunt scolded her kindly for being so long from her. Sir Benedict agreed. 'You should attend your aunt, Lavinia. You know she is not able to move about freely enough to come to you.'

'Oh, do not scold me so, Uncle, for it was not my fault! I am sorry Aunt, but I was not allowed to leave the dancing, not even for supper, until now. Lord, it is tedious indeed to have to dance with so many different partners that one cannot even remember their names! Lord Winchester has quite claimed my freedom and insists on his not leaving my side, whenever I am not dancing!' She gave him her prettiest smile, and sighed happily.

Charlotte fully expected Lavinia to announce their engagement, but no conversation on this subject was forthcoming. Lord Winchester was gay and attentive to Lavinia, but Charlotte found herself suspicious of any symptoms of attachment. He was at once both attentive and disinterested. She observed him on one occasion staring at a rather handsome woman across the room, and on another, exchanging sly looks with his friend, Captain Williams. She could not but help remember the first time she had seen him in the town, and the way he had looked at her in so improper a manner. She also remembered how he had received money then too, as well as from Captain Williams only a week later.

She sighed. It was perplexing. She yearned to speak to Sir Benedict but did not want to endure his accusations of interference again. She had no real evidence to present to him if she did. She had learned nothing of note from Captain Williams. Perhaps she was being over cautious, and Sir Benedict was right. However, it seemed that an engagement was imminent. People appeared to observe the pair, and converse in lowered tones behind open fans. Charlotte determined to speak to Lavinia if her uncle did not, and make enquiries as to an engagement, for it seemed that all the room expected such a development!

After supper, more dancing was to be had, and Charlotte had all the gratification that a young woman could ask for, by being approached by no less than three gentlemen, to request her hand for a dance. She had the dubious pleasure of dancing with Sir Frank, who bowed and bobbed his way through the sets so that she had to conceal a sigh, and then with Mr Weatherby, whom Charlotte decided was not so very dull after all, but rather had a serious demeanour which might be taken by some as insipid.

Sir Benedict hovered on the periphery of her vision, and danced only infrequently — once with Miss Smart, and once more with Sophia Latham. Miss Annabelle Latham sat with some other ladies on the sidelines, looking quite put out when Sir Benedict went down the dance with her protege.

Sir Benedict scarcely spoke to Charlotte for the remainder of the evening. It seemed to Charlotte that he disapproved of her dancing with other partners, and yet, he did not ask her to dance again himself. Was he jealous? But it seemed impossible to Charlotte that he could be, and she remained puzzled as to his ever-changing moods around her.

At last the evening gave way to yawns and tired farewells, and the crowd dissipated, leaving Lord Winchester and his own overnight guests alone. Lavinia was strangely quiet in the carriage on the drive home, absorbed in memories of the evening, thought Charlotte, and she expected keenly that Sir Benedict would now enquire of his niece as to the situation between herself and Lord Winchester. Sir Benedict, however, remained silent and brooding himself, and it was left to Eliza and Charlotte to fill the silences with generalities and comments upon the evening.

Charlotte slept deeply, and woke very early, her head aching. She regretted the punch from the night before and wished she had kept to water! She rose almost as soon as she woke, and dressing in a light morning dress and shawl, decided to walk off her headache before church.

Outdoors, the morning mist was just lifting and she set off over the hills toward the woods and the worker's cottages. She went over the events of the evening in her mind, still puzzled by both Sir Benedict's behaviour towards her, and Winchester's motives regarding Lavinia. She had not walked more than a few minutes when she noticed a figure coming towards her. A minute or so more revealed it was Tom Wilcox. He walked quickly and broke into a run when he saw her.

'Miss,' he panted. 'I was just coming to the great house to find you. I must speak with you. It is very urgent.'

She laid a hand on his arm. 'Stay, Tom, wait until you have caught your breath.'

'Miss, it is bad news, very bad. Where is Miss Markham?'

Charlotte was astonished. 'Why, she is still asleep I expect, in her bed.'

'But have you seen her this morning, Miss?'

'What do you mean, Tom? It is very early. She is not yet

risen.' Charlotte was beginning to be alarmed. 'Tell me all you know!'

Tom shook his head. ''Tis very bad, Miss. My friend, who knows one of the footmen who works for Lord Winchester in town, says Winchester is in a bad way, up to his eyeballs in debt. He says Winchester lives on borrowed money, that he ain't rich at all, Miss! They say he has gambled everything he has, and that Winchester's younger brother and he have cooked up a scheme for Winchester to marry money. Winchester heard about Miss Markham's inheritance from town gossip and decided to try his luck. He took the house here and made as if to become friends with the Master, to get close to Miss Markham. 'Tis said Miss, that Winchester has come to Wythorpe solely to catch Miss Markham. 'Tis the talk of the servants at Winchester's town house. My friend says he heard all this on good authority from the footman, who is very good friends with the butler there.'

Charlotte gaped, her worst fears coming true in a moment. 'But, Tom, are you very sure?'

'Yes, Miss. If I weren't sure, I would not have come to you. But, 'tis true, every word. My friend is not one to make up stories. He says Captain Williams has lent Winchester money to cover his expenses, on surety of repayment with interest on his marriage to Miss Markham.'

Charlotte was in shock, remembering how she had come upon Captain Williams in the lane with Lord Winchester after church, counting out pound notes, and what she had seen on the first day she had set eyes on Winchester in town. It all made more sense now. The furtive way he had taken the money both times, and his haste in attaching Lavinia's affections. But she could not understand his position. In debt? She shook her head in confusion. 'So he has no money of his own? But the estate in Norfolk! Surely there is money in the estate?'

'They say he has gambled away half the estate already, Miss, since there is no existing entailment. The brother is in a rage and insists on Winchester's getting money somehow, or they will be forced to divide the remaining land up and sell it off. See, Winchester has a reputation as a gambler, Miss, 'tis no secret in those parts. That's why he came down here, where they don't yet know him, to find himself a rich wife.'

'A rich wife whose fortune he will gamble away like his own. Oh Tom! My poor cousin!'

'It gets worse, Miss. There is some talk over at Wythorpe, that Winchester has talked Miss Markham into eloping.'

'Great God! You cannot be serious?' Charlotte held a hand to her mouth. 'When, Tom? Is that why you wanted to know if I had seen my cousin this morning? Do you mean they have eloped already?'

Tom said nothing but his countenance was all pity for Charlotte. She cried out in horror.

'But that would mean — but yes, of course! That was why — her gowns! All over the floor! She was packing her trunk! Oh stupid, stupid girl! Pray heaven we are not too late! I must go at once! I must find Sir Benedict!'

Charlotte turned and ran down the hill towards the house, leaving Tom watching after her. She plummeted as fast as she could down the slopes until she came, panting, to the small gate into the kitchen garden. She yanked open the gate and was about to push through it when Sir Benedict rounded the corner of the garden. He looked up as she abandoned the gate and ran to him. He looked quite astonished to see her in such a state. 'Miss Milton! Good God, are you unwell? Has someone had an accident?

'Thank God you are here. The worst has happened,' she panted, trying to catch her breath and hold back her tears. 'My cousin and Winchester! He is not what he appears, Sir! We must find her at once, at once!'

She made as if to run to the house, but he stood motionless, frowning in puzzlement.

'Confound it, girl! What do you mean by this? Calm

yourself. I'm sure you have simply mistaken things, as I told you before. What has happened? Try to calm yourself! We will go into the house and I will call some of the servants to bring you something for your comfort.'

'No, Sir, I thank you, but I beg you to hear me! I suspect Lavinia has eloped with Lord Winchester! He is in great debt, from gambling. He has gambled away his entire inheritance! He has come here solely to ensnare my cousin in marriage. If he is allowed to marry her, he will gamble away her fortune in the same way! You must do something, Sir! Even now, she may be going to her fate with this man!'

She left him gaping at her, and ran in some urgency towards the side gate, and was gone into the house. She heard his footsteps behind her as she ran through the kitchen, much to the surprise of Cook, and two kitchen maids who stood wide-eyed as first Miss Charlotte passed by, then the Master!

Charlotte reached the stairs and ran quickly up them, with Sir Benedict close behind her. He closed the gap between them and grabbed for her arm. She swung around, her eyes blazing. 'Sir! My cousin, at this moment, may be throwing her life away on this worthless man. Allow me to go to her room and see for myself if it is true.'

Her eyes spoke her anxiety and distress. He relented, and released her arm, and she ran to her cousin's door. Sir Benedict was behind her. 'I am sure, Miss Milton, that you have been vastly misled, but if it will set your mind at ease, do enter and wake my niece.'

His voice was laced with disbelief, and yet was not without compassion. She put her hand on the doorknob, turned it, and entered the darkened room. Her eyes went immediately to the bed. It was as she had feared. Her cousin was gone!

Sir Benedict strode into the room, and pulled apart the drapes, allowing early morning light to flood the room. There were signs of Lavinia, but her nightgown was unused, still under her pillow, and her bed had not been slept in. Charlotte flung open the closet doors. 'Her trunk is gone.'

'The Devil curse him!' Sir Benedict turned to Charlotte. 'How many hours do you think she has been gone? Did you hear anything last night? Your room is adjacent — did you not hear her leave?'

Charlotte shook her head. 'I heard nothing. But she cannot have moved her trunk without help. Perhaps her lady's maid?'

Sir Benedict nodded sharply. 'Yes. I shall call for her.' He strode to the door and called down the hall loudly. 'Stokes! Stokes! Where are you, man?'

A few seconds later, the butler appeared, his arms full of silver for cleaning. 'Sir?'

'Stokes. Forget the silver for now. Send Rose here to me immediately. Keep it discreet, will you?'

'Sir.' Stokes departed quickly and obediently, and Sir Benedict turned back to Charlotte who was sitting on Lavinia's bed, her eyes damp, and her countenance pale. She felt all the force of guilt combined with anxiety for her cousin. She ought, she really ought, to have said something to Sir Benedict earlier! She ought to have made him hear her! These thoughts had occupied her for the last few minutes, and their effects were telling, for anyone who could see. She looked extremely ill.

He observed her in silence for a moment, and then asked in gentler tones, 'On whose authority did you learn of this information? Are you sure of this source?'

Charlotte turned unhappy eyes on him and nodded. 'I am sure, Sir.'

'Who told you of all this?'

Charlotte paused, then sighed. 'Tom Wilcox told me.'

'Tom Wilcox!' exclaimed Sir Benedict. 'How could he know any of this? On what does he base his intelligence?'

'He works for Lord Winchester, as you know. He came to me this morning early, while I was out walking. He says he has a friend who knows the footman at Lord Winchester's town residence. There has been some talk among the servants. Lord

Winchester's vices are well known, I collect.'

She quietly related all that Tom had told her, and waited for his reaction. She half expected him to be either disbelieving, or angry, but to her relief, if he was feeling any of these emotions, he hid them from her and remained calm. Rose peeped around the door and bobbed a curtsy, waiting with her head down. She looked guilty, thought Charlotte.

When Sir Benedict began to question her, she quickly broke down. 'Yes, Sir, it is true, Sir. I had the young footman help with my mistress's trunk,' she explained tearfully. 'I know it was wrong of me, but she said you would not allow the marriage, Sir. So I thought to myself, I must help my mistress. Lord Winchester's footman came with a carriage and took the trunk and my mistress away.'

Sir Benedict cursed again. 'Damn stupid girl! Not you Rose, although you too, have behaved badly! What time do you say she left?'

Rose dashed tears from her eyes. 'Around three o'clock in the morning, Sir. You was all home so late from the ball, but everyone went to bed direct, and my mistress waited only a half hour or so before the carriage from Wythorpe came.'

'Where did she go, Rose? Gretna Green I suppose!' Sir Benedict's face was thunder. Rose did not look at him.

'Yes, Sir. I believe Lord Winchester and she was to go to Gretna Green direct from Wythorpe.'

Sir Benedict nodded. 'That will be all Rose. I shall deal with you later, girl. In the meantime, speak of this to nobody, and if asked, say that your mistress is tired from the ball and sleeps late. We may be able to prevent this from getting out, at least for the time being.'

Rose nodded sadly, tears welling up again. 'Very good Sir.' She left the room, sobbing quietly.

Charlotte leapt up. 'Could not you follow them, Sir?' she asked eagerly. 'They must not be *so* far along, only three hours or so.' Her eyes pleaded with his. 'If only my cousin can be brought back in time, if only we can prevent a marriage from taking place!'

Sir Benedict looked grave. 'I shall go at once. Speak of this to nobody. I shall send word as soon as I can.'

He reached for her hand, and, astonished, she did not resist. Emotions passed over his face, as he looked into her eyes, but although he seemed nearly about to speak to her, to console her wretchedness, to allay her fears, he did not, or could not. After a few moments he dropped her hand and was gone, and she was alone in her cousin's room. Minutes later, she heard the sound of hoofbeats on the gravel outside and after they died into the distance, she sat for a long time in the empty silence that surrounded her.

Twenty Five

'My dear, do not worry yourself. My brother will find her. You will see.' Eliza patted Charlotte's hand kindly, although she was just as worried about her niece. They had found a seat in the shade of the garden and Belle sat at Charlotte's feet, resting her silky head on one of her shoes. Charlotte had taken Lavinia's pup under her care and was grateful for the distraction.

'Benedict has connections in the city. He will be able to locate them quickly, I am certain. They cannot have gone further than the outskirts of London before stopping. The road to Scotland my dear, is most unpleasant. It is three hundred miles or more! I cannot see your cousin, who hates travel in any form, being able to bear more than four hours in a carriage before wishing to be out of it!'

'Yes, true. But her desire to be married, her wish to make a match which will elevate her in society, may overcome any objections she has to the journey itself,' Charlotte argued unhappily. 'And even if your brother can find them, her reputation is now surely ruined, beyond redemption!'

'Yes,' agreed Eliza quietly. 'She has been very foolish. I cannot see how she can recover. Unless she marries Winchester now, she cannot —will not—recover her name. And yet, to be married to such a man! We must see what Benedict can do.'

It had been almost a full ten hours since Sir Benedict had left, and both women were anxious to hear of any developments from London. Eliza had taken the news from Charlotte with some shock and yet, Eliza owned, she was not so very surprised, knowing as she did Lavinia's impetuous nature and strong-minded ways. Both women had felt they could not sit in church, while waiting so anxiously for news from London, so they had forgone devotions, and sat quietly at home, waiting for the hours to pass without a message from town. Now it was late afternoon, and the two women eventually agreed that they likely would not hear from Sir Benedict until the next day.

'And the cost of the journey!' continued Eliza, 'They must stop to change horses, and surely they will stop overnight. I doubt she has that kind of money in her purse, for my brother never gives her more than five pounds at a time, and from what you say, the gentleman surely does not, if he is so much in debt. Nay, they will stop in London, I fear, even if it is to procure more funds to travel onward.'

Charlotte considered how badly her cousin wanted to be married to Lord Winchester, and rather thought that her cousin was certain to have procured the funds herself beforehand. Or they would make the trip on borrowed monies, from Captain Williams or whomever else of Lord Winchester's friends was so foolish as to lend to him!

Now that she had had a day to consider and reflect on all that had taken place, she had realised that the elopement must have been planned carefully. Surely it was this that had taken Lavinia on her errand the day before the ball, to Wythorpe! It must have been to plan the details of the elopement, sealed with a kiss! What shocking things that gentleman must have led her cousin to believe, in order to convince her that elopement was the only option! With Lavinia needing only six weeks to turn seventeen, Lord Winchester must have realised that, even had he approached Sir Benedict for permission, Lavinia's uncle would have denied the couple and made them wait at the very least until her seventeenth birthday! Charlotte surmised that Lord Winchester would not have been willing to wait several more weeks to be married, or perhaps even another year, for fear of his debts being discovered, and Sir Benedict's permission withdrawn. That must have been why Lord Winchester had convinced Lavinia to elope in secrecy.

Nay, she thought it very much more likely that the couple had carried on through London for fear of being overtaken. With very good time, and no mishaps on the way, they might arrive in Scotland within three or four days, if they did not stop often. Unless they had relied upon Lavinia's absence not being discovered until much later. If Tom had not come to warn Charlotte, she thought, it might have been hours more before Lavinia was discovered to be missing! Even so, they had had a good four or five hours start on any pursuit. Surely Sir Benedict could not possibly overtake them before nightfall! But she did not share these thoughts with Eliza, for she did not want to make Lavinia's aunt, of whom she had become fond, even more anxious about her niece.

Charlotte still felt periodically overcome with guilt at having not tried harder to persuade Sir Benedict of Lord Winchester's motives for attaching himself to her cousin. She still felt wretched that she, Charlotte, could have prevented this reprehensible event from taking place, if she had just pressed her case more urgently upon Sir Benedict! As often as these thoughts returned to torment her, did she give way to sighing and occasional dampness of the cheeks. Charlotte was not able to fully conceal these melancholy thoughts from Eliza, and the older woman tried to comfort the younger, thinking her distress was all for her cousin.

'Oh Eliza,' said Charlotte, turning unhappy eyes on her friend. 'It is all my fault! I knew there was something wrong, something amiss, in the way Lord Winchester attached himself so speedily to my cousin! And I saw that Lavinia was determined to have him at all cost. Why did I not press my case for caution more urgently to your brother? I ought to have related to him all that I have seen—' She stopped abruptly, realising that Eliza was unaware of Lavinia's improper visit to Wythorpe.

Eliza raised her brows. 'My dear, if you know anything… anything else, that is, that you have not told my brother — anything that might help him in his search for them, you must tell us!' she encouraged kindly.

Charlotte shook her head. 'I do not think there is any such intelligence, except that I saw Lord Winchester on two occasions receive money, and in such a clandestine manner that it raised my suspicions. And the day before the ball, when Lavinia had gone out riding, I saw her visit Wythorpe, alone! Oh Eliza, had I shared this with your brother at the time, perhaps something may have been done then, to prevent this!'

Eliza digested this information thoughtfully and moved to take Charlotte's hand. 'My dear Charlotte, you are a good girl, a girl of the most excellent qualities and upright thoughts. No one could find fault with the way you have conducted yourself! Why, I know my brother, and I believe he can be stubbornly unreasoning on occasion. He mentioned to me himself that you had approached him regarding your fears for your cousin, and at the time we both agreed that such fears were unfounded. Yes, I am sorry, my dear, but I, too, believed your fears to be incited by youthful imagination. Ah, well, how wrong we both were.'

'But I could have been more forceful. I could have pressed your brother more urgently!' exclaimed Charlotte.

Eliza squeezed Charlotte's hand. 'There is nothing more you could have said or done to convince my brother of Lord Winchester's guilt. There was nothing to be done, other than what you did. You waited for more evidence of your suspicions, and it was not your fault that we were all too late to prevent this wastrel from absconding with my very silly niece. You must not forget, my dear, that Lavinia was determined to have this man, and even had you convinced my brother that Lord Winchester was to be suspected, it would have taken time to investigate him, and no one knew of the planned elopement, not even yourself. We none of us would have been able to prevent the unhappy event taking place. We can now only hope that my brother finds them in time to prevent the second, and worse outcome!'

Charlotte was not much cheered by this speech, but she hung on gratefully to the kind words, and tried to compose her feelings so as not to upset Eliza.

They spent an anxious evening, with no word from Sir Benedict. Eliza was exhausted and begged Charlotte's pardon that she might retire early. Charlotte gladly gave it and retired to her own room with relief, wanting very much the solace of solitude and rest.

Sleep, however, eluded Charlotte and she restlessly turned in her bed, going over in her mind the last conversation she had had with Sir Benedict. The way he had seized her hand, and then stood looking down at her, as if he wanted to speak but could not. His eyes had penetrated her soul, and some strange emotion had passed over his face, but what it was, and what he wanted to say to her, was beyond her comprehension. He had wished to comfort her in her distress; she had seen this on his face, in his eyes, but she would never know what he had wished to say. Eventually, Charlotte fell asleep, and dreamed of a dark horse flying over moors and roads, its rider shrouded in shadows.

The following morning the two women waited anxiously in the parlour for the sound of hoofbeats which would herald a messenger. Around late morning they were startled by a rap at the door and shortly thereafter, Stokes announced the arrival of a visitor, Mr Weatherby.

Eliza at once looked both pleased and nervous, while Charlotte exclaimed, 'Mr Weatherby? Whatever can he be doing here? How inconvenient of him to arrive at such a time!' and then covered her mouth with her hand in mortification. 'Please forgive me, Eliza, I did not mean — that is, I was not expecting calls, but of course it is eleven o'clock, and I had quite forgotten — forgive me!'

She smoothed her dress and stood unwillingly with Eliza to receive their unexpected guest. She was dismayed that a visit at such a time would have to be borne, when all she could think of was Sir Benedict, and her cousin's fate. She hoped most keenly that a messenger would not chance to arrive during the call, for that would make things very awkward indeed.

Of course, Mr Weatherby had no knowledge of the events of the last forty-eight hours, and was unsuspecting as he was kindly ushered into the parlour by Eliza. Indeed, Charlotte thought, Eliza was most attentive to Mr Weatherby, and the two struck up a cheerful conversation for some time. Charlotte wondered that Eliza could be so composed, but quietly petted Belle, who sat devotedly at her feet, and then took up her needlework to hide her anxiety, glad that Eliza was able to converse without giving way to the distress she knew that they both felt.

Mr Weatherby did not ask as to the whereabouts of Miss Markham, perhaps being quite content in his present company, thought Charlotte. She perceived that their visitor was the most animated she had seen him, and was grateful that Eliza's thoughts had been happily diverted, at least for a short time, from her niece.

When Mr Weatherby left, the two women had only been alone again for fifteen minutes, when they heard the much looked for hoofbeats and a rider was seen from the window to dash from his horse and bang upon the front door. Seconds later, Stokes brought in a note on a silver dish to Eliza, and Charlotte waited anxiously for its contents to be revealed. Eliza took it up quickly and, reading the back, she nodded. 'It is indeed from my brother. Well, Charlotte, let us see what he has to say.' She opened it and began to read.

'My dear Eliza,

It is worse than I had hoped, and yet not much worse than I had suspected. Lavinia and Winchester have continued on to Scotland after stopping in town for refreshment and to change his pair. After enquiring at the most likely inns for them to change, I chanced upon two postillions who have sighted persons who answer to their descriptions. They are said to have gone on towards the north east, but I suspect that the roads in those parts will slow them somewhat and that I shall be able to overtake them with some hard riding. I have solicited the assistance of my good friend Thomas Harding, who will come with me. God help Winchester if there is any resistance! I shall send word the moment I have her in my care. Yours in haste etc...'

She put the letter aside. 'At least he has found their trail. I hope very much that he is right, and that he can overtake them before they reach Scotland. If anyone can, it is my brother. And Harding is a good man, one of the best. He will be of some assistance. While they are in pursuit, there is hope for your cousin yet.'

Charlotte gave her a wan smile. She was not yet reconciled to give up her own part in the affair, and each mention of it brought a new flood of feelings, guilt mingled with distress. If her cousin should marry Winchester and give up her fortune to such a man! She wondered too, what Sir Benedict would think of her, for not informing him immediately of what she already knew; Lavinia's indecorous visit to Wythorpe, unchaperoned, may have alerted him finally to Winchester's true motives!

She felt wretched at the thought of Sir Benedict's thinking badly of her, and suppressed a sob. Why should it matter what he thought of her? His good opinion had never been hers, but she still felt misery at the thought of being sent home, or worse, staying on at Delford, having to face him every day, if he was able to find Lavinia in time and bring her back. She felt confused and miserable and, only with some effort, did she manage to conceal the extent of her sadness from Eliza.

The day yielded the inconvenience of yet another call, this from the Latham females, without Sir Frank. Spying their approach on foot from the window, Charlotte begged Eliza to be allowed to retire to her room and beg a headache. Eliza excused Charlotte kindly and told her she would tell the Miss Lathams that she and Lavinia were out riding, so as not to arouse suspicion. Her brother, of course, would be said to be away on business.

Relieved beyond measure that she would not have to face Annabelle Latham's malicious looks and sharp tongue, Charlotte quickly disappeared up the stairs and took refuge in her room. She hoped that nothing had entered the Lathams' suspicions, since every inhabitant of Delford had been absent from church the day before, and now both she and Lavinia were not "in" for calls. But Eliza assured her afterwards that no word had leaked yet; Stokes and Rose had been as good as their word and been discreet. Charlotte hoped the young footman who had helped Rose move the trunks was either too stupid or too young to make out what might have happened, but it would not be long before the servants would begin to guess, when Lavinia was not seen at dinner two nights in a row.

She said as much to Eliza later, over afternoon tea, where both women attempted, without success, to do justice to Cook's pound cake. It was agreed upon that it would be difficult to conceal such an event for much longer, and that the best they could hope for was the timely rescue of Lavinia from the hands of Winchester, and to bring her home to nurture her reputation back to health.

The afternoon passed in slow, tormenting hours, but finally the message both women sought arrived, and once again, Eliza snatched up the note. She perused it quickly and uttered those words Charlotte wanted to hear the most.

'He has found them in time! Thank God!'

'Oh! Oh!' cried Charlotte, 'it is good news indeed! But Eliza, what does he say? How did he find them? Oh, it is very good news indeed!' Charlotte sagged in relief, and then, her countenance becoming concerned again, pleaded for details. Eliza handed the letter to her.

'Read it yourself, my dear. I myself feel quite ill with the affair and I fear I cannot relate all the details without some mistake, just now.' She put her hand to her temple and closed her eyes. 'Read it aloud, my dear, for I wish to hear the particulars over.'

Charlotte took up the short note and read aloud.

'My Dear Sister,

I am at last able to give you and Miss Milton some relief for your shared anxiety. I have found them in time. They are not yet married. Harding and I pursued Winchester's carriage and discovered them on the Great North road, not seven hours outside of London, with the wheel caught in a rut and the carriage dog near death from exhaustion.

Winchester gave my niece up with no fight and has taken flight on one of the horses, I know not where. I suppose he will return, eventually, to Wythorpe, to end his lease and return to town. He is lucky to retain his life, for I excessively wished to deprive him of it, but Harding prevented me from so foolish an action. However, I have hopes of damaging his reputation severely in town, so as to prevent him from preying upon any other young ladies of fortune.

Please be reassured that your niece is very well, although resoundingly verbal, and quite unrepentant regarding her misadventure. You, sister, will no doubt give her the chastisement she deserves. I have hired a post chaise and will return with Lavinia by tomorrow midmorning. Harding will accompany us as far as London.

Your affectionate brother,

B.M'

Charlotte tried to hide her confusion at Sir Benedict's referral to herself and scanned the letter again to take in the details. At last she looked up. 'My poor foolish cousin.' She shook her head, unshed tears in her eyes.

Eliza sighed. 'She is ruined, for we will be hard pressed to cover this up. My brother has prevented a marriage which would lead to her unhappiness, but the alternative is shameful for Lavinia. At least they did not spend the night at a public inn. Perhaps we can hide the worst. But who will ever have her, now?'

'Abominable creature!' cried Charlotte, her eyes bright with feeling. 'He deserves the very worst, the very worst!'

'Yes, my dear,' Eliza concurred. 'My brother would have killed Winchester if Harding had not been present to prevent a fight. As it is, Winchester is lucky to still have his head intact with his body! My dear, we can now rest more easily, until she is home. Although what I will say to her, I really have no idea. I hope she has learned her lesson!'

Charlotte retired to bed that night with more than a little trepidation in her heart. She would have to face Sir Benedict the following day, when he returned with Lavinia, and her feelings prevented her, on every point, from enjoying calm and tranquil repose beforehand. Her guilt at not having shared the intelligence which she had had in her power to share! Her misery at the thought that she could have spared Lavinia's family the suffering and anxiety for her wellbeing overcame her once again and she spent a miserable night contemplating how she would be received by Sir Benedict the next day. She must apologise, and she must expect the censure she deserved from one whom it would pain her most to receive it from!

And yet, he was not so angry with her when he had left. But the urgency of pursuing Lavinia may have driven all recrimination from his mind. When he found himself at leisure to speak with her, she suspected his anger would be formidable! She had lost his favour, if she had ever had it, however briefly. The idea of his thinking badly of her seemed, more than anything else, to put her heart into turmoil. Her pillow was damp for some time.

Finally, in the small hours of the morning, she fell into a deep slumber, disturbed yet again by images of shadowed figures on horseback and herself, driven out of the house and back to her father in disgrace.

~~*~~

True to his word, midmorning gave way to the sound of hoofbeats and seconds later a post chaise drove up to the front door. Eliza had been lying on the sofa with a headache, but bid Charlotte, who had been watching from the window, to run down to meet her cousin, and inform her brother that she was in the parlour, a little indisposed. Charlotte obeyed immediately, but with her heart pounding in her chest as she met first her cousin, and then Sir Benedict, from the carriage.

Lavinia looked tired and ill-tempered, and much out of sorts with her uncle. Charlotte greeted her seriously, trying to maintain a calm appearance, keeping her eyes low so as not to meet Sir Benedict's.

Lavinia was defiant. 'Good day, Charlotte. I suppose you are just as angry with me as Uncle! Well, I shan't mind anything you say to me, for I wish I was in Scotland with dear Winchester and you shan't make me say else!' She stormed up the steps, followed meekly by Rose and the footman, who had come down to carry up her trunk and hat boxes.

'Indeed, cousin, I wasn't going to reproach you at all. It is not my place to do that,' began Charlotte, running up the steps to catch her. 'But we have been so worried! I am just glad you have come home, dear. Your aunt is in the parlour, lying down,' she added.

Having indirectly discharged her duty to Eliza, she followed Lavinia into the house and watched her stalk up the stairs without wishing her aunt good day. Charlotte guessed that she would, in due course, be sent for by Eliza, although she knew that the censure which she would get from her aunt would be as gentle as her uncle's would have been harsh!

Sir Benedict followed Charlotte into the house and, aware of him behind her, she turned to face him, her stomach fluttering under his gaze. He regarded her seriously, his face unreadable.

She curtsied politely, her heart hammering in her breast. 'Sir, I wish to speak to you — that is, after you are rested from your journey. If you would be so kind...' she faltered, overcome with emotion, primarily guilt, and another that she could not readily identify.

He took in her tired countenance and red eyes. 'Miss Milton — Charlotte. Please do not distress yourself.' His voice was tinged with an earnest seriousness. 'I shall certainly grant you an interview, if you wish it — in fact, however, there is something — I do have something to say to you. Would you do me the honour of coming to my library before dinner? I would speak with you earlier but I must attend to some urgent estate business which will take me from home for most of today.'

Charlotte kept her head down to hide the crimson in her cheeks. She had noted his use of her first name, had been confused by it, had delighted in it, and yet she was not so naive as to be rendered complacent by it. It meant nothing, and certainly did not mean that he would not be angry with her when she confessed what she knew!

He had requested an interview and she had no choice but to hear him, and she must have the opportunity to express her sorrow at not telling him about Lavinia's visit alone to Wythorpe. How great his anger might be, she could not tell, but she must own her actions, and if he saw fit to censure her for concealing such information, she must humbly submit. For her own part, she could only try to show him that, had she thought it would make a difference to his hearing her at the time, she would gladly have revealed what she had known, but her hope of his rationally hearing her had been considerably lessened by his previous reaction to what he saw as her interference. She nodded, curtsied again, and ran upstairs, aware of his eyes on her back.

~~*~~

Lavinia was defiant and obstinate when Charlotte tried to speak with her later that day. She was now in the small parlour, having come down for private audience with her aunt. Afterward, Eliza had gone to her room to rest, and Charlotte ventured into the parlour to see her cousin, who was lying sprawled on the chaise in a most unladylike attitude, absently stroking Belle's head. The pup's tail thumped up and down when she saw Charlotte.

Charlotte entertained little hope of moving her cousin, for she seemed to be only angry at her uncle's interference, and not a bit mortified at her own behaviour, or concerned about the danger she had been in. Rather, when Charlotte tentatively began a conversation regarding the matter, she was obstinate and sullen.

'Really Charlotte, I do not understand what all the fuss is about. *I* was not so scrupulous about his motives, even if Uncle was! And if dear Winchester is rather a gamester, that is nothing new for young men of his rank! Why, he is ever so rich anyway; what can it signify if he wanted my fortune? I told you that I never intended to marry for love! He could have provided me with all that I desire of society, fashion, and rank, and if I used my fortune to buy such things where is the harm? It is too, too unfair of Uncle to interfere!'

Charlotte sighed in exasperation, and tried to reason calmly with her cousin. 'Lavinia, your uncle saved you from a marriage of misery. You ought to be thankful! It is said that Lord Winchester has lost all his own fortune to gaming, and half his estate! He would have spent your fortune in less than five years and then you would have none of the fine things you think you wish for! He may even have abandoned you after the money was spent! Yes, you would be Countess of Winchester, but is rank alone enough to make you happy if you are living in a loveless union?'

Lavinia was unmoved and obstinate. 'I don't believe he was so much in debt as you say. You are only trying to have your way because you are jealous that I was going to make match of more superior rank that you could ever hope to make!'

The words stung Charlotte. She was not so proud that she had ever thought of making a match above her own station, but she was the daughter of a gentleman and well educated, with the manners of a well-bred lady. She tried to forgive her cousin, but her feelings were insulted. She did not try any further conversation and allowed the subject to drop. They played with Belle, and Charlotte suggested a walk.

Lavinia was curt with her. 'I think it will rain, Charlotte, and besides, I am not disposed to go rambling about the countryside with you as my watch dog. I will remain here, thank you very much.'

Charlotte went to the window. 'Yes, it looks rather dull, but I think I will walk out, for it looks like it will only rain a little and not very soon. And I am not your watch dog, Cousin; far be it from *my* power to prevent you from doing anything you wished!' she added archly, but if her tone was apparent to Lavinia, the young woman ignored it and would not be drawn in.

Charlotte took her walk, but it soon began to shower and the showers set in quickly as heavy rain. She gave up her walk and returned to the house, damp and out of sorts, to compose her mind as best she could for her interview with Sir Benedict.

Twenty Eight

Charlotte smoothed her skirts nervously and knocked on the library door an hour before dinner. On receiving a murmured reply, she took a fortifying breath and entered the room. The scents of pine and cinnamon assailed her nose. Her heart skipped a beat. Sir Benedict himself stood at the window, silhouetted in its dying light, making him a more formidable figure than Charlotte had hoped to encounter at this meeting. She curtsied slightly and waited while he enquired politely after her health. She made some reply and waited for him to start. He gestured for her to sit, but remained at the window himself, brooding and silent, and her heart plummeted. She had hoped very much that he would be approachable, that her responsibility to lay before him the facts of the last week would be eased by the kindliness she had perceived in his previous address to her, but it seemed that he was returned to that state which made it harder for her to lay bare her feelings. And yet she must!

She began in low voice. 'Sir, I must lay before you the events of the last week, of which I had knowledge before my cousin came to run away with Lord Winchester, for I believe I must own to some accountability for my cousin's behaviour.'

He turned, his brow furrowed. 'How so, Miss Milton? You

— of all people! You cannot possibly take any blame for what has happened! When I think of myself, my own behaviour, when you tried to warn me — it is I who must take the blame for her wayward behaviour, which I did not take the trouble to check. How can you claim any of that responsibility as your own?'

Charlotte rejoiced that she was given a reason to hope that he did not think so badly of her, and yet when he heard what she had to reveal, surely he would be very angry with her! She nervously continued. 'Only the day before she ran away, she made a visit on horseback to Wythorpe. She was alone, Sir.'

He digested this silently for a moment. 'Alone? How do you know this? Why did you not inform me of it?'

'I happened to be walking that afternoon, on the hill from which you can see Wythorpe, and by accident saw her arriving there. It was from rather a distance, but I saw a woman in a scarlet riding habit met by Lord Winchester. He kissed her hand, and I thought — perhaps it was his sister, or a relative. But when I returned home, I observed Lavinia, who had arrived home just before me, and she was wearing a red habit. That is how I knew it was my cousin. I was shocked, but I did not come to you immediately. I now wish that I had!'

Her anxiety and misery were clear, and such was her distress, and her keen feeling of guilt at having kept this knowledge to herself, that she rose up from her chair in distress, but then fell back, her legs no longer able to support her. Sir Benedict at once sat in the opposite chair and offered to call for some salts. She shook her head, astonished at his kindness, and yet knowing she must continue.

'I concealed the information from you, because I felt that my cousin and Lord Winchester must have some understanding between them, that they must have been engaged for her to risk her reputation like that. I assumed that they would make known their engagement at the ball the following evening. I expected Lord Winchester at any moment to come here to Delford, to ask your permission! But nothing happened! They did not announce an engagement, nor did he come here to ask your permission! Oh, fool that I am, I could have prevented all these unhappy events had I shared this intelligence with you!'

Charlotte buried her face in her hands, full of remorse and self-recrimination, and Sir Benedict leaned towards her, about to speak. However, a violent rapping at the library door, and the entry of Stokes, prevented her from hearing what he was about to say.

Stokes strode at once to his master, with a note on a platter. 'Forgive me Sir, but this came for you just now, with the greatest urgency, from town. I hope you will forgive my intrusion, Miss,' he added, nodding at Charlotte, 'but I thought it best that you had the note immediately, Sir.' He bowed and retreated, while Sir Benedict quickly took up the note, tore it open, and read its contents.

'It is from Harding, my friend in London. He says — Good God — is there to be no peace? He writes that Lord Winchester has proposed to Miss Anne Smart!'

Charlotte was astonished. 'But Miss Smart was at Highfield! But stay, I am mistaken, for she said she was to remove to her aunt's in London and then join her friends in Bath. She must have left for London, and now Lord Winchester has lost no time in procuring for himself yet another prospect! Sir! You must stop them! She must be made aware, before it is too late for her, too!' Charlotte realised that she had placed her hand on his arm, in her distress, and she quickly removed it, colouring.

He appeared not to have noticed. 'Will you tell my sister that I have gone to town again? I must away immediately! Oh, what a scoundrel! I shall have his blood or ruin his reputation, before the night is long!'

He left the room, calling for Stokes, who had been lurking behind the door in readiness. Minutes later, hoofbeats struck into the oncoming dusk and he was gone from the house.

Charlotte was left, in the dusky silence of the library, to contemplate all that had happened. She felt ill with contempt for Lord Winchester. She must find Eliza and explain what had passed.

~~*~~

She found Eliza and Lavinia in the parlour with Belle, waiting for dinner to be announced, and she at once related to them what had passed only fifteen minutes ago. Eliza was shocked.

'Wicked, wicked scoundrel! Lavinia, I hope you understand now from what misery your uncle saved you! What a man is he! Such an abominable creature, indeed! Lavinia, you have enough sense, I hope, that you may realise now of what he is capable, and how narrowly you have escaped his clutches.'

Lavinia, however, was not to be worked on, and showed herself ever more irrational than Charlotte had thought possible. 'Why, that sly trollop! What Miss Anne Smart has to tempt him over me, I know not! Ugly, stupid creature! Now she has lured him in with her own paltry fortune, the brazen little hussy! How dare she presume to take what is mine! Mine!'

She was quite worked up with rage and stormed around the room, stomping her foot on several occasions to punctuate her words. Belle slunk under the table. Charlotte and Eliza raised their eyebrows at each other and Charlotte shook her head, beginning to lose her usually mild temper.

'Cousin! You must see what his character is, what his motives are! How can you continue to be so blind! You have no thought but for yourself, while your aunt and I have been worried sick! Your reputation has been ruined by your behaviour, and yet you have no remorse at all!'

Charlotte's usually mild temper was frayed, and when they went into dinner, she had little appetite. At nine o'clock they had had no word from Sir Benedict and the three women retired, to find what repose they could in their various states of emotion.

The next day, a heavy, comfortless rain persisted, accompanied by a sudden chill, so that Charlotte was doubtful that summer had not yet passed, and winter taken its place. Her usual cheerfulness had sunk and been replaced by low spirits occasioned by the emptiness that seemed to encompass her at Delford whenever its owner was absent.

Charlotte was not rationally sensible of this thought, and it only passed through her as a feeling, rather than a reasoned understanding. She felt ill-at-ease, and both dreaded and yearned for Sir Benedict's return, for her interview with him the previous day had been interrupted so that she had not had the opportunity she sought to make her apologies, whatever the reply might have been. And yet Sir Benedict had not seemed so very angry with her. Perhaps she would be excused, after all.

These thoughts were put from her mind at breakfast, for some news came to them shortly after sitting down. The servants brought in some dishes, and the younger footman, who was a garrulous chap at any time, made free to comment upon the weather, and then with an air of confiding, he addressed Eliza.

'And 'tis reported Ma'am, that his Lordship over at

Wythorpe is closing down the house! In this weather too! It will be a damp job, I'm sure, for the servants there. And then they will have to find themselves employment once again, after only being there a few weeks!'

Eliza and Charlotte exchanged glances.

'Are you certain, Cox?' asked Charlotte, watching Lavinia, who was sipping her tea without comment.

'Aye, Miss, Mary said so. She met her — a servant from Wythorpe — in the village early this morning, while on an errand for Cook. 'Tis said his Lordship came home all a tither early this morning, and is setting them all to close up the house again. I imagine he will be off to his town residence now, although what he bothered coming here for, after all that fuss, who knows, Ma'am! Tis a great pity for the servants,' he added helpfully.

Eliza dismissed Cox and waited until the door shut behind him. She put a gentle hand on Lavinia's arm, who shook it off immediately. Eliza frowned. 'It is a good thing that he is going away so soon. He must be aware, surely, that he cannot show his face in this neighbourhood again, without shame. Yes, it is much better that he is gone this day! Surely you understand that, my dear?'

Lavinia pouted and looked pointedly away, making no reply to her aunt. The women finished their breakfast and Lavinia went directly to her room. Eliza went to hers also, to write some letters, and Charlotte found herself alone in the parlour. The servant came and made a fire for her, for there was such a chill in the air as was quite unusual. She took up a book and waited for the sound of Sir Benedict's return, or at least a messenger.

Half an hour later, she got up restlessly and stared out of the window, although there was little to be seen through the thick mist and rain. She was just moving away from the wet glass when she caught a sudden movement of colour in an otherwise grey mist. A flash of scarlet and a hazy figure on horseback moved through the rain. Charlotte gasped. Lavinia could only be riding out in this weather with one intention!

Charlotte ran to the door of the parlour then paused. It would serve no purpose to call Eliza, for she was unable to ride, and there was no one else except herself. She ran upstairs to her room, knowing what she must do, however much she wished she could avoid it. She pulled on a pelisse and sturdy bonnet, and her outside boots. She lamented that she had brought no riding habit, certain it would not be needed. A habit would have protected her a little from the rain. As it was, her thin morning dress would be wet through in minutes! There was nothing to be done, however. She raced down the stairs again, and out the front door. There was no sign of Lavinia. Charlotte ran to the stables, and found the first stablehand she saw.

'Saddle Ariadne, Mrs Granger's horse, please. And hurry!' she cried. The young stablehand's eyes were wide but unquestioning as he did as she bid, and then helped her mount.

'Have a message sent to your mistress, that I am gone after Miss Markham! To Wythorpe!' she cried. The boy nodded in wonder. She trembled as she sat side saddle on the big grey mare, but she put her fears from her mind. Lavinia must be stopped! If she threw herself at Lord Winchester, or was even seen there, her reputation would be in ruins, they would *have* to marry, and her fortune would be spent by a worthless wastrel! There was no time to lose! She urged Ariadne forward and they cantered out of the yard, Charlotte gripping the reins firmly in her in nervousness.

Immediately the cold assailed her and wet her thin gown through. She rode determinedly out of the yard and tried to decide which way her cousin had taken.

'Stupid foolish, girl! Oh, Lavinia, the trouble you have caused, and the danger you are in!' Charlotte cried to herself, as her horse began to canter across now muddy fields. She clung on, nervous of the huge beast, and tried to keep her foot in the stirrup. She could not see far ahead of her, but she trusted that the animal would sense where to step. Her bonnet barely clung to her head, and in another moment, it flew off in a gust of wind! She cried out, then sank low in her saddle as Ariadne climbed the hill which led to Wythorpe. Coming to the top, she reined in the horse for a moment and, breathing hard, searched the grey mist ahead for Lavinia. There! A flash of scarlet showed through the driving rain, and she urged the animal on again, down the hillside that led toward Wythorpe.

Her pelisse now drenched and heavy on her back, she clung to the horse's mane, almost losing her grip on the reins. Ariadne charged, almost of out of control, and broke into a gallop. Charlotte let out a scream, and the horse started suddenly at the sound, shying sideways a little in fear. As it did so, Charlotte's water-logged pelisse dragged her sideways, and she lost her balance, toppling from the horse, falling heavily. Something hit her head with a dull thud, and she found herself dazed, and lying on the ground near the base of the hill. The grey of the rain and the green of the grass so near her face grew hazy, and she slipped into unconsciousness.

~~✳~~

From time to time, she rose up from the darkness, to become dimly aware of the cold rain still pelting onto the skin of her face, and the chill which had set into her body. She shook, then stilled, drawn back into the comfort of oblivion. The third time she opened her eyes, she became aware of a dark figure bending over her, and the shadowy figure of a horse behind.

Familiar eyes, as if from a strange dream, caught at her own, and, barely aware of herself, she whispered weakly, 'Benedict, you have come!' Gentle, sure hands wrapped her in a cloak, then picked her up and held her against a hard chest. Fragments of sound, 'Charlotte, my silly, brave Charlotte', and something else which she could not understand, drifted past her ears. Now that she was lifted off the ground she felt as if she was floating, but the rain was running down her face, hot and salty on her cold skin, and she could not ask if they were really flying, although she tried.

'Hush,' was the reply and she closed her eyes and slept. Again, she woke to find herself being jolted gently as if on horseback. She tried to see the face of her rescuer but could not. She closed her eyes again, against the chill in her bones, and stayed asleep for a long time.

When she opened her eyes, she found herself in her own soft, white bed, gentle early morning light shafting through the half-open curtains. A rocking chair and an empty tea cup on a small table stood at the end of the bed, evidence that someone had watched over her in the night. Her limbs ached a little, but not as much as her head, and she felt so tired that she was tempted to drift back to sleep. Then the events of the day before came back to her, and she put a hand to her mouth to stifle a gasp.

Memories came to her, of riding through the rain, the fall from the mare, and then of Sir Benedict bending low over her, murmuring something comforting, although she could not remember what it was. Her mind strained to hear what her memory could tell her. Then, all at once, her own words, her calling him by his first name, came tumbling back. The memory came with an emotion. The feeling was as if she was drowning, but in candle light and music. Sensations rose up in her which she had never known, and yet, she had always known. Nay, not always! Since the night of the ball, of his taking her hand for the first dance, since she had become lost in a still, waiting moment! Now she knew herself, knew the meaning of every moment she had looked into his eyes and been held there, in those dark depths.

'I love him.' She said the words aloud, to the empty room. 'I love him!'

This thought, which ought not to have shocked her so very much perhaps, given her feelings in the last few days, shook her very core, and kept her silent and entranced for several minutes. Then, as this thought was replaced with others, her eyes widened. The distressing thought occurred to her, that she might have spoken to him in her weakened state, that she may somehow have exposed her secret when she was half conscious! If she had spoken aloud anything at all that might cause her embarrassment, if she had uttered anything in her delirium, she would never be able to face him again! But she must compose her feelings, she must conceal her emotions. She must leave Delford at once! She must leave as soon as she was well enough to get up. Mortified, agitated, and in awed wonder, she rose from her pillow, intending to stand up

At this moment, the door opened and Eliza appeared. Seeing that Charlotte was awake, she came immediately to Charlotte's side. 'My dear! You are awake at last! How are you feeling?'

Charlotte lay back against her pillow. 'I—what happened, Eliza? My head is a little ill. Have I been here long?'

'All night, my dear. Mary and I took turns to watch you, you know. You have taken a nasty bump to the head, the physician says. Nothing more serious, thank heaven! But I must tell my brother you are awake. He has been most concerned for you!'

She rang for a servant before Charlotte could stop her, and seconds later Mary put her head around the door. 'Oh Miss! You are awake! I'm so glad, for we were all so worried, although the Doctor said you were just chilled.'

Eliza interrupted. 'Mary, please tell the Master that Miss Milton is awake. That will be all, thank you Mary. Now, Charlotte, you must rest, for the doctor will be here presently to see you. You had quite a fall, my dear. Do you remember anything at all? You were very foolhardy indeed to go out in such weather, but,' she patted Charlotte's pale hand, 'you were very brave. My brother said it was very brave indeed, for he says you do not very much like to ride and are nervous of horses. We know what Lavinia did, you know,' she added.

Charlotte listened with puzzlement to this speech, but when Lavinia was mentioned, she tried to sit up. 'Lavinia! Oh dear, Eliza, what happened? Did she — was she found? She went to Wythorpe! I followed her to stop her!'

Eliza shook her head. 'Calm yourself, my dear. All is well. Lavinia is found. Winchester refused her entrance and had her thrown out, like common trash. Poor, stupid child!'

'She went to Wythorpe,' insisted Charlotte, dredging her memory for details. 'I guessed that she was going to try one last time to throw herself on the mercy of Lord Winchester, and there was no time to lose. Oh, poor, poor Lavinia! To be thrown out, after all! I do believe she loves him in her own way. I went after her, on Ariadne, you know. Oh, gracious! Ariadne! Is she found? Did she come home, Eliza?'

'Yes, my dear, that horse is an intelligent creature, and came home last night, on her own accord. You must not upset yourself, Charlotte. The mare is home and warm in her box now. There is no harm done.'

Charlotte frowned a little. 'But what happened? Did my cousin not ride to Wythorpe? Did she see Winchester? And how came B — your brother — to find me? I thought he went to town to stop Lord Winchester from proposing to Miss Smart? What happened to everyone? Is Lord Winchester to marry Miss Smart?' she asked anxiously.

Eliza laughed. 'My brother might be the best person to reveal the answers to your questions, for he was there, and I was not. Ah, but here he is now!'

At this moment, Mary entered, to announce 'the Master, just for a moment or two, Miss.' Charlotte's heart began to pound, and she felt her colour rise. She had not time to calm her feelings, before Sir Benedict was standing just inside the room. Charlotte looked away, and blushed deeply, which she hoped he would attribute to self-consciousness at being only in her night gown. If he ever guessed her true feelings!

Eliza spoke, warning her brother. 'Benedict, do not tire our patient, for the doctor must see her yet. A few minutes only!' She smiled as she spoke, but her good temper did not allay her seriousness of purpose. She exchanged a look with her brother, and left the room, leaving the door open.

Sir Benedict ventured a little further into the room, and stood there, looking rather awkward. He enquired after her health, and the state of her head, in the greatest of politeness.

She answered briefly, hardly knowing what she said, or where to look, for her feelings were in tumult. Glimpses of a memory of Sir Benedict bending over her, and her own, "Benedict, you have come", made her blush with embarrassment, and she could not look him in the eye. His tone was all compassion and solicitude however, and she hoped with all her heart that his kindness would extend to not mentioning the incident, to her embarrassment. However, he must remember it! Would he attribute such familiarity to fever? What must he think of her! She attempted, half successfully, to calm the agitation in her breast, and rose up a little on her pillow to address him in a low voice. 'I believe I have you to thank for bringing me home, Sir. I am sorry to give so much trouble, but I am indebted to you.'

Her earnest tone was met with such a look that she was unprepared for, a look of most kind and compassionate feeling and regard. He shook his head and his eyes caught and held hers. She looked away immediately, for fear he might read with ease the emotions she was most earnestly trying to conceal from him!

He seemed about to speak, then thought better of it, and then began once again. 'It was nothing at all, truly nothing. Please do not think anything of it. But, Miss Milton, do you have any recollection of your fall? Of your rescue?'

He could only be asking her if he remembered her words, her familiarity with his first name! Charlotte had not the presence of mind to speak. Her heart pounded, and she turned her face away. She hoped he would assume that she was thinking back on the events of the previous day. She shook her head.

'I'm afraid I remember little, Sir. I— I recall falling from Eliza's mare, and I think I hit my head. I'm afraid I cannot remember anything after that.' She hoped she would be forgiven the little untruth, but she must conceal her newly discovered feelings for him! She must hope that he would assume she had been delirious with a fever, and not in her rational state of mind.

He seemed himself fraught with some emotion which passed over his countenance. He struggled, overcame, and spoke. 'I was lucky to find you, such as was the dullness of the day and the heaviness of the rain. I am only relieved that I found you in time, that no worse damage had been done to your person — if you had lain in the rain longer, I can hardly think of the outcome! And yet, you are out of danger now, thank God.' He shook his head. 'That you went out after her, though you dislike riding, and are ill-at-ease with horses! Yes, your cousin owes you much, I think. If it were not for your going after her — I dread to think — yes, Miss Milton, your cousin owes you more than she will ever have the sense to realise.'

Charlotte was one minute joy, and the next misery, at this small speech. *It was nothing at all, truly nothing.* Was he moved, that her person had been in danger? Or was it that the emotion that appeared to run through him was motivated by gratitude that she had gone out after Lavinia? That his thoughts were all gratitude for Lavinia's safety and her narrow escape from ruin? His kind comments about her own safety were sincere, she thought, but seemed motivated only by the gentlemanly manners which duty would dictate to a lady. Her spirits plummeted and she forced herself to answer.

'I was only fortunate enough to see her leave the house, or no one would have known it until it was too late. I do not regret my going out after her, but, in the end, it does not seem to matter, for Eliza tells me that Lord Winchester refused to admit her,' Charlotte replied. 'But, how came you to know I had gone out in the rain after Lavinia? I thought you were in town, gone after Lord Winchester. And where is my cousin? Is she ill?'

'Do not alarm yourself, she is quite well. She is not at home. She is at Highview, for the present.'

'With the Lathams? But whatever is she doing *there*?' expostulated Charlotte.

Sir Benedict ventured a little further into the room. 'Perhaps, if I explain further,' he offered, 'you will understand. It is true, you saw me leave in the greatest urgency two nights hence, on my errand to town. I rode hard, straight to the address that my friend Harding had given me, arrived at around nine o'clock, and was granted an audience with Miss Smart and her aunt. They informed me that Lord Winchester had, indeed been there, and made a proposal of marriage to Miss Smart. He had been refused by the lady.'

'Refused!' cried Charlotte. 'Did she have information regarding Lord Winchester? But I suppose it does not matter, so long as her fortune is safe from such a man.' Charlotte did not harbour any fondness for the young lady, but she was not so unkind as to wish Lord Winchester's deceit and greed upon any woman. 'Please, go on,' she nodded to Sir Benedict.

'I believe Miss Smart had suspected Lord Winchester of being the scoundrel that he is, when she was with the Lathams. She informed me that one week ago, she had received information from her aunt that Winchester had made enquires in London, among her own relatives, as to the sum of her fortune.'

Charlotte gasped. 'So he was making enquiries after Miss Smart, while paying his addresses to my cousin! Profligate libertine!' she cried warmly. 'To openly and shamelessly treat my cousin, to treat *any* lady, as he has done! I presume he chose my cousin on the basis of the sum of her fortune. How is such a man to be brought to justice? The deceit of it! But that means Miss Smart knew his character, and said nothing to my cousin, or to you! Shameful girl! But I suppose, she cannot have told the Lathams, or something would surely have been said. Dear God, my cousin has had a fortunate escape from such a wastrel,' added Charlotte, angered on behalf of her cousin.

Sir Benedict frowned. 'Quite. But you must not excite yourself, Miss Milton, you are not yet well. Please, do calm yourself or my sister will scold me!'

He half smiled at her, and Charlotte pulled the sheets up to her chin, to hide the blush that coloured her neck, which a mere smile had incited. 'I am quite calm, Sir. Please do go on.'

'I went to the address I had for Winchester in London but was informed by the servant that Winchester had returned to Wythorpe. It was late, and the weather severe, so thinking the crisis averted, I took lodgings at my club, and left London early the next morning for home. I was just arrived when the stableboy addressed me urgently. He gave me a somewhat confused story that not an hour past, Miss Markham had demanded to go out riding in the rain, and that you, Miss Milton, had shortly afterward demanded the same. When I heard that you had gone riding, I knew that there was something wrong, for I know you fear riding, and would only venture out in terrible weather on horseback if you were once again interfering in some business not your own,' he concluded drily.

Charlotte pressed her lips together in anger, but when she looked up at him, his eyes hid laughter, and she could not but help smile back. 'Mock me all you like, Sir,' she replied, 'but it is quite ungentlemanly to laugh at a lady who finds it out of her power to leave the room! And I cannot ask you to leave, for it is your house!'

Sir Benedict gave a slight bow. 'I am at your service and will leave whenever I am ordered. You do not wish to hear the rest of my tale. So be it.'

He made as if to leave, but his laughing eyes caught Charlotte's startled ones, and her spirits lifted a little. 'You mock and tease me mercilessly, Sir,' she scolded, smiling despite herself. 'You know very well that I wish to hear the rest of your story, if you would be so good as to tell it.'

He seated himself in the chair at the foot of her bed, much to her sudden consternation, and continued. 'When I heard you had gone after Lavinia, I knew immediately where she would have gone, for I guessed that you would have ridden after her only in the most urgent and pressing of situations, considering your dislike of horses and riding. It was a brave action, if not excessively foolhardy! I immediately spurred my horse in the direction of Wythorpe with the greatest misgivings for your safety and the reputation of my niece.'

Charlotte watched his face as he spoke, struggling with uncertainty. One moment, she was close to joy, and another, she was plunged into misery, with each changing word. He had then, truly feared for her safety! He had ridden after her, and yet, not for her alone! He lauded her bravery! And yet, he spoke of it so rationally, that it was plain to her that there was no other motive for his actions than mere gentlemanly manners and general fears for her safety. After all, he was her host. It was nothing, as he had said. Nothing more than he would have done for anyone.

He continued. 'I ordered one of the stablehands to ride immediately over to Highview, to summon Latham at once to Wythorpe and to bring back my niece. Latham must have ridden out immediately on receiving the message, for he arrived there in time to find Lavinia huddled at the gate in the rain, having been refused entry to the house, and thrown out by one of the servants on Winchester's orders.'

Charlotte was shocked. 'Poor Lavinia! How she must have

been humiliated after such an effort! But how did she think her visit to Wythorpe would change anything? Lord Winchester would never take her now, not with you, her guardian, to stop any alliance. He would fear the repercussions of such a course of action, I think.'

Sir Benedict looked grim. 'He is lucky to be alive, I own. He has ruined my niece's reputation beyond repair!'

Charlotte spoke hesitantly. 'If the marriage had taken place, she would have been a little redeemed, at least, and yet – the outcome of such union, without love, for my cousin!'

'He may have married her,' Benedict replied after a moment, 'if I had forced the point. The thought did occur to me, I confess; a marriage would go some way to restoring her reputation. But then he would have her money, and she, a mere title, and a life of misery to accompany it. She is lucky he refused her, I think, fearing my reaction to such a development. As he ought to have done!'

Charlotte struggled with the sensations in her heart. She was misery one moment, happiness the next! She thought herself as foolish as her cousin and took a deep breath. 'So you rode to Wythorpe, and found me lying at the bottom of the hill? That is where I remember falling. I think I hit my head, and after that, I woke up here,' she lied, feeling guilty but knowing she could not reveal to him that she was conscious and rational when she had spoken his name that day.

He nodded. 'Yes, I found you lying in the rain, and brought you back here immediately. Eliza was ready, for she knew a little from the stableboy, and gathered correctly that I had ridden out after you.'

'But,' asked Charlotte with a puzzled frown, 'that does not explain why my cousin is at Highview.'

'Ah, yes,' he replied. 'Frank took her there, for it was nearer to carry her on his horse, and leave his groom to deal with her mount. He felt that it was right to bring her away where his sisters could nurse her and cheer her. I have had her clothes sent over, and she will remain there for a few days I believe.'

Charlotte was thoughtful for a few moments, but said nothing. She could guess why Sir Frank had taken her cousin back to Highview, and she was not sure she approved. But she would be well looked after there, and much attention paid to her, if more than she deserved. She wondered at Sir Frank's generous spirit, and thought that perhaps she had misjudged him more than she realised. She wondered, too, what the outcome of such a visit might have on Lavinia's weakened mind and spirits, after the events of the past few days.

Just then, Eliza knocked at the door and put her head around. 'Benedict, Charlotte needs to rest, and the doctor will be here shortly.'

Sir Benedict stood. 'We will talk further when you are feeling more yourself, Miss Milton. My wishes for your speedy recovery.'

He made the briefest bow and left the room. The space where he had stood just a moment ago, now seemed as empty and forlorn as her heart. *It was nothing at all, truly nothing.* Opening a box on her night stand, she withdrew a scrap of fabric and traced once again the letter B it boasted. A tear slipped and slithered its way down her cheek.

The doctor came and went, leaving her a sleeping draft, should she need it, and recommended bed rest until she felt well enough and strong enough to leave her room. She spent the remainder of the day in bed, and half of the next. In part, this was due to a feeling of weakness which pervaded her limbs, but she also acknowledged, she felt such agitation at the thought of confronting Sir Benedict again, of hiding her emotions from him, that she could not bring herself to leave her room. Surely, she could not hide her misery from his eyes, which seemed to see all of her thoughts! He did not visit her room again, and she did not hear his voice in the house, although she strained her ears to catch the sound of it.

By the morning of the second day, the bad weather had cleared, and the day was bright and warm once again. At around ten o'clock, Charlotte, who had been sitting quietly in a chair by the window, heard a faint knock at the door, and muted voices. Surely that was not Mr Weatherby, come calling again? But indeed, it was, for as Charlotte listened, she heard the unmistakable timbre of his voice. She mused quietly for some minutes, and after a decent time, she heard the caller depart.

She was just turning the page of her book when once again,

Charlotte heard a knock, and voices in the hallway, one of which was the rather sharp tone of Miss Annabelle Latham, and the other the softer tones of her sister. Charlotte gathered that their customary morning call was being paid to Eliza and was glad to be upstairs for the call. They had probably come to gloat! She supposed that everyone in the neighbourhood had now learned of the events of the last few days, for it could be concealed no longer, and Lavinia, she was sure, would apprise the whole of Highview of the grim details with no shame at all!

She felt mortified for Lavinia but knew her cousin would have little awareness of the inappropriateness of her own conduct, and care even less. Charlotte was just glad that she did not have to be downstairs to watch Miss Annabelle Latham gloat. Although, thought Charlotte archly, the lady had better take all care not to smirk over Lavinia's folly in front of her *objet d'amour* for she thought that Sir Benedict would not be at all forgiving if his niece's actions were openly ridiculed.

But Sir Benedict was probably out on the estate, as was his habit, and only Eliza would have to endure the visit. She was not certain of Eliza's opinion of her future sister-in-law, but she rather thought both women more than a little dissimilar in attitudes, opinions and understanding, although her hostess was unfailingly polite to the Lathams and took their calls with a calm equanimity that gave little indication of anything near dislike.

At the thought of Sir Benedict and Annabelle Latham, she felt a pang in her breast and put the distasteful image from her mind. She was not so naïve, she told herself, that she expected Sir Benedict to have noticed her as more than the companion of her cousin, nor did she seek actively to engage his attentions or his affection. She knew that would be impossible. After all, his object was Miss Latham, and try as she might to wish it away, she must face the truth that his heart had long been engaged elsewhere.

She had had time to think, while in bed. Over the course of

a day and half of solitude, she had come to some resolutions. She could not compete with the Miss Lathams of the world, and she refused to try, she told herself sternly. Sir Benedict had made his choice, and in Sir Benedict's eyes, Charlotte was only the interfering, inferior relative of his niece. He could dance with her, either out of pity or as a pawn to make his intended jealous; he could rescue her from a fall from a horse, as his duty; he could speak kindly to her, and make her feel that someone shared her sadness, but from common decency alone.

Although the day of the picnic had revealed some softness in his character, and she had felt comforted over the loss of her mother, he had given Charlotte no other indication that he thought of her as anything more than his niece's relative. He had, in short, supplied all of the common decencies that manners would expect. But as for anything else, any other token of his esteem and good opinion, he had never given her such a thing, and the idea that he might harbour a deeper regard for her than this, she knew was impossible! Her love, in short, was unreturned.

It tore her heart, and she had resolved that morning to go home, as soon as she could consult her cousin. She would say she was homesick, for this was partly true; she yearned for the familiarity of her things around her, her peaceful days restored to her once again.

She stood and went to the window. The day was cheerful and sunny, so different now to the dark clouds and cheerless rain of four days ago. And yet, the cheery warm day seemed a stark contrast to the pain in her heart. She stood there a moment, feeling so low in spirits, that she longed to be in her own home, yes, even with her new stepmother, if she could be far away from this place.

Perhaps at home she could bury her wretchedness in busying herself with familiar routines, and trying to make a friend of her new stepmother. 'Oh Mama,' she said sadly to no one, 'How I do miss you!'

Thirty Two

Determined to dress and put her resolution to Eliza, she rang for Mary, and then stood to look out her window. Then she startled and drew back from the glass with a gasp, for Sir Benedict stood in the driveway below, talking to none other than Tom Wilcox. She drew back further, guiltily, for she did not wish to spy, and yet she drew forward again almost immediately, unable to help her curiosity. A moment later, and the two men shook hands in the most amiable manner, and the younger man strode away. Charlotte was most astounded at this change of heart in Sir Benedict, for she thought that Tom Wilcox was most certainly not a favourite, and was not even permitted on the grounds at Delford. Something must have occurred to change his mind, and she was all curiosity to discover it.

Rose arrived to help her dress, since Mary was detained in the kitchen. Charlotte washed and dressed, glad to be moving around. Her headache was gone, and the small bruise at the back of her head was tender only when pressed. Rose brushed out Charlotte's golden-brown tresses and put them up gently. 'There Miss, you look quite yourself again!'

Charlotte looked in the glass, and gasped with some surprise, for she saw a different woman to the one who had arrived here only three weeks prior. Her figure had filled out a little under the delicate yellow and rose sprigged muslin, and she was not so thin in her person as she had been when she arrived here. Her face, although pale from the events of the last few days, was animated with a tinge of pale rose about the cheeks, and the eyes that looked back at her were a darker green than ever, animated with the blushing knowledge of first love. She looked away quickly, afraid that Sir Benedict would notice the same look in her eye, and worse, the cause. He had a way of seeing straight into her heart, and detecting her emotions and thoughts effortlessly, as if her soul was bare to him!

She left Rose tidying up, and, feeling quite strong enough, resolved upon immediately walking over to Highview and consulting her cousin about leaving Delford. She went quietly downstairs and peeped into the drawing room. There she found Eliza on the chaise, in the sun by the window. There was a letter lying in her lap. Eliza opened her eyes when Charlotte entered and put the letter aside.

'My dear, are you well enough to be walking about? I was going to have Mary take you up some tea. How are you feeling?'

'I am much improved, thank you. Almost my old self,' she added. *I will never again be my former self,* she thought, her heart desolate. 'I think I will walk to Highview, as I want very much to see my cousin, if you think it wise, that is. I wish to consult with her on something.'

Eliza smiled. 'I think you will find your cousin a little distracted, today. We did not tell you immediately yesterday, my dear, but,' she put a hand on Charlotte's arm, 'Sir Frank Latham has proposed to Lavinia, and she has accepted him. The Latham sisters brought a note from her with them this morning.' She indicated the letter she had put aside.

Charlotte was astonished for a moment, and yet, astonishment gave way quickly to a new feeling. She considered Sir Frank in this new light, and found that she admired him more than she had ever done before. He truly loved her cousin, if he would take her under the circumstances that would now make her unmarriageable from the perspective of all polite society. And for her cousin's part, she was not surprised. If her cousin wanted anything, it was to be married to someone with rank. Charlotte was sure Lavinia did not love Sir Frank, and yet, she had seemed to have admired him before she had met Lord Winchester. Charlotte rallied herself.

'Why, that is good news, Eliza. Truly. I am very happy for Sir Frank, for anyone could see he admires her excessively, and his heart was so downcast when he thought she preferred Lord Winchester. Frank Latham is truly the best of men,' she added warmly. 'But how can he be happy with her when he knows that he is not her first choice?' she added, with a pang in her heart for the gentleman.

'Why, it is true that Sir Frank might be full of foppish silliness, my dear, but at heart he is a good man. He cares not for Lavinia's history, I collect. She is vastly fortunate to have met such a man, I believe.'

'True,' admitted Charlotte thoughtfully, 'but do you think she will make him happy Eliza? My cousin has but a few small requirements for happiness. If she is only to be addressed as Lady Latham, and can be seen in London every Season, I think she will be content. But for the gentleman! She is pretty, and rich, but he must know that she does not love him!'

Eliza shrugged. 'Only time will tell, but I think they will make something of it. After all, love is not the only requirement for a successful marriage, although I believe on his side, it is the only requisite! No,' she added rather thoughtfully, 'there have been good unions based only upon esteem and respect – and I think, for my niece's side, no want of money will pave a smooth path to marital bliss!

'Well, there will be no want of money at least,' smiled

Charlotte, 'for she is rich and he has Highview. Does Sir Benedict give his consent? I suppose he must, for he was never against the match!'

'Why, you can ask him yourself, my dear, at dinner tonight. But if you insist on calling at Highview, you shall have the carriage, for I think you should not walk such a distance.'

At the mention of Sir Benedict, Charlotte's heart skipped a little. 'I am perfectly well, Eliza, and the walk will do me good,' she insisted.

Eliza continued. 'I have some other news for you, and I rather think you must not approve. But stay, shall we walk in the garden? If you will allow me your arm? Thank you my dear.'

Charlotte was almost sure of what Eliza would tell her, but she said little and merely took Eliza's arm as they went through the open windowed doors and out into the garden. It was a beautiful day, and they strolled to a seat in the shade of the large oaks at one side of the house. The green lawn spread before them, throwing into relief the great house, and the little shrubbery, rose gardens and arbour which were now so familiar to Charlotte. She quelled her sadness. She did not wish to leave so prematurely and yet she knew she must. She waited for Eliza to divulge her news.

'I have some news of my own, Charlotte, happy news, but perhaps you will not think it so. I, too, have received a marriage proposal, my dear. It has been accepted.'

Charlotte turned to her hostess, and smiling, took her hand. 'It is Mr Weatherby, is it not? Oh Eliza, I guessed his attachment, this morning, after his call here. I am very happy for you! It is truly good news! Do you — do you love him?' She was almost afraid to say the word out loud, lest she give way to her own emotions.

Eliza looked over the lawn and out towards the fields beyond. 'I have been a widow for ten years, and semi-invalid for most of this time, dependent on others. As good as my brother has been to me, I long for my own establishment again, however humble, and for the companionship of a partner in life. Benedict has given me a home for the past ten years, here at Delford, and I am very grateful, but it is time for him to marry, and to have children. I do admire and respect Mr Weatherby, Charlotte, and I feel myself lucky, at my time of life, to have found such a person. George wishes to marry in three weeks, as soon as the banns are read, and I will remove to his parish, and be very comfortable and happy indeed.'

Charlotte was very quiet during this speech. She felt sunk in spirits at the thought of Sir Benedict's marrying, and knew that Eliza was referring to Miss Annabelle Latham. She rallied herself and smiled weakly at her friend. 'Mr Weatherby is an amiable, kind man, and I wish you both very happy.' Charlotte felt even more urgently after this news that she must leave Delford as soon as would not be considered rude. She shared her resolve with Eliza, and endured the older woman's reluctance to let her make so premature a departure. She had expected Charlotte to be with them at least six weeks longer! Charlotte shook her head.

'Now that my cousin is to be married, and you yourself have much to do in the next three weeks, I shall only be in the way. No, please do not try to change my mind. You are too good, too kind, Ma'am, but I feel I must leave — it is most pressing that I do so—' She stopped short, unable to continue for fear of revealing her inner state. She would not for all the world have Eliza guess at her more urgent reasons for leaving Delford. As it was, tears made her eyes very bright, and she looked away, pretending to brush something from her skirts as she composed herself.

'I must put myself in the power of yourself and your brother,' she continued in a broken voice, 'and ask if you will allow me one of your carriages, to take me to the nearest coach. Today or tomorrow, if you would be so kind. I am truly sorry to ask, but I must depend on the kindness of friends—'

Here, again, she was forced to stop, and this time was not

able to contain her emotions, but such was the extent of her misery that her face crumpled and she muffled the desolate sound of her distress in the folds of her dress. Eliza looked on, startled but quiet. She did not utter a sound, and waited until, at length, Charlotte's sobbing abated, and she had dried her eyes. Charlotte could not speak, but she did not have to. The older woman leaned forward and took her hand.

'My dear. I do not like to see you so wretched. I do not wish to pry, but if you wish to unburden yourself, my dear, you can be sure of my discretion, and what small advice I might be able to offer.'

Charlotte felt in a panic. Did Eliza guess her secret? She must not allow it. She twisted the handkerchief she had pulled from her dress pocket, then quickly hid the insignia. If Eliza had recognised her brother's kerchief, she gave no sign. Charlotte put it quickly in her pocket.

'I am sorry. I am still somewhat in shock, I think, from the events of the last few days. Perhaps I left my bed a little soon. And I am melancholy to return to my friends in Sussex, without the presence of my dear Mama. But Eliza, I *must* go, today, or tomorrow. I am firmly resolved. You have been so kind, and I have grown to love your home. But please say I may borrow the carriage? If not today, then first thing tomorrow morning, after breakfast? I shall walk over to Highview this afternoon, and take my leave of my cousin and the Lathams.'

Eliza looked thoughtful, but gave way to Charlotte's earnest entreaties, and granted her the use of the carriage for after breakfast, tomorrow morning, on the condition that she take a maid to travel with her and take the Markham carriage the entire way. *One more day and I shall be gone*, she thought. Relieved in her mind, if not her heart, Charlotte ate a small luncheon with Eliza, and set off in the early afternoon to call at Highview.

She was glad to be outdoors again. It was now midsummer's day and the heightened energy of the day seemed to swell the breasts of the little swallows and finches who flung out their excited chatter over the languishing afternoon air. The unusual warmth penetrated Charlotte's bones, and she found it curiously soothing. She found that her emotions, which for the last few days had been buffeted this way and that, like a small boat on a storm-tossed sea, began to calm, and she found a comforting solace in the deep blue of the sky, the gentle bowed heads of the pink hedge roses, and the soft greenness around her. In nature, with such beauty surrounding her, she could begin to fortify her heart and mind, and to face what must be done, with something like equanimity.

Her path led downhill and on to Highview. She avoided the mud where it had not been dried by the hot hand of the sun, and when she arrived at Highview, was pleasantly tired, slightly dirty, and calmer than she had been for three days.

She was shown into the parlour and greeted with cold disdain by the older Miss Latham, with indifference by Sophia Latham, and genuine gladness by Sir Frank. Lavinia jumped up at once when her cousin appeared, and ran to kiss her cheek warmly, all previous ill humour now clearly abolished by the news she had for her cousin.

Charlotte sat by her cousin on the sofa, which was arranged opposite a second, on which the Latham sisters had artfully spread themselves. Annabelle Latham eyed her silently, as if she was something the dog had brought in, and spread her fan, indifferent to Charlotte's presence. Charlotte ignored the woman and congratulated her cousin and Sir Frank on their news. Lavinia talked incessantly of nothing else, as if her previous shocking behaviour were nothing.

'And we shall be married in the small church in the village, Charlotte, and have the breakfast here, and then Frank says he will take me away, to Scotland, which is amusing, for — Oh but no, I must not talk of *that*!' She put her hand to her mouth and giggled. 'But Sophia is to come with us, are you not, Sophia? And Charlotte, you must help me buy some new gowns, for nothing I have is decent enough for going away, and we will go up to town, once we are married, you know! Will we not, Frank?'

Frank Latham, who sat very close to his betrothed, nodded his powder-laden head. 'Most certainly, my dearest love. If you desire it. If you desire as much as seven trips to town in a month, we shall go!' he announced grandly.

Charlotte smiled. 'Indeed, Sir Frank, if you make as many as three trips to London in a month, you will soon be so tired of the place that you will never go again, and my cousin will be in very downcast spirits!' she noted drily.

'Oh yes,' added Sophia Latham, 'one must not have too much of a good thing! But if you do go up to town, Frank, you must take Annabelle and I, for we long to show our new sister-in-law where the best dressmakers and milliners are to be found.'

Lavinia squealed in excitement and clapped her hands. 'Oh, but I do need something now, for Scotland. And I must have a new bonnet. We should all go up to town tomorrow! Oh, do say we shall, Frank! Uncle can have no objection now, I am sure, since I am soon to be a married lady! Charlotte, you must come with us, for you need new gowns, I am sure!'

Charlotte smiled her thanks at this uncomplimentary inclusion, but shook her head. 'I am afraid I cannot come with you, for I have resolved upon returning to Sussex tomorrow, after breakfast.'

There, she had said it, she had committed herself, and now there was both the comfort and the anguish of knowing she could not turn back from her course. She did not look at Miss Latham.

Lavinia was merely a little put out, pouting, 'But I thought you were staying for at least three or four more weeks! Oh well, I dare say I shall be so busy preparing for the wedding, and having gowns made, that I shall not be very good company for you anyway. You had much better go, Charlotte, than sit around here feeling sorry for yourself.'

Charlotte, long used to what she was coming to view as her cousin's ill manners and unfeeling treatment, said nothing, but she could not now help glancing at Annabelle Latham. The lady smirked into her teacup and looked as if she would like to purr. Charlotte looked away, a pang of distress threatening to disrupt her much fought-for composure.

Meanwhile, Sir Frank was all kindness and polite nothings. 'Why, Miss Milton, such sad, such cruel news! Are you sure you must leave us so soon? We are miserable indeed, at such a thought! Are not we, my dear Lavinia? But you could not trifle with us, and cause us the misery of your absence, unless you were obliged to leave us, forced into action by some fancy not your own? Is it your father? Has he returned from abroad so soon? And you have not yet come to dine with us — surely you can extend your visit with your dear cousin a little longer? It is a peculiarly unfortunate moment to lose you, just when you could have attended the wedding, but you will return soon, will you not? And you must not stand on ceremony with us, Miss

Milton, for you may consider yourself a guest here any time you can make the journey, and your dear father can part with you, you know.'

This small speech was given without need for reply from Charlotte, or pause for the giver, and Charlotte waited patiently until Sir Frank had punctuated it with a profound bow and a small puff of hair powder. Charlotte thanked him very much, conscious of the hostile looks of which she was the recipient, from the sofa opposite.

'You are very kind, Sir, although I cannot say when I may leave Sussex again, for my father cannot often spare me,' she replied with gratitude tempered by her being sensible of the unlikeliness of the proposed visit. If she could help it, she would never again come into Hertfordshire, for it held nothing but sadness and heartache for her now.

'You must be very helpful to your father to be so indispensable to him,' noted Miss Annabelle Latham archly. 'I suppose, you go to his calls with him, and tend the sick,' she sneered. 'You must be invaluable, holding his instruments, administering hot water, soothing the feverish brow.'

Her smile was a thin line, full of ill-concealed contempt. Lavinia and Sir Frank were so engrossed in chattering to each other, that only Miss Sophia Latham had attended to her sister's words, and she busied herself with the tea things, no doubt embarrassed by her sister's open hostility, thought Charlotte.

At once humiliated and provoked by Miss Latham's indirect insinuation that she was good only for manual labour, Charlotte suppressed the outward signs of her resentment, and raised bright eyes to the lady seated opposite her. 'Not at all, for you must know a physician has no need of an assistant, Miss Latham. But I keep my father's medical notes, and pack his bags, and translate a little Latin and Greek for him, when needed, since his eyesight is poorly in the evenings.'

'Greek and Latin! Your talents know no bounds, Miss

Milton,' Miss Latham drawled, her voice dripping with sarcasm. 'With such accomplishments, you will have no problems finding a husband — as long as you do not expect to marry a gentleman! Gentlemen you know, do not wish for wives who can speak Latin. Oh, but perhaps you can find a husband if you go up to St Bart's... I'm sure they are not particular *there!*' She sniggered at her own joke, and Charlotte, quite speechless at the woman's insufferable rudeness, prepared to take her leave.

'My father,' she replied coldly, 'saw fit to have me taught those accomplishments, including Latin and Greek, which might fit the life of a physician's daughter, Miss Latham. Therefore, my governess taught me no less and no more, than what was needed to be useful in society. I would sooner be educated in Latin and Greek, and make use of my God-given powers of reason, than become merely a fashionable object, to be picked out by some man who wishes to decorate his parlour! And I would far rather continue my life as a useful spinster than to become a shameless husband-hunter as *some* women do!' She rose in anger, and realised that the whole room was now silent, having overheard her remarks.

Lavinia, rather startled at the outburst she had barely understood, cried warmly, 'Why, you will never get yourself a husband, Charlotte if you are happy to become a spinster! Good heavens!'

Miss Latham darted glances of pure evil at Charlotte and she, unused to such impolite manners and threadbare hospitality, excused herself, barely able to do what was polite. She bid good day to Sir Frank, kissed her cousin briefly, promised to write, and left the house simmering with anger and humiliation.

She had not walked more than a few steps before she gave way to angry exclamations, and spent the rest of the walk home fighting the misery which must be her fate. Intolerable woman! How dare she insinuate that Charlotte was not gentlewoman enough to find a husband her equal in society! Was it not enough that she, Miss Latham, was about to become the mistress of Delford, without gloating over Charlotte's lesser fortunes? Charlotte would go home, alone, leaving pieces of her heart in Hertfordshire. She had only dreary days to look forward to, with a stepmother who did not want her, a father who was too busy for her, and empty spaces where her mother's good-natured kindness used to dwell, where her love had made Charlotte feel wanted and cherished. She wished bitterly that she had never come into Hertfordshire, that she had never visited Delford, and had never met Sir Benedict Markham!

She spent an hour wandering the hills, keeping at some distance from Delford, as if distance could ease the pain that she would feel on returning. She dreaded and yet longed for the morning, the taking of leave, and the long carriage ride home. Not yet ready to return to the house, she wandered some more, until the sun was low and the light dimming. Eventually, she came to the little folly on the edge of the lake situated some distance from the house. Here, she sat forlornly on the steps and looked out over the lake. She had never felt so wretched. The image of Benedict, now so dear to her, visited her in her mind, and she relived each conversation they had shared in the last few days; each little kindness she remembered pierced her heart, and made her departure seem even more unbearable.

She put her hand in her pocket and withdrew the scrap of fabric which she treasured, and again, traced its embroidered 'B' with her finger. She would never see him again! He would marry Annabelle Latham, and she would return to Sussex to try to mend the pieces of her shattered heart. She stood at last and leaned against the cool stonework of the little folly. Soft midsummer's eve light settled over the water, painting the lake with unearthly gold and apricot hues. She thought she had never seen anything so beautiful.

'Alone and palely loitering, Miss Milton?'

Charlotte swung around. The man she loved stood a little distance away, and she stood still as if in a stupor, as if it was all a dream her heart had conjured. He stood still also, silhouetted against the pale blue and gold of the sleepy evening sky.

'Keats,' he explained. ' *"Alone and palely loitering, The sedge has withered from the lake, And no birds sing"* ', he quoted lightly.

She looked away to hide her face. She heard his footsteps come closer, but she was unable to speak, such was her agitation at his sudden appearance.

' *"Oh what can ail thee, so haggard and so woe-begone?"* ', he misquoted gently.

Charlotte dried her eyes with her hand, having stuffed the kerchief into her reticule, so he would not see it. She continued to look out over the lake. 'I did not know you knew Keats so well.'

'I did not read him at all, until recently,' he said mysteriously.

She did not reply at once, but after a moment she found her voice. 'You find me giving way, once again, to a little melancholy, Sir. It is a bad habit of mine. One of many, as I think we decided. But you quote inaptly. The birds sing yet.'

'Ah. So they do.' He paused, listening. 'But I collect we decided you had only three faults, not many.'

She did not reply.

He looked out over the water. 'You are fortunate to have only three faults, Miss Milton. I myself have many faults, and wish it were three only,' he went on thoughtfully.

Charlotte wished him gone, and yet yearned for his nearness. She roused herself. 'I hope I am not late in to dinner? I think I lost track of time. I walked for some hours after I left Highview. I did not realise it was near dark. It must be near six o'clock.'

'Yes. My sister sent me out when you did not return. I walked this way, to find you. You do not wish to know my faults?'

She shook her head, confused at the direction of this thoughts.

He continued. 'You shake your head. And yet, I must lay them bare, if I am to be forgiven them,' he said seriously. 'But first, my sister says you are to leave us?'

He turned to examine her face, but she would not meet his eyes. Instead, she said nothing, barely able to make sensible replies to such a speech. Her whole soul was in profound agitation, first joyful that he was here, the next miserable that she was to go. 'Tomorrow, Sir, if you would be so kind as to take me.' He did not answer her request, and she wished he would leave her.

He seemed not to notice her distress. 'Your walking to Highview and back has tired you. Walk back to the house with me. Please, let me offer you my arm.'

'No!' she cried, before she could help it. Blushing wildly, she walked a few steps away from him in utter consternation and humiliation. She struggled to contain her feelings. 'I— I am very well, I thank you, but I shall return to the house soon. Please apologise to Eliza, but I think you are right, I am a little fatigued. If she will excuse me from dinner, I shall remain in my room. I will walk back presently.' This speech left her weak with the effort of holding in her wretchedness, and yet he still would not go! She could not tell from his face, which seemed wooden, if he was angry or puzzled, but she bobbed a curtsey and turned to walk away from him.

'Charlotte.'

His voice stopped her, and suddenly he was before her. 'I have many faults, some of which you know, and some which I must lay bare before you. If you will hear me.'

His voice was urgent and she hardly knew his meaning. She

was not to be delivered from her misery yet.

He strode away from her in the dusk light, then turned sharply and strode back, to look out again, over the darkening lake and sky. His silhouette was dark, framed against the livid gold of the sunset. 'Before I left for London five days ago, to find Miss Smart, we began a conversation. Do you remember? A letter arrived about Miss Smart, before I had time to say what I will say now.'

Charlotte remembered, and was unable to let him continue. 'Nay, stop, Sir! Do not go on! It was my fault, my own fault, that led to Lavinia's shameful behaviour!' she cried. 'I, who knew what Lord Winchester was! I saw Lavinia with my own eyes, visit Wythorpe unaccompanied, and yet I did not tell you! Even Miss Smart was in danger due to my silence. I am truly sorry that I did not press my concerns more urgently. I, who had not one, but several reasons to suspect him, and yet I did not tell you! It is my fault alone, that she was not stopped sooner!' she cried passionately.

Sir Benedict uttered an oath. His eyes were dark. 'The fault was mine, and mine alone,' he replied, his voice low and full of emotion. 'Your behaviour in this matter was faultless. If I had not derided you, if I had not mocked your concerns and turned you away, you would have come to me! I did not believe in the power of a woman's ability to sense. We men have none of your sensibility and feeling! We do not see things that are before our eyes.' He laughed humourlessly. 'Even my sister has laid before me what I failed to see! I did you a great disservice, for doubting you, and I wish to God I had not insulted your more developed powers of perception. I, only, am in the wrong! Never you! Say it no more, and be at ease. Charlotte, can you ever forgive me? One word, and I will never mention this again, but please say you forgive me my faults, for I have been a great fool!' He took her hand without thinking and kissed it tenderly.

Charlotte stood in wonder, and thought she might still be

delirious with fever and would wake up in bed, after all. She was unable to utter a word, and yet, Sir Benedict held her hand most gently, his eyes burning into her soul. 'I have been proud, and haughty. I have been an arrogant cad to you, and a bacon-brained fool! Can you forgive me?'

Charlotte barely managed to incline her head, her eyes wide with unfeigned astonishment and joy. He cared for her, she knew he did!

He drew her hand to his lips once again and kissed it tenderly. After a moment, he put her from him, and looked deeply into her eyes. They were very bright, and he squeezed her hand. 'Tell me I have reason to hope? The day I rescued you from the rain, and brought you home, you called my name. It gave me hope that I might win your affections, that you did not just think of me as Lavinia's uncle, that you might care for me as I have come to care for you. Please tell me I have a reason to believe you care for me? Dearest Charlotte!'

Charlotte could no longer hold back her brimming emotions, and she sobbed into his hand. Pulling her close, he muffled her tears in his shoulder. His scent was spice and cinnamon and she breathed the scents in deeply, like a drug which should numb her senses, and yet made her more alive than ever before!

After a moment, she pulled away and looked into his eyes once more. 'When you found me, that day in the rain, I— I know that I called your name, for I remember it, even though I was fevered at the time. I saw you coming, out of the rain, and you bent down, and I was hardly sensible of what I said then, but— I knew you would come! And you did! But why you should care for me, I know not! How can you care for me when I have so many faults? I interfere in your business, and tell you what to do, and I judged you unfairly and—'

He put his finger to her lips and stopped her. 'You are all contradiction and spirit, Miss Charlotte Milton, and I love you the more for it! One moment you are melancholy and quiet, the next you are all passion and fire and argument! I will take you as you are— if you will take me, as I am! Here I am, laid out before you, with all my faults exposed. Will you take me, faults and all?'

'Oh, Benedict!' Her answer shone from her eyes.

With a tender smile, he tucked her arm in his and they turned away from the now-dark lake. 'The light is almost gone, and now we will have to walk back in the dark.'

In half wonder and half delight, Charlotte revelled in the feel of her arm firmly held by his. Together they began to walk slowly toward the house in the dusky light.

'What did you mean when you said that Eliza could see what you could not?' asked Charlotte as they walked. The ground was uneven, but she clung to Benedict's arm as much for the novelty of having him close as for support over the rough ground.

'My sister has suspected my feelings for you for some time. I believe she was alerted more fully, while you lay in bed for two days, recovering,' he chuckled. 'I was inconsolable. She guessed then, I think, but did not press me for more information. Then, when you were out of danger and resting, something else happened.'

Charlotte looked up at him, puzzled. 'Yes?'

'I informed her that I had allowed Tom to court Mary.'

Charlotte gasped! 'So that is why you were shaking hands with Tom in the stableyard two days ago! But how came you to change your mind?' Charlotte was all astonished happiness.

Sir Benedict shook his head. 'I was a fool, Charlotte! I hope you can find it in your heart to forgive me, for I allowed my stubbornness to blind me, once again, to your wisdom and better judgement! I said once that you knew nothing of love. I have been a fool! You, of all people, know more of love, of human nature, than I could! I ought not to have separated two people in love, but I was hardened to it. In part, my own pain from the past played a part, and made me wary. I had lost in love, and I wanted to protect the girl. But I let my stubborn prejudice against Tom blind me. When I found out that he was the source of information which allowed us to save Lavinia before it was too late, I went to find him. I apologised and gave him my permission to court the girl. He has accepted my offer of employment on the estate, and he promises not to poach my pheasants in return!'

Charlotte's countenance was joyous, and she sighed in contentment. Everything had worked out for the best! 'But how did Eliza guess? Oh, I see! She knew you had done it for me! You *did* do it for me, did you not? Benedict Markham, are you trying to win me over?' she teased.

He laughed abashedly. 'I'm afraid I am obliged to admit that I *perhaps* wished to win you over. But I hope I have proved my reformed character!'

'But, did Eliza guess my feelings for you? Was I really so open?' she asked, mortified that her efforts to conceal her feelings had signified nothing.

He chuckled and squeezed her arm gently. 'My sister suspected earlier. Then, when she spoke to you today, she guessed that your desire to leave Delford was not so much due to your cousin's impending nuptials, but to your feelings for me, which she believes you thought unreciprocated.'

'I did! I did think you did not care for me! I thought that you only saw me as Lavinia's cousin, someone to pity, that your kindness was born of pity, not love! When did you begin to care for me?' she asked curiously.

He shook his head. 'I cannot name the day, for I think it has come upon me gradually. But about a week after your arrival, one Sunday, we attended church, and I came downstairs to see you standing there, the sunlight from the window lighting you up like some kind of angel, and I think I fell a little in love with you just then.' He laughed, and she smiled with utter joy. 'But when I found you, lying in the rain that day, I knew what my heart had been trying to tell me for days.'

Charlotte's eyes were bright with emotion. 'I was so wrong about you. I considered that you were ruthless and uncaring, judgemental, and harsh. But then, you were so kind to me on the day of the picnic. You know, I still have this.'

She stopped and pulled his linen handkerchief from her reticule and held it out. He took the scrap of fabric, fondled it a moment, and laughed. 'I knew you had not returned it, and it gave me a tiny reason to hope, even then, that you might have begun to care for me.'

She shyly took the kerchief back, and put it away again. He made no comment. She could no longer see the expression on his face for it was too dark, but she felt him pull her closer against his arm and smiled to herself in contentment.

'But it was not only that day,' she went on as they made their way towards the house. 'The day of the ball, you asked me for the first two dances. I was so puzzled, for I was certain that you were to marry Miss Latham, and yet you asked me for the dances she ought to have had as your intended. I could not make out your purpose at all! Do please tell me that you do not still intend to marry Miss Latham?' she asked lightly, 'for I am afraid she does not like me at all, and if you wish to marry us both, I must warn you that I think the lady will offer some resistance!'

Sir Benedict chuckled. 'I suspect she told you she had reason to believe we had an understanding? In the church that day? Ah, yes, I suspected as much. You came out of that church door like a rabbit with the hounds after it, and she with the blackest looks! I suspected she had been warning you off. There is no understanding, not that but she might wish it.'

He paused to consider his words. 'I have been on intimate terms with that family since I knew Frank Latham's father, but I have never paid Miss Annabelle Latham any more attention than I would to any other lady of my acquaintance. My only crime has been to be too polite, too attentive, at times. Do not unrest yourself on that score. She will be a little put out, but I do not believe her heart to be much moved.'

Charlotte felt sorry for Miss Latham, for she would be most agitated when she discovered her favourite was to marry her rival!

'I was so sure you were to marry her, that I could not dance the second dance with you at the ball,' she confessed. 'I was sure you were only dancing with me to make her jealous.'

'Was that what made you unhappy on the night of the ball?' he asked. 'I wondered. I knew you were not ill, and I could tell you were not faint, for you danced again that night, and appeared to be in good spirits! I confess I was angered to see you dancing in such good spirits with Lord Winchester's friend, Captain Williams. You looked so beautiful that night, you know. I thought I might have a rival!'

She blushed. 'I only danced with Captain Williams to discover more about Lord Winchester. I wished very much to have some solid evidence to present to you, for I could not go to you with my concerns again, if I did not have good reason,' she explained. 'Did you really think me beautiful?'

'It is some weeks now that I have considered you to be the most beautiful woman I have ever met. Nay, do not hide your face Charlotte! It is true. When I led you out for the first dance, I felt like a schoolboy, as if it were my first ball and that I had never stood up with a lady before. You took my breath away,' he told her earnestly. 'Did you have no idea of the effect you had on me that night?

She shook her head. 'But I felt something of it, I think, something similar. Something I cannot describe,' she said shyly.

They approached the house from the front, and paused some distance from it under the trees. 'Do you think my cousin will be happy, Benedict? I believe she was as much in love with Lord Winchester as she could be, given her youth.'

'I believe my niece to be quite content with the outcome. She will feel the sting of rejection for a time, but I believe this will pass quickly.'

Charlotte sighed. 'Her engagement to Sir Frank will go some way to restoring her reputation. And yet, how I wish we had been able to prevent her from such a course of action, and such a rejection! I wanted so much to confide in you, but I felt prudence was the right course. I hope my cousin has not suffered too much as a consequence. I would spare her pain, even after all this!'

'You are too good, too kind to your cousin! And I have been a fool, Charlotte! If I had listened to you when you came to me before! But it was your going after her, on horseback, which alerted us, and it was you, my brave, sweet girl, who saved her from sure ruin and unhappiness in the end. My dear Charlotte, I can never part with you again! Say we will be married as soon as I have the license!'

She could only lift her head to his, and offer her silent reply. He bent his head and met her answer in her lips, while the night enclosed them in its private, tender arms. His warmth pressed against the delicate muslin of her dress and she marvelled at the feeling of him, the scent of him. It was cinnamon mingled with pine and it left her heady and breathless. In the distance, the nightingale sang, and Sir Benedict paused and lifted his head.

' "My sense, as though of Hemlock I had drunk" ', he quoted softly.

'*Ode to a Nightingale*', she observed quietly, when he at last released her. 'How do you come to know Keats so well? I would not have thought you a romantic... that is until now,' she added, smiling in the darkness at him, her heart full.

'I do have a volume or two in my library,' he returned. 'I am not completely an oaf, you know! But I confess, I have been reading it again, although I refuse confess my motive,' he added roguishly.

She laughed and they walked on, and presently they felt the crunch of the sandy driveway on their shoes.

'Benedict? Could we — I mean, would you mind very much

if we do not tell Eliza tonight? I wish to treasure this time a little longer. Until tomorrow, if it pleases you?'

Benedict's eyes glimmered. 'I would give you anything you asked of me, dear Charlotte. Of course. We shall tell Eliza in the morning. But you must go in first, if that is the case, or I am sure the servants will talk, even if Eliza does not see us!'

'It is past dinner time! Cook will be cross! Shall I join you and Eliza? But I do hope I will not give anything away, dearest Benedict, for I am not yet ready to share our happiness.'

She glowed like an angel, her face lit with joy.

'No indeed, with a look such as that you have on your face at present, no one will ever guess!' he said drily.

She chuckled and put her hands up in mock defeat. 'I must give in to your greater wisdom, and defer dinner then, since I shall never be able to keep myself from smiling like I have won the whole world! And I have, I truly have!'

Benedict bent once again to silence her with his mouth, and a few moments later, he gave her a little push. 'Now go, sprite, and stop tempting me with those eyes,' he admonished. 'I shall come in at midday tomorrow, and we shall tell Eliza our news then. I shall send a letter to Highview tonight, to Lavinia, but I shall direct that it not be delivered until after breakfast. She may, I am sure, wish to come home, and at any rate, she has stayed long enough and ought to return to her aunt.'

Charlotte nodded her agreement. 'Then please excuse me to Eliza, and tell her I will see her at breakfast,' she said, thinking hard. 'And I must write to my father at once. You must write too, you know, for you must ask his permission! Oh, how shall I ever sleep tonight!' she exclaimed.

'I will write to him this evening, if you will give me the direction. Write it for me and leave it on the table in the hall by my room. But Charlotte, will you come to me in my library before luncheon? I have something else to tell you, and I wish it to be private.' His voice was grave, and she was suddenly anxious.

'But what—?'

He silenced her with a kiss. 'Not now, dearest. Tomorrow is soon enough. Now, go, be off with you, before I carry you off myself! Farewell then, my love, until tomorrow!'

Benedict gave her one last look, and strode toward the stables. Charlotte watched him disappear and slipped inside the garden gate, where she found the kitchen door open and Cook bustling around in the kitchen.

'Lord, Miss, I did not expect you down here at this time!' cried Mrs Ransom. 'Dinner is already served up, so you had best go upstairs 'afore it gets cold!'

Charlotte tried to erase the glow from her countenance, but could not. 'I will take something in my room, if you could manage it, Mrs Ransom. Could you send Mary up with a tray for me? I will only take soup, if you please. I have not an appetite for anything else, I think.'

The older woman narrowed her eyes as if personally affronted, but nodded, and Charlotte went directly to her room. She felt dazed, as if it were all a dream she could scarcely believe. She wrote the direction for her father in Italy, and slipped out to place it on the table near Benedict's bedchamber. Returning to her room, she found Mary arranging her tray.

'Oh Miss,' cried Mary when she saw Charlotte. 'I am so happy! The Master has said Tom can court me, every Sunday! He has even given me a half day on Sundays, for the courtin'! Why Miss, I never did think he would ever let us, and now everything is better!'

Charlotte smiled her joy and took Mary's hand. 'Yes, Mary, everything is better now! I am very happy for you.'

The maid left the room with a curtsey and a fond smile, and Charlotte was left to spend the evening holding *his* cherished kerchief, and hardly touching her soup and bread. Over and over she relived the cherished moments of only a few hours previous. She fell asleep clutching the little piece of cloth to her breast.

Eliza was not present at breakfast the following morning, having remained in her room with a headache. Charlotte was somewhat relieved not to have to face her friend, since she did not think she could hide her feelings for long. Consequently, she spent the first part of the morning alone, in the coolness of the drawing room, book in hand but untouched, as she eagerly waited for Benedict. She felt occasional anxiety when she pondered what it was that he had wanted to discuss with her, but she felt that nothing could mar her happiness, and felt equal to anything he had to tell her.

It was not long before eleven o'clock when she heard a carriage draw up outside, and moments later, Miss Annabelle Latham was shown into the room. Charlotte sprang to her feet and gave a nonplussed but polite curtsey, but Miss Latham, forgoing the common courtesies, did not curtsey in return, and sat without being asked. Charlotte viewed her arrival with surprise but could have no misapprehensions about the purpose of the woman's visit.

A newly engaged woman, in love and full of contentment, overflows with good will and can magnanimously wish all others, even her rivals, some equal amount of happiness, even though in *her* mind, her own degree of happiness will always be just a little more than that of her fellow creatures. Charlotte, so full of contentment and unexpected joy, found herself quite equal to the task of entertaining one disgruntled Miss Latham. She sat waiting quietly, her inner tranquillity, her complacence in the sure knowledge of loving and being loved, enough to impart a delicate glow to her countenance. The other woman cast her calculating glance with narrowed eyes and began.

'So, Miss Milton, you insist on carrying on this mockery, do you? Yes, I heard your news, when the letter for your cousin came. You think you have drawn him in, you, who are the daughter of a nobody, with your fits of melancholy and your prating over your dead mother! Yes, Miss Milton, you may well look like that! Your cousin has told me everything, and if you have used your allurements to capture his interest, it is only because he is sorry for you! He always did have a soft heart for the weak! But he forgets what is owing to *me*, what he has promised to me! I will have you know, that we are most certainly engaged, and I have the proof!'

Charlotte, in all her magnanimity, could go no longer without losing some of her calm, and she sprang to her feet in cold disdain. 'Engaged? Really! Miss Latham, I must ask you at once to leave me! If you have anything to say, you ought to say it to Sir Benedict, for I can no longer hear you.'

She walked quickly to the door, seething with anger, but she was halted in her steps.

'If you do not believe me, Miss Milton, I have a letter, in his own hand, addressed to myself, giving the particulars of our engagement. It was written only weeks ago.'

She held out a paper, the seal broken, and Charlotte could see a strong male hand on the parchment. She paused, then turned back and unwillingly took the letter. She opened it out and began to read in silence.

'My dearest Annabelle
This letter will be bought to you by Frank, for as you know,

he is in town with me, and I must conclude our business here before I can return to your side. I hope your wait will be of short duration, but it may be as many as five days more, for my business takes me also into Kent before I may return to you. As you see I am much engaged, and yet all I long for is to be back in Hertfordshire, before my own fire, and to see your face.

You know how much I shall dislike a long engagement, my dear, but in the meantime, I am of the hope that once we are together again, the time will pass relatively quickly. You know that my own desire is to have you at Delford immediately and yet, due to my sister's illness, it seems we must wait. The fates are cruel, but we shall be united yet.

Until I return, I remain your devoted

B.M.'

Charlotte thrust the document back at Miss Latham, unable to speak. She sank to a chair, unable to support herself. Confusion and distress marked her countenance, and swelled in her heart. This must have been what Benedict wished to speak to her about! But what was he thinking? If he thought she would submit to an engagement when he was already engaged to another, he was mistaken! And if he planned to break an engagement off with Miss Latham, she would not willingly be party to such despicable, ungentlemanlike behaviour! He was bound by his status, by his honour as a gentleman, to abide by such an engagement!

Nay, there was nought to be done, but to admit she had been taken in, that she had been horribly used, that he had preyed upon her feelings for the purpose of inciting Miss Latham's jealousy! She slumped in her chair, bent over like a reed in a strong wind, which can no longer stand straight. Rivers of silent tears ran over her face and dripped down upon her dress.

Miss Latham gloated. 'Now, do you wish you go ahead with this sham engagement? He has only engaged himself to you, to inflame me, to excite my jealousy. Yes, Miss Milton, he does not love you and is engaged to me! For himself, of course, he can do no lasting harm to his reputation, for the agreement between us has been longstanding and it is only I who have held back from the union, on the basis of his sister's still being at Delford and an invalid. I have no wish to share my place as Delford's mistress with another, which he full knows. He has berated me for it and wishes us to marry immediately, and I confess his mock engagement to you has had the required effect. I wrote to dear Benedict this morning to agree to a union immediately. Now that his sister is to marry, it will be easier for me to be mistress of Delford. My advice to you is to leave now, before any more harm is done to your reputation. A lady cannot be spurned without her reputation being burned, for who would want a lady who has been rejected by another?'

Charlotte had nothing to say. She was consumed by a misery so great that all she could think of was that she must leave the house, before he came back and found her. She could not confront him; she would leave now. Miss Latham was standing.

'I am sorry for you, Miss Milton but there it is. I tried to warn you, with your best interests in mind, but you would insist on pursuing him. Now you have learnt the truth and I am sorry for your disappointment. Perhaps you feel it might be best for you to leave this house immediately?' she added with insincere sympathy.

Charlotte, full of confusion and despair, nodded unhappily, unable to make any intelligible reply.

'Well, then, perhaps I might offer you the use of my carriage. If you will have your maid pack your trunks, I can carry you as far as the village, then return to Highview. I shall make your apologies to dear Lavinia on your behalf. Tell your maid to hurry. Nay, let me.'

She rang the bell and Mary appeared. 'Pack Miss Milton's things,' she instructed imperiously, 'just her most important things, for her other gowns can be sent on later. Hurry girl, for I am very busy today.'

Mary met Charlotte's unhappy gaze with questioning eyes. Charlotte nodded miserably. 'Yes, please Mary. Just a few gowns and my personal belongings. I shall come up directly and change gowns, to the grey travelling dress.'

Mary, looking most confused and unwilling, left to do as bid and Miss Latham sat on the chaise, drumming her fingers, and tapping her foot in the most agitated manner. Charlotte, consumed by misery, went upstairs after Mary, and terrified of Sir Benedict's appearing suddenly, she hurried Mary to help her change, and gather her bonnet and reticule.

'Miss?' asked Mary shyly, after some minutes of silent endeavour. 'I just want to say thank'ee very kindly, on behalf of both Tom and me, for I know it was you who put the Master in mind to let my Tom court me, and I am very grateful, Miss. Tom would thank you himself, but you will not see him now as you are to go away.'

Charlotte did not answer her, for fear of giving way to tears. Mary reluctantly carried on packing Charlotte's trunk, and within another fifteen minutes, Mary and the footman had carried down her things, and the footman had put her trunk on Miss Latham's carriage. The unhappy girl handed Charlotte her pelisse and bonnet, who took them, hardly knowing what she did. Miss Latham led the way outside to the carriage.

Charlotte turned to Mary, who had followed her out in some agitation. 'Mary, please tell Eliza that I am sorry I did not say goodbye, but I will write—' Here she stopped, unable to continue without breaking down entirely. She turned away and made a fuss of gathering her things. Mary, seeing her mistress in great distress, was even more confused. However, she nodded and curtsied and Charlotte suffered herself to be helped into the carriage by the footman.

Miss Latham was about to step up into the vehicle, when the sound of hoofbeats hammered on the gravel of the drive and Charlotte was transfixed in her seat, for Sir Benedict was riding in all fury towards them. Miss Latham gave a little gasp.

Sir Benedict swung from the saddle of his beast and strode angrily to the carriage. Miss Annabelle Latham pressed her lips together, defiance upon her countenance. Sir Benedict took in the carriage, and an astonished and red-eyed Charlotte seated within. 'What is it you have you done?' he bit out, turning towards Miss Latham. 'What is the meaning of this?'

He stepped towards the nervous woman and she lifted her chin defiantly. 'Nothing that ought not to have been done before now,' she answered. 'How can you engage yourself to *that*,' she shrilled, pointing to Charlotte who was frozen to her seat, 'that toad-eating, ingratiating, petticoat! She has lured you in, and you, all the time you know you are engaged to *me*!' she cried in a little shriek. 'You are bound to our engagement! You know you are!'

Benedict gave her a look of withering disdain and grasped her arm in a most ungentlemanlike manner, astounding Charlotte, who could hardly believe the scene playing out before her eyes.

'Miss Latham, you broke our engagement eight years ago!' continued Benedict in a low, angry voice. 'You threw me over, in favour of another, and I have only ever congratulated myself for a fortunate escape! I have never given you reason to believe that I might renew those addresses. That I ever loved you, I can hardly believe, but I certainly do not love you now! You drew me in with your beauty, but you killed my feeling for you with your callous betrayal! If you yourself were thereafter jilted, it is your own fault! Perhaps that fortunate gentleman also saw you for what you really are!'

Benedict released the sputtering woman's arm, and turned to the carriage, leaning in to offer Charlotte his hand. She held out her own small one, and he gently drew her from the dim carriage. She stepped down and out into the golden light.

'How dare you sully my name, my reputation!' Annabelle

Latham turned several shades of crimson, and dashed her reticule to the ground in anger. She stalked to carriage and turned to Charlotte and Benedict. 'You were engaged to me, do you hear! Me! She is nothing compared to me, nothing! She is the daughter of nobody! She wears pattens to town! She reads Greek and Latin! She is not even a gentlewoman by birth! You lower yourself to address yourself to that person! She is nothing compared to me!' she cried angrily.

'Excuse me one moment.'

Benedict dropped Charlotte's hand and strode to the hysterical woman. Taking her by the arm, he compelled the ranting woman into her carriage and shut the door, as she continued to hurl insults. He removed Charlotte's trunk from the rear and set it down on the drive. Picking up the now-soiled reticule from the ground, he handed it to its owner through the window, and nodded to the coachman, who at once set the horses off down the drive. As the carriage departed, Miss Latham's head was seen protruding from the carriage window, calling all manner of insults down upon them both as the vehicle moved out of sight. Finally, there was silence.

'Is it true? Was Annabelle Latham the woman who jilted you eight years ago?' asked Charlotte, her eyes bright.

He nodded and continued to grasp her hand. 'I should have told you sooner. This is what I wished to tell you today, in private. I did not want you to think that I had concealed a friendship with the woman whom I once loved. I was afraid you would think me in love with her still. It has been a curse that our land is positioned so near, that we must be neighbours! And yet, I am an intimate acquaintance with the family, and once enjoyed a great friendship with old Frank Latham, their father. I felt that it would be churlish of me to hurt Frank and Sophia, so, some months after my engagement with her ended, I put my feelings aside and continued my intimacy with the family. I thought all was at an end, and that she had reconciled herself to that. She has never indicated to me until now that she harboured hopes of regaining my affections.'

'But she does everything in her power to gain your attention! Did you not think her behaviour suspicious? She warned me off on more than one occasion!' cried Charlotte warmly. 'She told me from the first that you had an understanding.'

He paused, considering his words. 'I was aware of her peculiar attentions to me at times, but this I put down to her need for attention in general. I suspected she had insinuated certain things to you, but I had never thought she would go this far! I have been a blind fool! But my sister will confirm for you that I have never given Miss Latham any hope of renewing my addresses to her, for Eliza knows of the whole affair and has been at Delford since the engagement was broken.'

Charlotte shook her head in puzzlement. 'But how came you to be jilted? On what grounds did she break it off?' she asked, eager to understand.

'I had been taken in by her beauty, but soon learned to understand her cruel heart. She pretended to be free, and gained the attentions of a man of higher rank. He proposed, being unaware of the understanding she had with me, and she failed to tell him she was already betrothed. She accepted his addresses, and his proposal, and subsequently broke off her arrangement with me.'

'But Benedict, why did she change her mind and break the engagement? Was it really the lure of fortune and rank? If so, she is a despicable woman!' Charlotte marvelled at how many common ideas her cousin and Miss Latham shared about the pursuit of happiness in marriage. She thought they would make fine sisters-in-law for each other!

Sir Benedict shrugged. 'I think it in part due to my insistence that we wait until my sister was recovered from the illness that left her an invalid. When I did not marry her immediately, at her insistence, she set her heart against me and threw herself at other men. Perhaps it was to make me jealous. But, whatever the reason, when the gentleman discovered she had played us both against each other, and understanding her to be engaged to me, he broke it off with her, and went away. She came back to me, as if nothing had occurred, demanding — indeed, expecting — our engagement to be renewed, but I refused to play her cruel game.' He passed a hand over his eyes. 'I was but twenty-eight, Charlotte, and I felt all the force of my pain. I was bitter and wounded, but I soon came to realise that while I had thought myself in love for a time, it was my pride that had been more wounded. The pain of being jilted was cruel, but the pain of being duped was worse. I had to admit that I had judged her wrongly. I had thought her capable of love and fidelity, but I was wrong.'

Charlotte thought she understood. 'So that is why you did not allow Tom Wilcox to court Mary! You thought he would jilt her, as you had been! Oh Benedict, I am so glad you have allowed them to marry. But tell me, was it not awkward to be in the same room with the woman who had humiliated you? You have remained on good terms with the family all these years!'

He inclined his head. 'It was awkward yes, but due to my friendship with old Latham, and now with his son, I put aside my feelings. At first, she would not speak to me, then she began to be more easy in my company, and I grew less anxious about her renewing her demands. I felt she had put the matter entirely to rest, as had I. Again, I have misjudged her character! I never harboured any suspicions that she seriously wished to renew our intimacy.'

Charlotte considered. 'She wanted me to think you still have an understanding. She showed me a letter. I think it must have been written very long ago, but it was not dated. In my misery, I allowed her to convince me otherwise.'

'I made clear my intentions never to renew my addresses to her years ago. Any correspondence I entered into with that woman began and ended eight years ago. I suspected her jealousy shortly after you arrived, but my dear girl, I had no idea she would carry it this far. Forgive me, sweet girl, for again, I have been much mistaken on matters of a woman's heart. I do now bow to your greater wisdom on such matters!' He kissed her hand tenderly.

'You have great forbearance then, if you have suffered her company so politely for the sake of her friends,' noted Charlotte, smiling. 'I think I could never show such forbearance. You are a saint, but I am not surprised.'

He laughed. 'Not a saint, but very forbearing, perhaps,' he replied, amused. Directing the waiting footman to return Charlotte's trunk to her room, he took Charlotte's arm and tucked it under his own. They began to walk toward the house.

The midsummer sun grazed her skin gently, and she felt in that moment, bathed in the light and heat of that perfect summer's day, that everything she had been through had led to this moment. Her heart felt peaceful. As they walked, she momentarily felt a strangely familiar, yet fleeting brush of lips on her forehead. *Mama.* She smiled to herself.

Benedict stopped suddenly, and looked down at her. 'Do you really read Latin and Greek?' he asked with fascination.

She nodded, smiling.

He bent his head to hers, and nothing more was said for a very long while.

THE END

I hope that you've enjoyed this book!

After the About the Author section you'll find a preview of

Beauty and the
Beast of Thornleigh

About the Author

Kate Westwood is the author's pseudonym. Kate has a background in academic writing and holds a Master's degree in English Literature. Having had a life-long dream to write, she finally turned her pen to regency romance when she turned fifty.

Kate is a huge fan of Austen and her contemporaries, and strives to recreate an authentic 'regency' experience for the reader.

Kate's hobbies, when she is not writing or reading Regency romance, include playing classical piano, and walking and hiking the beautiful Gold Coast Hinterland. Kate lives with her three teen sons and one cat on the Gold Coast of Australia.

Connect with Kate

Facebook:
https://www.facebook.com/katewestwood.net/
Sign up to Kate's email newsletter at :
www.katewestwood.net
to receive the subscriber exclusive story *The Gift* as a welcome gift!

Here is Your preview of
Beauty and the Beast of Thornleigh

Prologue

1812

Captain Asher Brandt had come into Derbyshire with less enthusiasm than a mutineer walking the plank, and now he felt just like one, as he sat on a hard chair, too close to the fire in Lady Selkirk's drawing room, on this unseasonably cool April day. The cold pierce of that lady's gaze was powerfully chill enough to quell the perspiration rising under his linen shirt, from his close situation to the fireplace. He tugged at his cravat which felt too tightly tied. In that chill look, he felt all the force of Lady Selkirk's disapproval, and yet, he must ask for lenience, and for time; he must ask an indulgence for which he dared not hope.

Neither lenience nor indulgence looked promising; they did not signify upon Lady Selkirk's stark countenance as she sat opposite him. In her eyes he divined only stern disapproval, the same disapprobation he had encountered on the last visit, twelve months previously, when he had first come, upon his own inclination, to put his supplication forward.

But he remembered, that the cut of her jib concealed an unexpected kindness which lay below her surface, and for which he had been grateful then; this remembrance now gave him some hope. If he could but draw out that human kindness once again, he would be willing to humiliate himself as he was about to do, for he needed Lady Selkirk's good will, and perhaps even her pity, if he was to accomplish his object. His course had been, until now, nothing but doldrum winds. His scheme had been brought up short, and he was now obliged to ask for help. Although his visit was this time at Lady Selkirk's summons, he harboured hopes of gaining her indulgence, through his opening himself to her and falling upon whatever tendency toward clemency might yet sit behind the chill glance of her eyes.

He shifted his weight uncomfortably, a testament not only to the determination of the chair beneath him, which was now asserting its authority against his *derriere* rather zealously, but to his inner mental and emotional state, which was ever more uneasy and troubled with each minute of his being there. He was half hope, half despair. He knew not what to think, or to hope for.

Lady Selkirk silently indicated to him to take up his teacup, which he did, and sipped obediently against its delicate bone china edge, as much to borrow time as to quench his thirst. He looked down at the fragile pink china against his own comparatively vast hand, and idly thought how incongruous the cup appeared. It was a tiny, feminine symbol which made mockery of his own distinctly male, and brutish, appearance. The corner of his mouth twitched, but it was not in humour.

His accuser sat opposite, waiting for an answer to the question she had just asked him, eyeing him with that disapproving stare which was her way, and to which he yielded after a short time.

Placing his teacup gently on its saucer, he met her eyes fully. His voice was hesitant, as it always was, these days. 'Ma'am. I have not yet resolved the matter. There have been — difficulties, with available choices. I find myself at a loss. I have made no advance towards securing what I promised in our last meeting, but, under the circumstance, I hope you will understand, it has not been easy. The situation is a rather delicate one.'

Lady Selkirk waited. There was pity in her glance, he discerned, and it gave him some hope, even while it stung, but he could also discern that it was mingled with annoyance.

He continued. 'I understand your terms, and the agreement we came to on our last meeting, but my circumstances are, shall we say, of a somewhat unusual nature. It is my personal circumstance, my lady, to which I refer. It has not been easy to fulfil the terms of our agreement. I require more time.' He looked away momentarily, self-conscious at having been obliged to make a direct reference to his personal situation. It was not that he was embarrassed, for he could not help his situation, but to admit that it was the cause of difficulty in gaining what it was he needed, and that this may forever prevent him from obtaining that alone which his heart required, to find peace and solace — he wished it were not so, and yet he must lay his pride before the woman who held his future in her power.

Her eyes were thoughtful, but still, disapprobation met his own gaze. She set her teacup down, her brown taffeta gown rustling in the quiet room as she did so. 'You refer, I suppose, to the problem of your appearance,' she said, not unkindly. 'You think that no young lady will want you. You are timid in society, my friends tell me. You do not go out, you refuse all invitations to card parties, dances, and public entertainment, you do not go to London for the season, and you shutter yourself up in that dreadful house of yours, keeping to your own company. Oh, do not deny it, Captain, for my friends tell me it is true. No wonder, you have not found it easy to accomplish your task, when you refuse to go about in society!'

He concurred. 'It is true, my lady. I do shun society. I do not go about in it as easily as I once did. I do not feel — out of respect for my brother, and, yes, due to my own shame, my pride, I do not go about in society any more than I can help. This circumstance has limited my ability to be introduced to young ladies.'

'But have you enlisted the support of your friends? Surely, *they* must know some well-bred young lady or other who might agree to an introduction? Perhaps you are too fastidious, Captain! The young woman need not be rich or beautiful, you know! So long as she is well-bred, sensible, and has a tolerable maternal instinct about her, she will meet all *my* requirements!'

He inclined his head. 'My good friend, Captain Townsend, last month set up private introductions with two eligible young women. The first young lady took one look at me, and fled the room in tears, without uttering a word. The other suffered hysterics on the spot, and a fainting fit, and had to be carried away! You can see my predicament, Lady Selkirk. They cannot even hold a conversation with me, let alone consider an offer. My face is my downfall, Ma'am; no woman will look at me.' He gave a short, bitter laugh.

'Then I am very sorry for you, Captain; this must be a material change from the kind of reception you have been used to from young ladies.'

He uttered a short, mirthless laugh. 'Only three years ago, I regularly moved in the best of society; young ladies fell over themselves to set their caps at me, to flutter their fans at me and flirt outrageously! Now, things are very different. I need more time, my lady, to locate the right prospect. I admit I am straightened, to my limit, to find somebody by the end of the year. I must beg for your clemency, while I devise a new scheme.'

'As you are aware,' replied Lady Selkirk ominously, 'my foremost concern must be for my granddaughter, your brother's child. She must be cared for adequately. If you cannot provide what I have asked, she must return to this house permanently, and be cared for here. She is of an age now where she is impressionable, an age in which her character and personal attributes are now being formed. If she is to remain with you, she must have a mother; she must have a gentlewoman's care. Her visits to me are of too short a duration to have any lasting influence over her. She will, of course, have a governess, but she must be schooled in the ways of a lady. She needs a mother's guidance – and a mother's love,' she added a trifle less severely.

Asher waited while his hope dwindled.

Lady Selkirk sighed. 'I am not a harsh woman, Captain, and it is my desire that, should you find a wife of whom I can approve, my granddaughter may remain at Thornleigh, her natural home. And despite my reputation for sternness, I am not insensitive to the difficulties, the complexities, of your—situation, as it were.'

She rose and Asher thought she meant to go to the window, but she stopped short at her desk, and reaching into the drawer there, she withdrew a letter, and held it out to him. He took it, puzzled. Before he had time to peruse its contents, she seated herself and spoke again.

'I have taken the liberty of procuring you an introduction to a young woman whom I think will meet your needs. That is the letter from her mother, giving her consent to the plan. You will travel down to London, where the family is in residence for the Season. You will find the details of the introduction in the letter. It has been arranged that you will attend one or two dinners, card parties and so on, as the guest of my friend, Mrs Fanny St. George. She is the girl's aunt. The girl herself is of good breeding, and meets all of my own requirements in this matter, which is all that needs to answer, for my part. Most importantly for you, Captain, I am almost certain she will accept an offer should you make her one.'

With these words, Asher's heart rose once again from despair to hope, although this was coupled with humiliation. He swallowed down his pride. 'I am at a loss, my lady, to know how to reply. You know it is my fondest object to have Rose live with me at Thornleigh. But what makes you think this young lady will accept my offer? How can you be so sure?'

'The young lady, Miss Georgiana Hall, is the middle daughter of three, the niece of my friend, Mrs Fanny St. George, who at present is in town for the season with her sister's family. The father passed away almost two years ago. It appears that he was a wastrel of sorts, according to Fanny, deep in debt when he died, and left almost nothing in the way of an income for his children or widow. There was the estate, of course, their current home, but that is entailed to a brother, a man - I will not say a gentleman - of trade, who can hardly be expected to support the girls and their mother indefinitely, along with his own family. The girls have a home at Loweston, here in Derbyshire, for their uncle has not yet turned them all out, but his son will inherit Loweston on his marriage, and as he is of age, they cannot have long.'

'But do they not have any means at their disposal? Are they really so poor that a daughter among them would accept a marriage proposal from a stranger?'

'The girls have no provision to speak of, and the oldest is beyond the age for marriage. The youngest is not yet fifteen. The middle daughter is three and twenty and has had no offers made her as yet, if my friend, Mrs St. George, has not been misled. As the most eligible daughter, she will feel it her duty to accept any offer which might be to the advantage of the whole family. But there is one more thing.'

Asher's countenance became guarded. "Yes?"

'The girl has a deformity herself. She has a wasted limb.'

He was still for a second, his face was ashen. He stood up. His voice was cold, full of barely checked disgust. 'I beg your pardon, but I cannot agree to such a scheme. It is a bad enough affair, that I must subject myself to... to *pity*,' he flung the word out, 'although my circumstances have obliged me to submit. For the sake of my brother's child, I submit willingly! But that I should also allow myself to be paired up with a… a… cripple! I may have lost my face, and yes, I may well inspire pity wherever I go, from all who look upon me, but, my lady, I refuse to subject myself to the insult that you have paid me, inferring that only a cripple would take me! I may no longer be considered handsome, but I have my fortune, I am a gentleman, and I am respected in the circles which matter to me. I *will* find a wife, and she will not be a cripple with no other prospects!'

Lady Selkirk had stared mildly at Asher during this outburst, not seeming to be affected by his anger. She smiled humourlessly and indicated the chair. 'Sit down, Captain. I thought this might have been your response. I recommend you calm yourself, for I did not intend offence, although it appears that I gave it nonetheless. Now, before you storm out of my drawing room, hear me out. I have something more to say on the matter.'

'What more could you possibly have to say on the matter, Lady Selkirk? I think you have made yourself quite clear.'

'Nonetheless, stay a moment. Now, Captain, I am not quite intending to pair you up with a cripple, as you put it. The girl has a wasted limb, yes. But it is not quite so bad as it sounded at first. There is no obvious defect, except a slight limp, and she relies on a cane. Unfortunately, this has affected her ability to marry, since her deformity makes any offer unlikely. It is a great pity, for I have heard from her aunt that she is considered a great beauty, and she has been brought up a gentlewoman. I am told that she is quiet, dutiful and would make a grateful wife. If an offer were made to her, I feel that she would all the more willingly accept if it were made from someone in, shall we say, a similar position? Stay Captain, hear me out,' she added commandingly, as Asher strode towards the door, unable to hear more. He stopped unwillingly and turned, the smooth portion of his face as angry and bitter as the other side was ugly and deformed.

Lady Selkirk continued, her voice placating. 'It is not my intention, I assure you, to offend, but to facilitate an event which by your own admission, has been difficult to bring about. Whatever your fortune, Captain Brandt, young ladies do not readily marry older men with, excuse me, disfigured features. Forgive my bluntness, but it is so. It is my firm belief that his young woman will accept you; you may find yourselves, shall we say, *simpatico*. Go to London, Captain Brandt. It may be your only chance to keep Rose.'

Continued...

Be the first to know when

Beauty and the Beast of Thornleigh

Is released!
Go to
www.katewestwood.net
and sign up to Kate's newsletter for release notices and more!

Other Books by Kate Westwood

Beauty and the Beast of Thornleigh (Coming Soon)

A Bath Affair (Coming Soon)